MEETING JOE

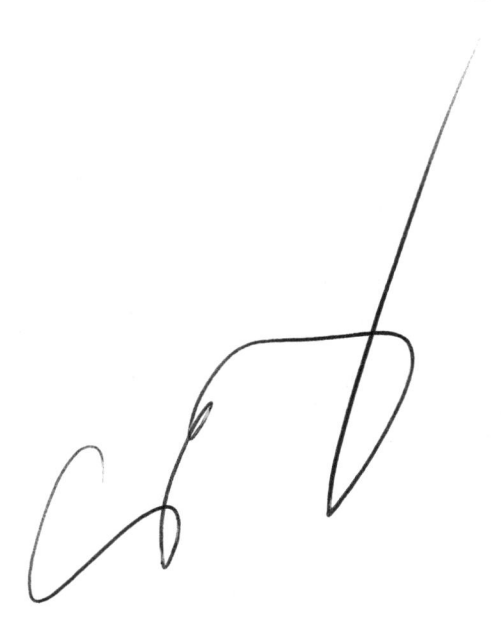

Meeting Joe

Shannon DuBey

© 2018 by 1107 Printing

All rights reserved. No part of this book may be used or reproduced in any manner what-soever without written permission, except in the case of brief quotations embodied in critical articles or reviews.

Printed in the United States of America.

For LeAnn - a promise fulfilled

Also By Shannon DuBey

Unconditional

Timmy Meets His Match

Many Thanks to

Jack Cairy, Monica Lytle, & Stacey Szenderski

Their input, reviews, suggestions, and proof reading helped to shape this story into the novel it has become.

Chippewa Nature Center, their board, benefactors, & staff

Many hours were spent here writing, proofing, and editing this novel. I posted on Facebook once that they deserved a writing credit, partly in jest. Truth is, sitting in the River Overlook, borrowing the free WiFi connection for hours on end, and gazing out at nature helped me find the inspiration required to continue working on this project more than once.

Stop by sometime and check them out!
400 S Badour Rd, Midland, MI 48640

PROLOGUE

An echo is defined as "a sound caused by the reflection of sound waves from a surface back to the listener." To hear one you must listen quietly and carefully. They are often muffled, muted, distorted. Sometimes though, if you are patient and listen close you can hear them as clearly as if the origin of the sound was speaking directly to you. I wouldn't tell most people that I believe in ghosts, or Earth bound spirits. To be honest, I'm not certain that I do. I mean I've never seen one, though I have heard stories from those who claim they did. I've never even had an experience I would consider a haunting. You know those typical Halloween movie scenes where lights flicker off and on, floors squeak under some unseen weight, and footsteps can be heard walking across the room though it's empty of all life but me. That sort of thing just never happens in real life as far as I know.

However, I have heard the voice of people I was close to before they died, after they were long since dead. Sometimes it seems like just a memory of some conversation we had in the past, before they died. Other times, and these are the more frequent of them lately, it's far more like a real conversation, with someone who is dead. Maybe it's just a mind trick where the conversation in my head uses a voice from the person I wish I could talk to about whatever is going on. Maybe it's not. I guess I have to believe in something after we pass from this life into whatever happens next. Otherwise, I must accept that I am in fact absolutely insane.

You may think or even call me crazy if you wish, I have labeled myself this a time or two in my life for sure. Maybe I am. Maybe I am not. What I do know is that if we allow ourselves to set aside the labels and baggage from our past that often clouds our present view of the world, amazing things can happen. My family taught me that, those both living and dead. And yes, for some of them that lesson was taught long after they died. Your thoughts about my sanity matter less than you may think at this point. However, I challenge you to keep an open mind and continue reading.

This story is not one about ghosts, or talking to people no longer with us, but it may come up again as you read on. For the non-believers out there, try not to get hung up on it and miss the real point of this story. In plain English, we all have a history. People we know, or knew, places we've been, things that have happened to us or around us that shape who we become. Like it or not, it is our past and though we may think we have put it behind us and moved in a new direction to prevent it from affecting our present, it always does. Our past is impossible to 'put behind us' because it's part of who we are. No matter how long it has been forgotten about in our present day lives, it's always there, just under the surface, tainting our view of the world and the decisions we make.

For nearly all of us, eventually our past will surface again. Refusing to remain buried in memories it has a way of catching up to us and forcing us to deal with things we left unresolved. In my case, it happened about two years ago with a chance meeting I never expected. In one ten minute encounter with someone I had long since left behind me, my past life slammed into my present full force. The fallout from that event rippled through every part of the life I had built for myself and of those closest to me.

The pages that follow explain what happened and the journey it led me on. There may be portions some find impossible or unfathomable. It is still my truth and part of my story. Before I can take you along for that ride though, I need to take you on the journey that led me to the event.

Part 1

May 1996

I've lived in this place and I
know all the faces
Each one is different
But they're always the same
They mean me no harm but it's
time that I face it
They'll never allow me to change
I never dreamed that home
Would end up where I don't
belong
I'm moving on

> Rascal Flatts
> *I'm moving on*

Chapter 1

The day I left town I was 18, had graduated high school only a few days prior, and hadn't seen eye to eye with my ol' man most of my life. He was a roughneck sort of man with a scruffy beard that had gone gray when I was in elementary school. His eyes were dark as coal yet had a shine to them in the warm North Carolina sun, sort of like highly polished black onyx. He'd left home at the age of 16, some town just outside Montgomery, Alabama I can't even spell let alone pronounce. He stumbled his way northeast through first Georgia, then Tennessee and the Carolina's picking up work where he could. From the few stories I have heard, all from Mother, he never stayed in one place for too long. Eventually he landed a job in the mill near my maternal grandparents' farm just outside of Thompson Station, North Carolina. That's where he met Mother and before he was 18 had a wife with a child on the way. That was me, Martin Joseph Taylor born November 21, 1977.

From what little I remember about my early childhood, my ol' man was a great father who worked his fingers to the bone Monday through Friday in Dickson's Mill & Furniture Factory. It was the only industry in Thompson Station and employed 80% of the town in some way or another. He was home for dinner every night by 6:30 and most Saturdays and Sundays were spent with family. Mother would always have supper in the oven when he came up the drive and holler for us kids to, "get washed up for supper, your father's home!" just as he stepped onto the front porch.

Like I said, weekends were family time and no matter how much I didn't want to back then, looking back now I actually enjoyed the time I spent with my ol' man in his wood shop on the weekends. I was learning his craft and helping to build everything from my own chest of drawers to the neighbor's dining room table. It was a wedding present for their daughter. She decided to cancel the wedding and run off with the boy instead just one week before their big day. Her parents kept the table my ol' man had built and sent their old battered kitchen table as their 'moving out gift' instead. My ol' man always got a kick out of that one.

Unfortunately, all those good memories stopped just after my 5th birthday when I began to see him through clearer eyes. Instead of a great father who could do no wrong in my eyes, I saw him for the angry, often cold man he really was. I have not called him Dad, Papa, or Father since. Instead, it was always my ol' man, Joe, and occasionally Sir, as in 'yes sir' and 'no sir', but never anything that would make someone think of him in that cherished role of 'father figure'.

Chapter 2

In the first real memories I have of my ol' man, you know the ones where you actually remember details not just the general idea of what took place, anyway my first memories of him are from when I was five. I mean I remember him from before then, or I guess at least the idea I had of him in my head, and now they just seem like a fantasy. By the time I was a teen, all the details were gone, just fuzzy clips of memories now that feel like they happened between us at some point, but I have no real proof of them.

My first vivid memory of my ol' man was on a family trip to a local zoo. It should have been a joyous occasion for all, yet my ol' man was angry. I was too young to understand why but I definitely remember his angry face, his raised voice, and his vicious words when I asked him why he wasn't having any fun at the zoo that day. It's the first time I remember his hand as it quickly flew from his side and violently struck me across the face. That slap sent me hurling backward into a nearby bush as I watched him throw his hands in the air and storm toward the front entrance through tear filled eyes. Mother helped me to my feet, brush the dirt from my clothes, and dry my tears. My ol' man just left.

It would be years before I would understand the impact

of this one event in my life or how it would set the tone for our relationship from then on. Unbeknownst to me at the time, it would be the cornerstone of the path I chose in life. It was all of those things and so much more. It was a single day, not long after my fifth birthday, when I should have been happy and having the time of my life. Instead, I was miserable and learning how miserable my ol' man was to be around.

Mother tells me I enjoyed that day at the zoo with her and the rest of the family. Kera and Kylee, my younger twin sisters were there laughing the day away in the sunshine. They were not quite three at the time and spent most of their day in the stroller being pushed around the park by Mother. I remember their faces all coated with cotton candy, strings of it hanging from their long blond curls, pink crystals stuck to their rosy cheeks. I remember their giggles as Mother and I stood next to them on the carousel holding tight so they didn't fall from atop the painted ponies. I remember all of these details, but none of the fun I supposedly had. I was bored out of my mind on that carousel holding onto Kylee. I wanted to go ride the train, or the bumper cars. I wanted to play in the arcade, to have the man guess my weight and get it wrong. I wanted to do what I wanted to do, but instead I was a good boy and stayed with Mother to help her with the girls. That was what my ol' man told me to do after he slapped me into that bush for asking him a simple question.

My ol' man was not always an angry man, but he

worked harder than most. He always said he wanted us to have a better life than he had when he was a boy, and I believed him. He had grown up on a farm outside of Montgomery, Alabama in the mid-fifties. He was one of four boys and three girls in their small three-bedroom house and, according to all the stories I have been told, had to walk to school in the middle of winter with no shoes. They weren't poor per say, my grandfather worked hard on the farm and there was always food on the table, but they certainly weren't rich either. It wasn't easy growing up in that time, working hard in the fields all afternoon after schooling all morning, but my ol' man wanted something better for us. I understood this meant I was college bound after I managed to graduate high school. That fact was drilled into my head from as far back as I can remember. Possibly all the way back to before I was five.

I had the same amount of respect that every five year old boy has for his father, he was my idol perched high atop a pedestal and in my eyes could do no wrong. At least that was the case right up to the moment his hand landed hard against my left cheek and my bottom slammed into the picky bush across the path. At that moment, the illusion I held of my ol' man as an unflawed idol came crashing to the ground and splintered into a million little pieces, never to be repaired. It was a tough lesson, one every child learns eventually. In my case it was only the beginning of learning who my ol' man really was.

From that day on, I approached my ol' man with caution, asked only what was absolutely necessary, and learned to duck and cover when needed. Throughout most of my early years, I managed to avoid his anger and frustration by sticking close to Mother. Unfortunately, three short years later, not long after my eighth birthday, that too would come to an abrupt end.

Chapter 3

Mother fell ill in the spring of 1985 and spent months going back and forth to the doctor's office first every couple of weeks, then weekly. I tagged along to tend to my sisters who were now almost five and into everything if left unattended. They were happy little girls, much like I was at that age I suppose, completely unaware that life was about to teach all of us a very hard lesson. I never asked Mother or my ol' man what was wrong, or when Mother would get better. I knew the answer to it already. Sometimes I could just sense when something bad was about to happen, a gift I suppose. I mean, it allowed me to prepare myself for the event in some ways, or at least to not be taken completely by surprise when it did happen. Though as a young boy to know that your mother was ill and that something bad was coming your way, I remember feeling so helpless and unable to enjoy the same unknowing bliss that those around me had. In that way I suppose it was much more of a curse than a gift.

To help me cope I bottled up those feelings, screwed the lid on tight, and tucked that jar up on a high shelf inside my heart. I put it completely out of my mind whenever possible. Every once in a while, I would pull it down from that dusty shelf and let it out, but only when I was in my safe place knowing that I was completely alone. I mean a boy was not supposed to cry, not even if he had driven his pocket knife deep into his hand accidentally while whittling a stick. My ol' man taught me that lesson the hard way too. Nobody should ever see a boy cry.

When the time was right, and I could manage a few selfish moments to myself, I would sneak off to someplace I knew I would be safe from the world. Following the path that began on the far side of the barn in our back yard I would hike to a place where the trees were low and it felt like I was on top of the world. I always checked the path in all directions to be certain I was alone, and then would find my spot out on the flat rocks that overlooked the valley below. It was here that I would finally allow myself to feel again.

After the tears, which always seemed to come first the anger would gradually rise up from that place I tucked it deep inside and eventually spill over. I had dealt with it in many ways before finding something that helped to release it without leaving me battered and bloody in the end. I now kept a pile of rocks next to my space on top of the world to help with this. The act of chucking rocks, some as small as a golf ball, others so large they required both hands to lift, helped me release those angry feelings about whatever I had tucked inside my little jar. Sometimes I would chuck all the rocks in my pile and have to go stomping off into the forest to restock. Other times, just one or two chucks seemed to do the trick. On those days, I found myself picking up a rock only to toss it up in the air and catch it with my other hand before sitting back down on the overlook.

It was then, after releasing all the feelings I kept locked inside that little jar, lid tightly sealed, that I was finally able to feel at peace. When I could, I would spend time asking metaphorical questions, some aloud, some just inside my own head. I would contemplate life's little mysteries and, when the mood struck, I would spend a little time talking to God. I don't recall much of those conversations but I definitely remember asking him to help me take care of my family, and to help my ol' man with his work so he could be a little less angry with the world. I know, pretty heavy stuff for an 8 year old boy but I have always felt and acted a lot older than I really am. Mother once told me I had an old soul. It took years for me to understand what she meant by that but, I believe she may be right. It explains so many odd things about me both as a child and the adult now writing this story.

When I was done, I would slowly wander back down from the top of the world to our back yard and eventually into the house. I would almost always run into Mother in the kitchen as I made my way back to my room and she would always ask where I had been. Without fail, she would always accept my answer of, "no place important" as good enough. I think she knew it was just something I had to do, something that helped keep me sane and calm even in the most emotional and difficult situations. It was my own way of dealing with the harsh realities life could throw at a little boy, and would be my saving grace after the death of Mother and the virtual disappearance of my ol' man.

Chapter 4

I don't remember what happened exactly, not the exact chain of events or explicit details of the day as a whole, but what I do remember is crystal clear in my mind. Even now some thirty years later, I can close my eyes and remember it so exact, so realistic it's like I have been transported through time back to that horrible day. Mother had been more seriously ill than I remembered her ever being when we went to her weekly doctor appointment. As usual, I sat in the waiting room with the twins to keep them quiet and out of trouble. We played with the wooden blocks in the corner, we read from our favorite book Children's Bible Stories, and we sat quietly on the chairs and listened to the conversations of old people.

It was then, while the three of us were sitting there quietly that a nurse came out and asked if I knew how to reach my ol' man. I nodded slowly and replied, "He is at work ma'am." She thanked me and then scurried off back behind the closed office door. Through the window I could see her making a phone call and knew right away that Mother had in deed taken a turn for the worse, though at only eight years of age, I didn't fully understand what that phrase meant. I had heard it used many times, and knew it was never a good thing, but I had no idea just how bad it could be.

I remember walking down the cold hall of the hospital hours later, this time alone. My ol' man thought that the twins were too young to be in the hospital and had called on a neighbor to watch them for the night. He tried to send me away too, but I refused to go. I stood up to him, one of the few times I can recall ever doing that in my early years, and Mother told him to let me stay.

The last time I heard Mother's voice was when she managed to whisper the words, "Let him stay, Stephen." Mother had a thing about using people's full first name when she addressed them. Most people called him Joe, even his own parents since his father's name was Stephen. I never heard anyone but Mother call my ol' man Stephen, but to her that was his proper name.

I had climbed back up on the bed next to Mother, kissed her cheek, and knew somewhere deep inside that I was kissing her good bye though none of the adults would admit just how sick she was when I was around. I lay curled up in her arms for a few minutes more before feeling so overwhelmed by the impending 'bad thing' that I left Mother's side to go for a walk. I needed a change of scenery and a little voice whispering inside my head told me that Mother and my ol' man needed to be alone for a bit.

I had been gone about 30 minutes when I thought I heard Mother's voice whisper to me telling me it was time to come back. I thought maybe she just wanted another hug before we left for the night. It would be years before I fully understood the significance of that event, when I would again hear her voice whisper in my ear. When I returned to her room, I saw my ol' man sitting quietly, head in his hands, on the empty bed where Mother had been when I left. In that instant the world around me began to swirl as if I was in the middle of a tornado standing perfectly still while the winds tossed everything else in circles around me. Though in my gut I already knew the answer, I remember asking my ol' man where Mother had gone. I did not get an answer. His only response was a very cold, blank stare from those black onyx eyes followed by a gruff, almost growl of his voice saying, "Let's go home."

Three days later I was standing with Kera and Kylee in the front row watching them lower Mother's casket into the ground. My ol' man was walking away from the ceremony in progress. He made no appearance at the viewings the previous two days and though he was technically there, he stood outside during the entire funeral. He claimed he hated cemeteries, gardens of stone as he called them, and something about work and already saying his good byes or something for the two separate viewings. Instead he made arrangements for Mrs. Maybelle to take the twins and me to the services. When he climbed into the limo to ride with us to the cemetery I thought maybe he had come around and accepted that my sisters and I needed his support today. As he patted my shoulder minutes into the burial service and whispered "stay here Marty" before walking away from the service, from his family, I realized I had been wrong. He was too selfish to realize his children needed him, or too selfish to care at least.

That was the beginning of the end of my relationship with my ol' man. In one fell swoop I lost Mother to what I would later learn was cancer and my ol' man through the choices he made to all but abandon my sisters and me. It began with the funeral services and continued every day thereafter.

Chapter 5

A little more than ten years after Mother's death I'd finally had enough of the arguing, yelling, and attitude from my ol' man. With nothing more than a heavy gray pack on my shoulders and a worn brown leather guitar case in my hands I was leaving for the last time. As silently as I could, I opened the heavy oak door and set my guitar case on the broken concrete pad just below the single step outside my ol' man's front door. Without hesitation I stepped out of that house and quietly pulled the door shut behind me. I was extra careful to latch it without a single sound, not even the click of the metal bolt as it slid into place against the strike plate. Releasing the breath I had been holding, I let go of the handle, turned away from the door, picked up my guitar case, and walked away from the place I had called home for nearly all of my short eighteen years. With absolutely no intention of ever seeing the inside of its walls again, I took my first steps toward a new life leaving the past and my ol' man behind me.

A windbreaker and a ball cap were all I had to keep me warm on that crisp spring morning. My heavier spring jacket had been accidentally left at my friend Tommy's house the night before, the catalyst of last night's argument with my ol' man, and there was no time to retrieve it. Tommy lived five miles outside of the town limits, three more miles in the opposite direction than I was heading. With only my feet to carry me there, it would simply take far too long to retrieve it. Instead, I shivered a little in that pre-dawn morning chill but I knew it would be short lived as the sun would be up soon. In the meantime, I walked a little faster both to warm my body and to increase the distance between my former home and my new life as quickly as I could.

I had close to $500 cash in my front pocket, money I'd retrieved from a hiding spot in the ceiling of my bedroom closet before I made my final walk toward the door this morning. I had been saving it to buy a new car before I went off to college in the fall. After the way things went last night with my ol' man, another stupid argument that led to yelling, even a shove or two between us before he stormed out and went off to where ever he was hiding these days returning long after I ate dinner and went to bed, alone. It was how most nights went between us but something about the tone in his voice, the force of his last shove before he pulled his hands back and stormed off was the last straw. I knew it was time to go and I no longer cared about a silly car, my feet would get me where I needed to go for now.

The dimly lit morning sky grew brighter with each passing minute and it wasn't long before the once dark shadows I passed along the road side became fuzzy outlines of buildings and then what I could clearly make out as houses, barns, and garages. There were just ten or twenty of them stretched along both sides of the road between my ol' man's house and town. Thompson Station was a pretty small and rural town nestled on the edge of the Pisgah National Forrest northeast of Asheville, NC. My ol' man lived just a couple miles north east of town on a plot of land carved out of what was once a very large mountain farm.

Most of the properties I passed belonged to families whose children had already grown and moved out, or who were so much younger than me that I didn't know the family except by name. The one house I did know was Mr. and Mrs. Johnson's place. Their two story farm house sat way back off the road next to both an old post and beam barn built in the last century and a modern metal sided pole barn. Smoke rising from the chimney of the house was its only sign of life this early in the day. Their place was the last one in the row of houses before the half mile of terrain too rough to farm or build on, which lay between my rural neighborhood and the official limits of Thompson Station.

I had worked for Mr. Johnson last summer, helping him repair the porch roof and rebuild the top of the chimney after a strong July storm had blown a tree across the house. It hadn't been the first time I worked for him, and was where at least $150 of the cash in my pocket had come from. It now looked like it would certainly be my last.

"Thanks for the work Mr. Johnson, guess that'll be the

last I can help you out," I whispered into the chilly morning air as I passed the drive and continued toward town.

You're doing the right thing Marty, you know you are! It's time to get out of this one-horse town, away from that ignorant man, out from under his rule. It's time to be your own man! To Hell with his always telling you you'll never amount to anything unless you do it his way. It's your life, time to live it your way!

I was doing my best to convince myself I would be better off getting out of town for good, going out into the world, and finding my own way. I knew it was time to leave, and that this was the only way it could be done. Talking never worked when it came to the ol' man, not since Mother died at least, and even less since the accident last fall. I knew that leaving without a word was the only way this could be done, and that it would be the final act in our very rocky relationship. Leaving like this would be unforgivable in his eyes, that I was certain of. And honestly, was partly why I chose to do just that! It was the last blow I could strike against a man I felt had wronged me most of my childhood. I was legally a man, but at times it felt good to be a vindictive kid, even in the most subtle of ways.

Chapter 6

A little over two miles and close to 45 minutes after I took the last steps out of my ol' man's driveway, I turned right on Grove Street. It was the last street before entering the downtown area of Thompson Station, if you believed such a thing existed in that place, and would take me to my one and only stop before heading through town for the last time. There was just one set of good-byes I had to make. A few hundred yards down Grove I made another right turn and set my guitar case in the dirt as I reached for the latch of the thick iron gate. This was a two handed job for sure.

The black paint was cracked from years of exposure to the weather and large chunks of it peeled off in my hands as I grabbed hold of the metal rod that held the gate closed. I lifted the L-shaped rod up, freeing it from the hole in the cement that served as a latch, and placed one hand on the crossbar of the gate. Slowly I nudged it forward. The gate was heavy and groaned on its tired hinges as I walked it open just far enough for me to step through before carefully lowering the metal rod to the ground propping it open.

It was early, sun just barely peaking over the mountain tops to the east. The grounds keeper wouldn't be in for another few hours at least but everyone knew the gate was never locked just in case folks wanted to come by when he wasn't around. This was the first I had taken advantage of this opportunity. Fitting I suppose that it would likely also be my last visit here as well. Both a first and a last all at once. How often does that happen in life?

I dusted the paint chips from my hands before picking up my guitar case and stepped through the small opening I had created between the two large gates. I followed the old sand road as it wound its way toward the back side of the cemetery. I wasn't headed all the way back, just to where the road curved sharply to the right to follow a nearby stream that ran along just outside of the fence. It was about halfway back and probably the nicest section of the cemetery. The area was shaded by large hardwoods with open grassy places and had more of a park feeling to it than a garden of tombstones.

It was late spring and the tulips and daffodils planted along the fence were in full bloom as I walked up to pick a few. Normally I would bring roses, it was their favorite flower, but the short notice and early morning timing of my departure made stopping at the florist shop on the edge of town impossible.

"Tulips and daffodils will have to do, just this once," I said to myself as I lowered my guitar case onto the soft sand and gravel road.

I took a few steps toward the colorful fence row and

helped myself to a handful of flowers just beginning to shed the morning dew. There were yellow daffodils and both red and yellow tulips that I divided into two bouquets of about the same size. With one in each hand, I carefully picked up my case using just the tips of my fingers to keep from crushing the delicate flowers. My tennis shoes crunched along the gravel as I followed the road around the sharp corner to the right, then another equally sharp turn to the left before reaching my destination.

Beneath the shade of a tall maple tree sat a white and gray marble bench flanked by two angels carved of stone. I approached slowly, set my case down behind the smooth marble bench, and gently placed the two flower bouquets. I laid one on each side of the stone that sat in front and a little to the right of the bench before slowly standing back so the entire scene was in full view.

"One for each of you this time, so you don't have to share," I whispered as I wiped a tear slowly making its way down my cheek.

"I know it's early today, probably the earliest I've been out of bed in years I admit. I guess that alone should tell you something's up. I don't know if you'll understand this, any of you, but I won't be around for a while. I ... um ... I have to go. It's the right thing to do, and I'm done with school now so there is nothing standing in my way this time.

"I can't live with him anymore! And ... um. Well I guess I just ... I have to get out of this town before it suffocates me."

Turning my back to the stone where I placed the flowers moments ago, I looked to the marble bench now in front of me and continued, "Mother, I know you'll understand that, though Kera and Kylee may have been too young to ever feel the pressures of this little town weighing them down."

The bench had been placed at the foot of Mother's grave to honor her memory. Though I was young when she died I still could remember her saying she didn't want a headstone on her grave. She thought they were too cold and useless. She liked the idea of a bench instead placed where a passerby could stop for a rest, look over the beautiful flowers growing along the fence, or just sit in the shade on a hot summer day to cool off. That was why we had chosen this section of the cemetery, under the shade tree and overlooking the fence row filled with flowers most of spring and summer. My ol' man had arranged to have the bench made by a local sculptor who also carved "In Memory of Elizabeth Marie Taylor" into the top of the seat and both her birth and death year in the pedestals that the two angels flanking the bench stood upon.

Though memorial benches are common in cemeteries now, and even then in other parts of the country, Mother's bench was a first for Thompson Station. Some of the locals thought it was an odd choice, some a practical one, but it was the talk of the town for a bit after it was set in place all those years ago. Now it was one of a half dozen or so in the cemetery.

To my knowledge, Mother's bench was crafted and placed here before my ol' man ever saw it. Since he refused to set foot in this 'garden of stones' as he referred to it, it meant that my ol' man had never seen it at all. Fitting I guess. He refused to attend her visitations, walked out in the middle of her burial service, and hasn't been back there since I'm aware of. It seems only right that he never see the sculpture he commissioned to mark her grave site. At least he managed to do something for her after she died. The bench really was both beautiful and practical, just like Mother.

To the left of Mother's grave was a plot reserved for my ol' man marked only by a cement pad and a small headstone with his name and year of birth. I knew that eventually the task of removing that stone and carving in the year of his death would fall to me, his only living next of kin. After last night, I wasn't sure I wanted that responsibility and didn't care much how quickly the task had to be completed. I'm sure that some small part of me hoped that in time I would change my mind, but for now it remained silent knowing there was no looking back. Right now I wanted nothing more to do with him, ever.

To the right of Mother's grave was the double headstone where I had laid the two bouquets of flowers picked on my way in this morning. It was the final resting place of my two younger sisters, Kera Marie and Kylee Marie. They were identical twins born two years after me and should be getting ready for their final days of tenth grade.

It seemed like just yesterday I tossed them the keys to my car after a football game as we headed our different directions. I had been invited to a party at a friend's house to celebrate our winning season and had chosen to go with my buddies rather than drive my sisters home after the game. I remember their curly blond hair bouncing as they ran to my car and waived back at me while Kera called out, "I promise to keep it under 100!"

God, that was months ago! I can't believe they've been gone seven months already. I can still remember that night like it happened just last night. Hell I even dreamed about it again last night.

"I miss you two twerps! Your stupid cheerleader uniforms always hanging in the bathroom. Your curling irons and blow dryers in my way all the time. I even miss that high pitched squeal of a laugh you had Kylee. Ahh, and those shiny blue eyes Kera. They were always so bright and full of life. Not anymore I guess.

"I wish I could get THAT image out of my head," I said I as squeezed my eyes closed.

I shook my head violently trying to dislodge the image of my younger sister lying on the pavement, her lifeless blue eyes staring up at the night sky. That image had been haunting my dreams since the night of the accident, always popping into my head at the most inconvenient times.

"Someday! Someday I can think of them and not remember the horror of the accident that took them from me. Someday! I hope."

I was talking aloud to myself, convincing myself I was doing the right thing as much as I was trying to explain my actions to my family buried beneath the ground where I now stood. They were what was left of my family, Mother and my two sisters all taken from this world far too soon. Coming here to be near them helped me make peace with it all, and to finish high school like I promised them I would. Now, it was time to let go of that crutch. Time to stand on my own two legs. To walk away from my family, my home, my life, and find a place that felt more like me.

I spent a few more minutes standing quietly in the shade of the tree taking in all that was around me. The smell of the dew covered grass and spring flowers. The chill of the morning air, the gentle breeze swirling what was left of last fall's leaves across the park-like setting. I wanted to remember this moment, this place, and this exact scene forever. I knew this might very well be the last I saw of Thompson Station, and of the memorials for Mother and the twins. From here on out

I would only have my memory to rely on during those days when normally I would come here to feel better, to be closer to them. It would have to be enough.

"... Many places yet to visit, many people yet to know. But in following my dreams, I will live and I will grow, in a world that's waiting out there on the loose. On the loose to climb a mountain, on the loose where I am free, on the loose to live my life the way I think my life should be. For I only have a moment and a whole world yet to see. I'll be looking for tomorrow on the loose," I softly sang as I kissed the fingertips of my right hand and gently placed it over the names Kera Marie Taylor, Kylee Marie Taylor, and Elizabeth Marie Taylor one at a time. It was the second verse to *On the Loose*, a song I had learned years ago at Boy Scout camp one summer, and its theme seemed to fit the scene perfectly.

Still humming the last few bars through the tears now filling my eyes, I picked up my worn guitar case and headed back the same way I had entered the cemetery. This time I did not stop to pick any flowers and in fact, never even looked over in their direction as I made my way back to the iron gate at the main entrance.

Chapter 7

It was shortly after 7:30 when I passed under the large sign mounted over the entrance of the only bank in Thompson Station. A slight shiver ran down my spine when the display changed to the current temperature, a rather chilly 38 degrees. It was late May and a morning temp that low was not normal this late in spring, yet it seemed somehow fitting that my last memory of Thompson Station would fit the profile of a 'cold day in Hell' perfectly. It was a phrase I had heard my ol' man utter repeatedly over the few months that had passed since the accident. When he did, he was almost always referring to the day that I would do something for myself, make a decision about my life's direction, or do whatever was required to reach a single goal.

My ol' man was convinced that I was going nowhere in life. He believed that I would never make a decision and follow through with it or do something he considered 'productive' with my future. To him, productive meant going off to some elite college, taking on an apprenticeship or manual labor gig, or maybe the military. I made it clear to him I was not interested in any of those. So I fed his belief that I had no plans post high school.

This was partly to blame for his belief that I was afraid

to take risks, and at least partly why he thought of me as lazy. Unlike my ol' man, I was an avid reader and also loved to write. That last part he knew nothing about. I mean the kids at school gave me a hard enough time for enjoying writing poetry, essays, heck even term papers. My ol' man, a roughneck who spoke broken English with a Deep South twang in his voice would crucify me for sure. What he did see was me choosing to read books instead of do something more physical or labor intensive with my free time. Even when I would go off on my own for a hike it was always with a book in my hands, or bag. I was, heck still am willing to get my hands dirty and perform manual labor when required. I am by no means lazy as my ol' man believed, but my preference is definitely to work smarter, not harder. And to make time for a good book or two!

By the time he was 16 my ol' man had left home to make a life for himself feeling that he had outgrown the family home. He worked his way into Georgia, then north into TN, east into the Carolina's and eventually into Thompson Station, NC. By then he was just about to turn 19 and had worked his way from sweeping shop floors to running machines in the mill. Not long after, he met and married Mother, bought an old farm house outside of town that needing fixing, and started a family. He had gone places, picked a direction, followed it through, and made a life for himself by working hard. He also never finished high school, something I had just done. I guess finishing that goal wasn't enough for him to get over his belief that I was not doing things with my own life.

What my ol' man seemed to forget is that things had changed a bit since 1969. Back then the average man in North Carolina lived only to the age of 65 after spending much of his life with a 8th grade education working in a furniture factory or out on the family farm. Life was a lot different 27 years later, especially for those who managed to complete high school and planned to do something other than factory or general labor work. Life now required college, or skills training of some sort. I was headed to the former, unbeknownst to my ol' man.

My ol' man claimed he wanted the best for his children. All my life I could remember him telling us to pick a direction and move in it, never look back. He was a strong willed man, set in his ways, and pushed himself and his children hard to be somebody in the world. But, my ol' man and I seemed to have disagreeing views of what 'being somebody' meant. To him, it was finding a job and supporting yourself and your family. To me, it was so much more than that. I wanted to find a place where I was comfortable, could make a decent living, and get an education. More than any of that though, I wanted to do something that made me feel like I made a difference in the world. I wanted to die knowing that I had left the world a better place in some way. I just had no idea how to accomplish that and it drove my ol' man crazier than my lackluster grades in school.

My sisters on the other hand, they were his angels. From the moment they were born my ol' man was wrapped around their fingers. He would have given his life to save theirs, like most parents I suppose, but my ol' man honestly believed that the two of them were destined for greatness. Both Kera and Kylee were more book smart than I and my ol' man never let me forget it. All throughout school he would hound me to get better grades, telling me if I thought I was going to do something with my life besides 'grunt work' I had to pull my grades up, hope I got into college, and studied even harder. As I got older the more he yelled about them, the less I cared. I wasn't dumb. I managed to pass every class while doing the least amount of homework possible. In that respect I guess I was a bit lazy. I knew which teachers would let me get away with the most, and I always managed to pull nothing less than a B- in every class even without really trying. Most of the time I would pass my tests without ever cracking the cover of my text books. I was intelligent for sure, but I wasn't interested in school. Except for English class.

My ol' man, furious about my grades had no idea I was putting in such little effort on my school work, he simply assumed that I was too dumb to pull all A's. He never bothered to ask any of my teachers a single question when he would go in for parent-teacher-conferences. Instead, he would sit for hours talking about his precious Kylee and Kera and what latest AP classes they were taking. He was proud of them, and he had every right to be. They were brilliant at school. Unfortunately for me, it meant I was always third fiddle. I was the only son who was going nowhere in life. After the accident, it only got worse.

He never outright said it but I could tell that he blamed me for their death. And all he was left with now was his disappointment of a son. A son who always preferred to spend time with Mother when he was younger and stepped into her vacancy in the family after her death. A son who raised his younger sisters, took care of them until their last breaths. Hell it was his son who had to set aside his own grief to plan their funerals and pick out their grave markers. My ol' man couldn't even bother to take care of their final arrangements and of course attended neither their visitation, funeral, nor burial services. But then why would he? They were his angels going off to do great things in life ... right up until they died on him.

Sometime in my sophomore year of high school I mentioned I wanted to study either English or Psychology at the University of North Carolina. My ol' man laughed in my face. He told me it was a waste of time to think I could even get into that school and if I did, wanted to know what the hell good a degree in English was in life. I never mentioned it again and my ol' man had no idea that not only had I been accepted at UNC Asheville, I had a two year full tuition scholarship to the English program. It took a simple recommendation from my Junior and Senior English teachers, a short story submission, and an application.

That was it. And, I did it all without uttering a single word about it to my ol' man. As far as he knew now that I was done with school I would just be looking for work around town while I decided what I really wanted to do. He just knew it would be a 'cold day in Hell' before his son got off his ass and did something useful with his life. At least that was what he told me last night. That thought made me laugh out loud as I closed the distance between where I was, and the far edge of town less than four blocks away.

"You're right Ol' Man. It certainly is a cold day in this Hell!" I shouted into the wind on my way out of town.

Chapter 8

Just over a mile outside of town Main Street came to an end at an intersection that locals called 'The T'. Thompson Station was a place where directions were often given to out-of-towners with landmarks and even the most hopelessly lost travelers could easily understand what was meant when they were told to "go straight all the way to The T, then take a right." It just made sense.

When I arrived at The T, I followed those exact directions heading south on Highway 80 walking along the gravel shoulder. 80 was the main highway passing by Thompson Station just to the southeast and led the way to my future, wherever it may be. I walked maybe a mile along 80 while the sun rose above the ridge line and quickly removed the chill from the morning air before stopping for a short break to get more comfortable. Setting my worn leather guitar case down in the gravel as far off the roadway as I could safely get, I dropped my pack on the ground in front of it. I could feel the sweat dripping down my spine and pooling in the small of my back as I carefully sat down on top of the guitar case and began to remove my windbreaker.

"Don't need this anymore! My sweatshirt will be plenty warm now. Feels like it must be close to 40 out by now," I told myself as I packed the windbreaker into its built in storage pouch.

I sat for only a moment or two before tucking the small rectangular pouch that contained my windbreaker securely into the elastic cargo pocket on the front of my pack. I knew I had to keep moving and put as much distance between myself and Thompson Station as I could to avoid my ol' man eventually finding out which direction I had gone. There were only two ways out of Thompson Station, southeast to Highway 80, the route I had taken, and west up the winding mountain road that would eventually get you to NC-16. That route is a climb and downright dangerous to take on foot with all of its blind hairpin curves and switchbacks. Knowing my affinity for hiking and camping, my ol' man might assume that I had headed up that winding mountain pass toward NC-16, especially when he realized my pack was gone from the shelf in the garage. There was a spur trail that connected to the Mountains to Sea Trail (MST) not too far up the road. I had solo hiked it a few times in recent years and my ol' man would likely assume that after our latest blow up I had gone for a trip into the woods and would be back in a week or so after having time to cool off.

However, he may find out the truth much sooner than I would like if someone from town spotted me out here heading in the opposite direction. It was less of a risk this early on a Saturday morning, but still a possibility since Highway 80 was the most common route followed by those who live in Thompson

Station but work in larger communities like Marion, Morgantown, and Asheville.

With a little stronger sense of urgency now that it was quickly becoming daylight and prime commute time I hoisted my pack to my shoulders, snatched my guitar case from the gravel, and headed off toward my new destiny. I managed to put another mile between myself and my past before my pace slowed from a brisk power walk to a casual stroll. Tired from the seven miles I had already walked this early in the day, and wanting to reduce my exposure to those who might recognize me, I finally turned around to face traffic, reached out my right arm toward the road, and stuck up my thumb while continuing to walk backward slowly. I had never hitch hiked before and was well aware of the dangers it could pose but I was tired and figured that it was a greater risk for me to be seen and recognized by someone from town than to accept a ride from a well-meaning stranger heading in the right direction.

Be smart about this Marty! No scary looking dudes driving beater station wagons or pickups. No rides where you are outnumbered either. Maybe you can get lucky and flag down a trucker; they pick up hitchers all the time on television and nothing bad ever seems to happen.

It took about ten minutes of being passed by car after car who never even slowed down before my luck kicked in. I managed to thumb down a big rig with Ontario plates on the front headed south. The scruffy yet friendly driver offered me a ride to his next stop and with little hesitation, I accepted. He was a big burly man with long gray hair pulled back into a tight braid that began at the base of his skull and went on for at least 12 inches. Wearing a camouflage baseball cap and a blue flannel shirt to go with his dirty blue jeans and tattoo covered forearms, he seemed to fit the stereotypical truck driver image I had in my head perfectly.

"Where ya' headed dis time a da mornin' Sunny?"

His accent was thick, so thick I strained to separate the words into a sentence my brain could understand.

"Where am I headed? Nowhere really, just out of town as far as you can take me I guess," I cautiously replied hoping that was in fact the question he had asked me.

"You old 'nuff to be runnin' from home?" the trucker asked.

"Plenty! Graduated high school a few days ago, finally. Now it's time to move on to something better."

Anything is better than living under his roof for another second! Even if it means a cardboard box on a street corner in Asheville, it HAS to be better than with him.

"Well, we're headed south, hope dat works fer ya sunny."

"Works plenty Sir. And, thank you for letting me tag

along for a while," I said as I shrugged off my pack.

"Sure thing. Comp'ny be nice fer a bit."

I passed my pack and guitar case up to the driver who stowed them behind the seats in the 'sleeper cab' of the truck before climbing into the passenger's seat. I wasn't much company. Not long after our journey together began, I fell asleep! When I awoke the sun was fully up over the tree tops and we were pulling into a truck stop for fuel. I had no idea where we were exactly, but I knew it was not Thompson Station and for now, that was all that mattered to me.

"Hey-dare seepy-head! Wakie, wakie! Time ta rise-an-shine, git sum food in yer belly eh?"

I'd woken up just after 4:00, grabbed the bag and case I packed the night before, and left the house with no time for breakfast today. The clock in the dash, just above the CB and radio said it was now just before 9:00 and my stomach was grumbling with the thought of bacon, eggs, and a stack of hotcakes.

YUM! Definitely time to get some food in this tummy! I thought to myself as I gently patted my belly and searched for the door handle near my right knee.

Attached to the fuel station was a hole-in-the-wall diner that reeked of bacon grease from the back of the parking lot. That only fueled my hunger pangs! Walking through the door behind my new trucker friend, whose name I still had not asked, we strolled up to the counter and each took a seat on a worn vinyl covered metal stool. Looking around the mostly empty joint reminded me of a television show I use to watch in re-runs as a kid. All it needed was a cocky sarcastic waitress named Alice.

The wood paneling on the walls began at the floor and stopped about half way up leaving only a cream and gold designed wallpaper straight out of the 1970's. The table tops were white laminate with gold flecks mixed in and were chipped at just about every corner and along most of the almost straight edges. The booths and counter stools were chrome with redish-brown vinyl seats and backs and, in many cases had been repaired with silver duct tape in places where they had obviously split open. Even the floor was a throwback to the 1970's with its alternating black and white checkerboard vinyl tile job that had clearly seen better days.

"You eat here much ... Sir?" I asked my traveling companion.

"Jus bout ever time I'm in dis part a da state. Best bacon-n-eggs you'll ever git."

"Sounds good to me ... Sir. Toss a stack of hot cakes on that plate too and I'll be a happy man," I replied.

"Was dat? Baccon, eggs, n cakes?"

I looked up from my newspaper menu to see a tall blonde waitress standing over me with pencil and paper in hand. She too reminded me of that show I use to watch, but her hair was curly blonde and pulled up in a tight pony tail on the top of her head. Her silvery blue eyes reminded me of Kylee instantly.

"Um, yeah bacon, scrambled eggs, and hot cakes, please. Ma'am."

"You betcha' cutie, and for you Bob? The usual again?"

Bob, is that his real name? Better find out soon, I don't suppose I can get away with calling him Sir for too much longer.

"Usual be jus fine sugar. And bring my partner here some a that coffee, looks like he'd use some eh?"

"One special wit cakes, one usual, and two black coffee's comin' right up," she shouted toward the opening in the kitchen wall and turned on her heels to fill our cups.

I wasn't much of a coffee drinker up to this point in my life, but since this was the first day of my new life, my life in the real world, I was game to take a risk on my beverage choice. I had finally done what my ol' man was certain I was incapable of, making a decision and seeing it through. I was on my way to becoming my own man and in my past life, men drank coffee.

Chapter 9

Breakfast arrived and was eaten in silence, except for the clinking of dishes from the kitchen and the roar of the diesel engines outside the diner. So far it seemed that my traveling companion was a man of few words, something I greatly appreciated today. While we ate, my head was filled with doubts, what-ifs, and thoughts I dare not repeat here. Suffice it to say that I was both excited and scared to be out on my own in a world I knew little about. I had been born and raised not far from a major city and yet had no recollection of ever going there except for one or two school field trips many years ago. Now I was headed to that city in the fall for college, at least that was the plan for now, and had no idea where I would find myself over the next few hours let alone days between now and then. I was as lost as you can get with absolutely no safety net to catch me should I make a wrong move. And yet I was also the happiest I had been in months!

My decision to leave Thompson Station had come quickly, too quickly maybe, but it had been made and I was already far too invested in its outcome turn back now. For the first time in my life I was standing on my own two feet out from under the shadow of my ol' man. Though inside I was absolutely terrified I still intended to keep moving forward into whatever new life awaited me. I knew the cash in my pocket wouldn't get me very far and that eventually I would have to find someplace to settle for a bit and figure a way to earn a living. I had a place to go in the fall, if I chose to, but it was still spring and the whole summer lay before me now. An entire summer of possibilities and decisions to be made.

So you left home, now what Marty? Where are you headed? Could go look up Mikey in Tennessee. Spent so many years writing letters to him after that summer at camp I know the address by heart. Could head out west, maybe be a bum on some beach in southern California. Isn't that what everybody does when they run away from home? Run away, is that what this is? Am I running from –

"Hey there Slim, ya'll done wit the chow?" the deep voice of my new trucker friend interrupted my internal debate and dropped me back into reality. There was a moment of silence between us while my brain processed his question. Then, "Uh ... Yes Sir. Couldn't eat another bite," I replied as I slid the plate forward on the counter.

"Guessin' we'd best be hittin' the road then Slim, eh? Headed south to I-40 an west to Asheville fer the next load. If'n ya' wanna tag long wit me that is."

"Got no place else to be right now Sir. I would love to keep you company for a bit, at least into Asheville," I replied. It was true, I had no place else to be and Asheville was at least in the right direction for me.

We made a quick stop at the register on our way out the door to pay the bill, all $8.25 of it, and headed back to the truck waiting in the back of the parking lot. I climbed back into the passenger's seat of the large cab while Bob walked around to the driver's side and climbed up into his seat. Bob, that was in fact his name. I learned that on our way back to the truck when another driver waved and called out, "Hey Bob, catch ya' next run!" from the window of his truck.

Bob, plain but fitting I suppose. Rolls of the tongue easy enough. Sort of like Marty instead of Martin like Mother always used to call me. Nobody's called me Martin in a long time. Nobody gets to use that name. Last time I let my ol' man get away with it I was 8. Nobody has ever tried since, well not more than once anyway.

It wasn't long before Bob and I were back on the road again headed south to I-40. I had learned from the short conversation before breakfast that he had been up in Wilkesboro last night picking up part of his load and used this road as a shortcut to pick up I-40 just so that he could stop at the diner for breakfast. He ran this route about once a month and every time he did, he managed to be at that diner around 9 or 9:30 for breakfast. Having just eaten there, I could understand why he would take a little longer on his run to hit that diner for a meal. The food was excellent!

"So what's yer' name there Slim? Don't believe ya ever did tell me for ya' fell sleep."

"Martin, but everybody calls me Marty," I replied

"Well nice ta meet ya' there Marty. Marty, that's a good name fer a strappin' youngin like yerself. Bet Yer mamma picked it out for ya'. Eah? My Pa named me Robert, too formal fer me. That why I jus go by Bob. Everbody kin member Bob."

"Ya' I suppose it's an easy one to remember. And, yes Mother named me Martin. Martin Joeseph, middle name is the same as my ol' man's. I was the first, only son. I guess she wanted to be sure somebody carried on his name for him, or maybe she just liked it I suppose. She died before I ever thought to ask," I replied. I was rambling, talking out loud more to myself than to Bob and the truck was eerily silent when I stopped.

Minutes went by before Bob said another word. I think he was surprised at the ease with which I talked of Mother's death. Finally, he managed just a simple "Sorry to hear 'bout yer Mom Marty. Too young ta' have to deal with that stuff."

I decided to let it go with a simple, "Thank you. I've had a few years to cope with it by now," and hope he didn't ask too many questions about it. Mother's death was still painful after all these years and knowing I had just walked away from the only place I could be close to her was already bringing a tear or two to the surface. Lucky for me, Bob was as uncomfortable asking about the subject as I was, or maybe he sensed how much I didn't want to talk about it in the tone of my reply. He drove the big rig on in silence and in all the time we spent together over the next few days, never once brought it up again.

I appreciated that more than you can imagine. I had been young, and it had been a long time ago, but it was a wound that had never healed. So much of my childhood had ended the day she died and though every child who loses a parent is changed by the experience, the loss, not all are changed so drastically by the fallout from the death. I was forced to grow up quickly, to care for my young sisters. It took a small distance between my ol' man and me and turned it into a chasm so deep it appeared to grow wider with each day that passed. Yes so much of my life changed with her passing that I can't imagine what kind of man I would have become had it not happened. It certainly would have been different, that's for sure.

Chapter 10

The remainder of my time with Bob was filled with pleasant conversation that steered clear of any mention of Mother, or death. I learned that Bob was 46, had been a truck driver with the same freight company for the last 22 years, and loved the freedom of setting his own schedule. He traveled mostly across the southern United States on his routes but on occasion, would take a run to Colorado, Maine, or Oregon allowing him a chance to see the entire country at one time or another. In fact, the only states he had not yet been to were Hawaii, and Rhode Island. He'd even been to Alaska a few times, but I guess that's not so surprising for a Canadian born truck driver who works for a Canadian based freight company. I always did wonder why Alaska belonged to the United States when it was surrounded by ocean and Canada. I'm sure they taught that back in high school geography once upon a time but I must not have been paying attention that day. All I remember is that we got the land cheap and some guy named Seward was involved.

While Bob was more or less an open book, I was a little more reserved with my story sharing only what I knew wouldn't reveal too much about me, where I was from, or why I had been hitch hiking along the shoulder of Highway 80. I told Bob that I had just graduated from high school and was bound for college in the fall. I decided against telling him where I had graduated from or what school I had been accepted to. I told him I had made the decision to leave home and stand on my own two feet, a quality he respected having joined the military at 18 for the very same reason. We discussed the fact that I was not cut out for military service, though I respected those who made that decision and appreciated all that they did for the country as a whole.

Bob shared some stories form his time in the Canadian Army and I listened intently. I had heard similar stories from my ol' man growing up, he too was in the military at one point but not because it was a choice he had made. My ol' man had been drafted in January of 1971 at the age of 18 less than a week after the now infamous invasion of Laos by the South Vietnamese, under heavy support of US troops, began. With hundreds of soldiers being killed almost daily, the Army was still drafting heavily to maintain their ranks and by March of that same year, my ol' man was stationed somewhere in the jungles of South Vietnam with an infantry unit attached to the 101st Airborne Division. I remember some of his stories about time he spent with the Vietnamese people, the friendships he made over there, and what little good he could find while in a war torn country for just shy of a year of his life. I know there were bad things that happened to him, that he lost many friends and came home scarred from wounds both physical and emotional. I had also learned about the mental scars that tend to haunt soldiers long after their war experiences are over in a high school psychology class and wondered if that might be partly to blame for the ol' man's temper from time to time. I know that he saw more death in that short eleven and a half months than most people see in a life time. Deep inside I know it was to blame for the way he handled deaths in our family, but I never believed it was a valid excuse to abandon us. I guess I just don't think there ever is a good enough reason to do that.

My ol' man stopped talking about his experiences during the war not long before Mother died. It was about the same time she began to visit the doctor's office more frequently. After her death he would become enraged if any of us asked him to tell some of our favorite stories about the Army. I often wondered why, but I knew better than to ask. My ol' man's temper had resulted in many incidents of his hand meeting my face rather harshly over the years. I learned to keep my mouth shut most of the time rather than light his fuse. I understood not wanting to talk about the bad stuff, but there were fun stories from his time there. Funny stories of culture differences and misunderstandings, birthdays he helped to celebrate, meals he shared with local friends, even a baby he helped to bring into the world and his grateful parents who spoke no English but thanked him and his buddy with hand carved Buddha statues. My ol' man still had his gathering dust on the mantle. I suspect he forgot it was there or it would have been destroyed in one of his fits of rage over the years like so many other things in that house.

My ol' man was full of rage after Mother's death and for that I could not blame him. Abandoning his family though, now that I could, and I did. I still remember watching him walk out of Mother's service. He never once stopped to look back, just kept his head down and maintained a steady pace as he walked away from our family.

In so many ways, that was the day he walked out of my life! That's the first time I remember hating him, truly hating him! He left me there to take care of Kera and Kylee, then all but disappeared from our lives right after. Always working, never around for anything. I had to finish raising those two myself. So much for being a father!

There were frequent lulls in the conversation between Bob and I. It was obvious that we were both hiding things, or at least wondering how much we could safely say to the other without opening up a huge can of worms to explain. I respected his privacy and appreciated that he too respected mine. It seemed that whenever the cab of the truck would get too quiet, Bob would come up with another story to tell or a series of questions he felt safe in asking. Each one brought me out of my shell just a little more. It was the first time I could remember since Boy Scout camp, back when I was a kid, where I actually had to get to know someone new.

I never was very good at this!

Growing up in Thompson Station, population 983 meant that I didn't have to get to know many new people in my life. I had been in school with mostly the same group of kids since the early days of elementary school, had lived next to the same people my entire life, and could only think of a few times in recent memory where someone new moved to town. More often than not, people were moving out of Thompson Station rather than into the sleepy little hole in the map. Our main industry was the mill and furniture factory just outside of town and it wasn't exactly a growth sector. Every once in a while a family would move to the area because someone had gotten a job in one of the larger cities in the area and they wanted to live in a smaller town. That was typical of many families in Thompson Station actually, living there because it was smaller while they worked someplace else. I guess that sort of makes it what they call a "bedroom community", I just called it boring.

Chapter 11

The last time I saw Bob he was sound asleep in the bunk likely dreaming of chasing his old hunting dog Champ down some two-track on an epic coon hunt. Of all the things we had talked about in our time together, that was the one story I enjoyed the most, and yet hated at the same time. It reminded me a little too much of just how unhappy my life had been over the last few years, and how much I missed some of the simpler joys in life like a good hike or fishing trip.

I had been riding with Bob for nearly a week by then along his route into Asheville and beyond. We traveled further south to Greenville, SC, the northern parts of the Atlanta, GA metro, back up north to both Chattanooga and Knoxville, TN and eventually headed back east toward Asheville again. Bob's next stop was back to the beginning of his route and would take him very near the place he picked me up outside of Thompson Station. The further we drove in that direction, the more agitated and withdrawn I became. I could feel a deep sense of dread growing in the pit of my stomach with each passing mile and found it almost impossible to sit still inside the cab of that truck. At one point, I nearly rolled down the window of that big rig and launched myself through it at full highway speeds just to keep from getting any closer to the past I was determined to leave behind. Clearly I came to my senses before doing something that drastic.

We stopped for a late dinner, it was sometime after 10 o'clock, and some shut eye just east of Asheville at one of the diners we visited on our way west. When I realized it was the diner where Bob and I had our very first meal together, a wonderful breakfast just a few hours after I first hitched a ride with him, I knew the time to part ways with Bob had arrived. We were far closer to my home town than I realized and I could not risk getting any closer. I had been gone long enough for even my ol' man to become suspicious, possibly even concerned about why I had been gone for so long. I needed to keep my distance now more than ever. In time they would forget about me, stop wondering where I had gone, maybe accept that I was an adult now and out on my own. For now though, I was likely a missing person, someone that even the police would recognize on sight and want to take me back to that place.

Uncertain of how to say 'thank you' and 'good bye' to a man I had only begun to get to know yet felt like I had known much longer than 6 days made me quieter than even old Bob had become accustomed to. Rather than asking questions to attempt to draw me out, he decided to leave well enough alone and we ate mostly in silence before retiring to the cab. Now that I look back on it, maybe he knew it was the end of the road for us as well and wasn't certain how to say 'good bye' either.

I crawled into my space in the front seat while Bob stretched out on the rack in the extended cab of his truck. We had done this every night since the beginning of this journey. The seat was not the most comfortable bed I had ever claimed, but that was exactly the reason it was my place and not Bob's. It was only fair that he get the best sleeping quarters since it was his truck and he needed the rest far more than I. Though his bunk could have fit two of us at one time, it was somewhere between a full and twin sized mattress, it was not a place either of us felt comfortable sharing. I was fine with the front seat rather than up close and personal with Bob, a nice guy but not someone I would ever claim to know very well. I think he likely felt the same though I never bothered to ask.

That last night in the truck I settled in, feet and legs spread across to the driver's seat and my head propped against frame around the passenger's door. Unlike previous nights though, I had placed my guitar case on the floor in the front seat and my backpack on top of it instead of leaving the pack behind the seat. I didn't think that Bob had noticed the change, he never mentioned it aloud at least, but thinking back on it now he may have. I was quick to quiet down hoping Bob would believe I was already fast asleep and drift off himself. I didn't have to wait too long, maybe 30 minutes before I heard his breathing change from a soft inhale/exhale pattern to a raspy snore that grew in volume with each breath. Certain he was now fast asleep, I pulled out the napkin and pen I swiped from the counter on our way out of the diner after dinner and began to pen a simple note.

```
Thanks for the ride but I think this
is my stop.
Stay safe!
Marty
```

I gently pulled back on the silver square handle of the passenger's door freeing the latch and pushing it open just enough for me to exit the cab. The engine was still running. Like most truckers Bob left it run while he slept to keep the batteries charged and the cab warm or cool depending on the weather. The noise from the engine masked any little noises I made in my exit as I hopped down to the pavement, grabbed my pack and guitar case, and left the note I had just penned in my empty place.

I am not a man of many regrets, but not finding some way to remain in contact with Bob is one of them. He was a good man. He offered me a ride when I was desperate for one, allowed me to share the cab of his truck for more than a thousand miles over the course of those couple days, and gave me some much needed time to settle on a direction for my life to wander off in. Our conversations had been brief in the grand scheme of things but they still felt like he was a man I could have spent many good times with if we'd had the chance.

I didn't realize it at the time to be honest, but the

moment he decided to pull over and offer me a ride was likely more significant a turning point in the direction my life would take than the day I decided to pack my bag and head out of Thompson Station forever. After all he had set in motion a chain of events that would change me forever, nudging my future into place with a simple random act of kindness.

Life can be funny that way. You think you are your own person, making your own choices in where to go, what to do, even who to befriend. You make plans and even act on them thinking you are the master of your own destiny. But, life has taught me over the years that while we do exercise free will over our course and destiny, often it is someone or something else that presents choices directing our course. I kicked the ball into motion by leaving my ol' man that day. When Bob stopped to pick me up along that highway he nudged it toward a new track. His usual breakfast stop, the diner that would also be the last place I saw Bob, would prove to be another crossroads in my life where a choice I was presented with would forever alter my future. I made the decisions, but the choices were put there for me pick from for a reason.

There are many more examples of seemingly random acts turning out to be major players in the direction life would take me. Far too many for me to continue believing that I alone make the choices of where my life will go. I am but the choice maker, someone, or thing provides the opportunities for me to make those choices.

Chapter 12

With nowhere to really be and honestly, nowhere to go, I spent the next hours of that lonely night tucked into a corner booth inside the diner while Bob slept in his truck. Luckily the diner was a 24 hour operation, had light customer traffic, and even lighter staff to cover the overnight shift. The waitress stopped by once in a while to be sure I still didn't want anything to eat or drink but seemed content to go about her business and forget I was simply taking up space. As a truck stop sort of place I guess they were used to people hanging out for hours on end without ordering anything from the menu.

I managed a few short naps with my head propped against the high seat-back of the booth, my feet resting on top of my guitar case tucked under the table sometime after 2 o'clock. When my eyes opened for the last time just after 5 o'clock, I quickly realized the sun was slowly beginning to light the eastern sky though I was by no means rested! As a teenage boy I was used to going a few days with little to no sleep and still being able to function, or at least muddle through my days semi alert and energetic. This skill would be put to use for sure as I gathered my things from the booth and headed for the door.

Knowing I shouldn't be in sight when Bob awoke, he

seemed like the kind of guy to come looking for me thinking I might be in some trouble, I quietly ducked out of the diner shortly after the sun began to rise above the peaks of the eastern ridge. I knew where Bob was headed and truth be told, since we had crossed the state line into North Carolina yesterday afternoon, I could feel something begin to weigh me down again. It started simple enough, a tightening in my chest that made my breath catch a time or two. It rapidly grew into a sense of dread getting stronger mile by mile as we continued east. By the time we hit Asheville I knew I had to begin putting distance between me and Thompson Station again. That place was suffocating me before I left and finally breaking free from it felt better than I had dreamed it ever could. As Bob and I drove closer to my past life, the deeper I felt that growing oppression and dread, like a dark hole in the pit of my stomach slowly consuming me from the inside. It was clear that distance was what I now required and Bob was simply headed the wrong direction now.

As the sun began to spill its orange light through the broken clouds, I ducked into a small wooded area that lined the parking lot. It provided a space where I was out of sight but could still see Bob's truck. Almost on cue, the driver's door to his truck opened at nearly the same time the sun spilled just enough light through the trees to bathe the parking lot in a warm orange glow. Day was breaking and the trucks needed to hit the road again. I couldn't see him well, mostly just a dark silhouette, but I could see him with a small piece of something in his hand. My note I assumed. He looked around, maybe a bit confused and walked into the diner returning only a few minutes later. He didn't have the object with him this time, but climbed into his rig and pulled out headed east toward his next stop without me.

I was in the clear. Now out on my own, out from under my ol' man's thumb, and starving! I checked my pocket to be sure I had remembered my wallet when I left Bob's truck and headed into the diner for some breakfast. It really was the best eggs-n-cakes I'd had in a long time.

"Back so soon there Sonny?" the breakfast shift waitress called to me as I entered

"Got no place to be, thought breakfast sounded like a good plan Ma'am."

"Sho is! Yer buddy Bob left this fer ya' Have a sit I'll get that chow ordered up."

Handing me what looked to be a folded napkin she turned toward the kitchen pass and ordered up two hotcakes, two eggs sunny-side up, bacon, and toast. It was 'The Usual' Bob ordered every time he stopped by here no matter the time of day.

Bob never got his breakfast today. He loves this place. It's time for breakfast. Why did he leave without eating?

I wondered to myself as I began to slowly unfold what I now realized was the same napkin I had left for Bob on the seat of the truck. Written below my words I read this:

```
Marty,
Was a pleasure to spend these last
few days with you. Hope you find what
you're looking for out there. I stop
by here every couple weeks, maybe
we can have us a sit down and some
breakfast someday. First one is on
me.
Bob
```

"Came in here looking for ya'. Told him you'd split a few minutes after my shift started. Night Girl said ya' spent the night in that booth over yonder," the waitress explained and I folded up the note and tucked it into my back pocket.

"Ol' Bob, he's a good one. Paid for your breakfast when he left that figuring' you'd be back in I guess."

"He is a good one for sure Ma'am. I think I'm going to miss him."

"Where ya' headed to now? Anyplace special?"

Anyplace away from Thompson Station! Direction doesn't matter, just miles from there!

"No Ma'am. Got no place in mind. Just someplace further west I guess. Suppose to be up at NC State end of August."

"Ahh a college bound youngin'. Good fer you. Betcha do well up there. If you looking fer work dis summer I could put in a word wit old Chester, he own dis joint. He always looking fer night cooks."

I can't stay here, it's too close! Got to get more distance behind me. But a job would be good. I can only walk so far, and hitchin' ain't the safest way to travel. Not every trucker is like Bob.

"Thank you Ma'am I appreciate that but I think I am headed further west for now. Maybe if I make it back this way."

"Well how you wit kids? My brother-in-law knows a guy always looking fer help up at his kids camp. Place about 20 miles up the mountain from here. A'int California if that what ya' was thinking fer west, but it sho is right pretty up there," she said handing me a bright orange piece of paper seeking applications for Camp Adohi.

"Seeking summer staff, June to mid-August for Camp Ah-do-hi –"

"Ah-doe-hee child! It's Cherokee for timber or woods I think," she corrected me.

"Camp Adohi. All positions include room and board and weekly pay. Sounds nice. I could use a place to stay. I'll think about it Ma'am," I said as I sat the flyer down on the counter and slid it back toward her.

"You keep that. Got me plenty more," she said sliding it back across the counter at me and pointed to a stack near the beverage center behind her.

Camp staff? Can I really be camp staff? I guess I could be qualified to work maintenance or something. Lord knows I can't cook and probably am not fit to be around kids who would look up to me and do whatever I asked them to. Hell, I doubt I have the patience for them anyway. Though I did raise the twins on my own mostly, and they turned out okay.

Kera, Kylee, I miss you two knuckleheads so much!

Stop, no tears here!

So Camp, maybe I could be a lifeguard or something. I think my certification is still good.

Finishing my breakfast in silence I was deep in thought. Since leaving Thompson Station I had worked very hard to keep my past from invading my present but as I sat there eating my eggs, images from my days spent at summer camp, and from picking the twins up from their weeks there every summer kept creeping into my head. I made my best friends there as a child. Maybe being a part of that for somebody else was not such a crazy thought. I did need a job, and a place to stay until I could move into my dorm in August. I had left with some money in my pocket but knew from day one it would not be not nearly enough to get me through the summer let alone the upcoming year of school where the essentials were covered but nothing else.

Maybe I'll head into Asheville and see about a place to stay for a few days. See what work I can scrape up. Might be something else to keep me busy for the summer.

Chapter 13

I'm not certain I remember much of my trip into Asheville other than it was a long walk. I opted to travel the 6 or so miles completely on foot, and even turned down a couple of rides offered by passersby. It just felt like the right thing to do, to be totally on my own as I charted a new way forward. It also gave me a chance to think more about what I should do next. I knew I needed a place to stay, and that the streets were a bad idea. I had enough cash on me to afford a few days in a cheap motel, maybe as much as a week or so if I went really cheap, but I had to eat too. With no skills to speak of, no references, no job history I was willing to give, I knew it would be tough to secure much for employment. I also really doubted a camp for kids would touch me if I had no address, or references. They tended to be a little more selective in hiring staff than some 18 year old kid off the streets who was mostly looking for a place to sleep and a little cash on the side.

Let's face it Marty, you are screwed! Who is going to hire you? Maybe you should take that nice waitress up on her offer to work the diner. It would solve one problem at least. Maybe it would pay enough for a room to rent in the area.

It was late afternoon when I finally reached the edge of Asheville and began to look for Help Wanted signs in windows. For each one I saw, I walked in carrying everything I owned in the pack on my back and spoke with someone about filling their opening. Everyone gave me the same reaction. They wanted prior job history, an address, a reference, something to prove I was more than just some kid who claimed to be not running from the law hoping to start life over in a new city.

The most positive thing I got out of that afternoon was a flyer for an open mic night where I could play for tips and a lead on an elderly lady who had a room to rent. That tip came from a local church looking for help mowing the lawn. It turned out to be a non-paying gig I landed, mowing their lawn, but the pastor gave me the name and number for someone he thought could help me out with a place to rent cheap. Both the open mic gig and the home of Beverly, the lady who had the room for rent, were over near the UNC campus, a solid 5 miles from my current location and further than I was willing to walk on a hunch. I set out in search of some place to eat cheap, take a rest, and maybe find one of the last functioning pay phones in the state to make a call.

Life on your own at 18 is not an easy thing to pull off. This was quickly becoming very clear to me and yet each challenge gave me more resolve to make it work and prove my ol' man wrong. I was an adult, I was a hard worker when I needed to be, and I would find a way to make it work. I had to.

Chapter 14

By the end of the third week after walking out of Thompson Station things had finally begun to look up. I'd been able to see parts of the country with Bob I had only heard about on the news. After parting ways with him, I'd managed to secure short term housing on a week by week basis, in exchange for a little money and odd jobs around the house to help out the lady renting me the room. I cooked her meals, and managed to not burn them too terribly, cleaned up the kitchen, kept the yard mowed, and did other handyman type things for her and her neighbors as needed.

She was very nice. She was also old enough to be my grandmother had she lived long enough for me to even meet, and didn't ask too many questions. The situation worked for now, but I knew it was temporary. I think she would have liked me to stay on. She seemed to enjoy the company and the help, but I had plans to head off to college in late August. It also looked like I might have summer employment at Camp Adohi after a one on one meeting I would not exactly call a job interview with the camp director David James.

Having little luck finding work around town that would pay more than just tips, I decided to take a risk and attend the hiring event for Camp Adohi. I filled out the application on the back of the flyer the waitress at the diner gave me. I did leave some key areas blank though. For employment history and reference I listed my current landlord. She was as good as anything I had and I knew would speak highly of my work. She didn't seem like the type to speak ill of someone in hopes of dashing their possibility for future employment. At least I hoped not.

Dressed in my best shirt, only tie, and a pair of khaki cargo pants that would have to pass as dress pants, I arrived early for the event. I was the first person in line when they were ready to begin going over the applications. In fact, I was so early it was the director himself who took my application. He smiled wide as he took it from my hand and said "So I see you know Julie," with an odd mix of southern drawl and an accent I could not place immediately but involved elongating his 'o's.

"Julie Sir?"

"Tall, blonde, thin as a rail with a strong Mississippi drawl. She's a waitress at a diner out on Highway 80," he explained.

The waitress!

"Oh! Yes, Julie. She's the one who gave me that application, Sir. Said she hands them out to anyone she thinks would be a good fit."

Way to drop that in there Marty. Maybe it can help that she handpicked me for a job here. Can't hurt, right?

"She does have an eye for the right qualities in my staff. I'll give her that. Never steered me wrong. Not once ever. What kind of work are you looking for Son?"

"Well Sir, I am pretty flexible there. I recently discovered I can cook without burning things, though being outside in the sunshine is probably more preferable. I am handy, can fix things. I am, or was, a lifeguard. I think that certification may have expired. But I could re-certify easy enough."

Marty SHUT UP! He asked a simple question, give a simple answer. You talk too much when you are nervous.

"Good enough. I need all of those for sure, but kitchen staff and maintenance workers are easy enough to come by. All my counselors need to be lifeguards. How do you feel about working with the kids?"

Kids? I like kids, but is a wandering 18 year old with no direction who has actually thought about not going to college in the fall even though it is fully paid for a good influence on kids? I bet their parents might not think so. Especially if they found out that I just left my only living family behind without a word of good bye and never intend to see him again as long as either of us is breathing. Let's be honest here Marty, you're a runaway and no parent wants a runaway in charge of their kids!

"Yes Sir. Kids. I helped to raise my two younger sisters since they were about 6 when my mother passed. I had to step in and be mother and father for them. Long story. But I am good with kids. Very willing to work with them this summer."

There you go saying too much again!

"Good. How old are they now? Proud of their big brother out making his way in the world I suppose. Says here you are headed to UNC here in the fall. What is it you plan to study?"

"English, Sir. Not certain what I will do with it yet but thanks to a couple English teachers I managed to land a scholarship to UNC so I can even make it to college. I always was good at English, the writing part of it anyway. Maybe someday I will teach it, or write a famous novel."

"Kid with a dream. I relate well to that," he replied with that contagious wide smile across his face. It wasn't one of those laughing silently at me smiles, more of a proud smile of remembrance or approval of my choice.

I spent the better part of an hour talking to him. In that time I learned it was his camp, his name was David James which seemed odd to me. He had no middle name or initial and both his first and last name were typical first names. He was a man with two first names. Maybe it was a custom where he was from which I also learned was Burlington up in Vermont. That helped to explain his long 'o' and 'a' sounds. He had set off on his own shortly after high school and walked his way south along the Long Trail and Appalachian Trail. As he made his way south toward Georgia he fell in love with the mountains of North Carolina and decided to stay. He was a true adventurer at heart and on some level I connected with him in those moments. His passion was spreading knowledge and self-reliance and his camp was the perfect way to reach that next generation. He spoke with an ease and tone that made people want to listen, made them stop and take notice. I hoped I would get the chance to know him better.

Chapter 15

On a chilly morning, the last morning of May 1996 to be exact, I finished packing all my belongings into my backpack and guitar case. I turned the key to my short term room over to the landlord and headed a few blocks away to the bus station where I would meet the man with two first names, David James for a ride up to Camp Adohi.

Pre-camp training didn't start for another week but I had been asked to come up early and help with a few maintenance things when he called the number I had given on my application to let me know he was holding a position for me. I still didn't know exactly what position I would hold for the summer, one of those questions I forgot to ask on the phone in my excitement of a job offer I guess. It honestly didn't matter what it was though. What did matter was that I had managed to secure work, work that would pay more than just a place to eat and sleep, and that would also provide a place to stay for the entire summer.

Being a kid out on my own with no place to go, no way to make money, and nothing to do with my days was not in my future. College was, for now at least. Though my education and living expenses were covered for the first two years at UNC Asheville, I still needed money for supplies, entertainment, and incidentals.

The $500 I left home with a few weeks ago was now more like $200 and even if I managed to not spend any more of it for the summer, it would not last more than a week or two once I began classes in the fall. Money isn't everything in life, but it is a requirement to live in society these days.

"Hey there Martin!" David James shouted from across the parking lot nearest the bus departure terminal.

I tried not to seem too eager, or reserved as I smiled and waved to let him know I'd heard him before I began to walk in his direction. I was excited, fearful, and a bit annoyed by the use of my full name, calling me by my full name definitely needed to stop, but I was also oddly at ease with the thought of spending the next week alone in the woods with David James helping to get Camp Adohi ready for the summer to begin. I was now a runaway with a purpose at least!

"This all you got for the summer?" the man with two first names asked as I took the backpack from my shoulders and placed it into the bed of his red and white Ford pickup truck alongside my worn guitar case.

"Yes Sir. It is everything I currently own. Long story. But I think it is everything I need for now."

Everything I currently own? Way to go Marty, tip him off that you are a runaway. Make him think twice about hiring you to work with kids. Moron!

"Runaway or orphan Martin?" he asked unfazed by my admission that everything I owned in the world was inside that pack and case.

"It's Marty, Sir and a little of both I guess. Mother and sisters are all passed. Not much left to call home or family though my ol' man still lives back in the little town I grew up in," I attempted to explain with as little emotion, good or bad, as possible. I hoped my hatred for the ol' man didn't show any more than the still raw emotions for my lost mother and the twins.

"Did I ever tell you how I came to be here in North Carolina Martin?"

What is with this guy? Nobody calls me Martin anymore. Not since Mother died.

"Marty. You hiked south on the Appalachian, Sir."

"That I did Martin –"

"– Marty."

"I Graduated high school and wanted to get out into the world. I packed everything I called my own into a pack like this and headed out on foot. I wasn't running from anyone or thing, but I sure wasn't sticking round any longer than I had to. Know what I mean Son?" he said as he slapped me on the shoulder and squeezed just a bit.

It was a gesture I had seen fathers do to their sons over

the years. My ol' man never once did it to me I could recall. Had he tried it in the last few years he would have found himself flat on the ground anyway.

My ol' man hadn't come close to touching me in nearly three years. Not since the last time he tried to get a point across while he was less than sober and it resulted in violence. Now don't get me wrong, my ol' man was not an abusive asshole like some fathers out there. He used physical punishment to get a point across when I was young, and it worked. That one night he'd had a little too much to drink from his favorite adult beverage. When I refused to listen to him tell me how to do something his way, he reached out in anger, blinded by the alcohol, and I defended myself. Well, I might add. It never happened again. It was partly because I never let him close enough to make another mistake like that and partly because he avoided me more than usual after that night. I suspect out of shame, or maybe I just hoped that was the reason. He should have been ashamed for how he handled himself.

All I could offer in response to David James question was a smile and slow nod of my head in respect. He somehow knew what I thought I was hiding, and I think maybe he respected me for setting out on my own like I had. Not many people would understand it let alone respect it. It was something I was prepared to hide for the summer, maybe the rest of my life if I had to, but definitely had no intention of telling my new boss I was a runaway. Yet, here he knew it all along and respected me for it. It was at that moment I knew there was something special about the man with two first names and that this was only the beginning of our friendship.

Chapter 16

The ride up to Camp Adohi took about 45 minutes along a winding mountain road that led us up, along, and over mountain ridges and deep into the forest. It was beautiful country, more beautiful than I think I had ever seen. I had traveled around a bit as a kid on camping trips with friends and for a short stint in the Boy Scouts. I had seen things along the road with Bob through the windshield of his big rig. But I had never seen things this beautiful or peaceful that I could recall. Early summer rains filled flowing mountain streams creating roadside cascades that would disappear as quickly as they were created once the stream levels dropped. Wildflowers were still in bloom, trees fully covered with leaves and foraging wildlife. There were even encounters with deer, turtles, and a quickly moving grey fox. Everything was perfect, and free.

I don't recall exactly what David James and I spoke about on the trip, thought I do remember it was not silent for long. I recall him telling me more of his adventures south bound from Vermont along the Appalachian Trail and asking me questions about what I was looking forward to over the summer. I also know he never did ask about my past. I think he understood that it was not something I wished to talk about nor was it very relevant to the present. He knew that I had left it behind me, or at least I hoped I had, and that was that.

It struck me as odd that this man, someone whom I had more or less just met and knew nearly nothing about me personally, had agreed to both hire me for the summer and give me a place to stay for the next couple weeks while I helped him to get camp ready for the summer. It also occurred to me that perhaps I was walking into some sort of danger placing so much trust in someone I had just met and knew very little of. Those fears were quickly dismissed by the very natural, caring demeanor of David James. He was unlike anyone I had met thus far in my life and his caring and trustworthiness was obvious to me, even from a distance.

Some people have an unconditional trust and sense of ease when they encounter a 'man of the cloth'. I'm not one of them, a 'man of the cloth' or someone who feels that trust and ease around them. I consider myself a Christian of course, and I believe some of what I was taught in Bible classes as a child. However, I detest religion and honestly don't trust many preachers these days. Maybe it's due to all the scammers, or the ones who use the pulpit to spread fear and hate. I don't know, but I do know that with David James I feel that sense of ease and unconditional trust. Something I'll never explain well, but a fact none the less.

I came to learn over the course of the next few weeks that David James was also a very well educated man who not only stocked authors like John Steinbeck, Dickenson, Faulkner, Hawthorn, Salinger, and Thoreau in the camp library, but also King, Koontz, Straub, and even a few Danielle Steel. I never asked if he had read those Steel books, but I do know that he had read most if not all of the others himself. He told me once that many of the classics had been required reading for his college classes and he liked them well enough to keep copies of them at the end of the term. Yes, David James was a college graduate as well. He had earned a business degree from a local community college after arriving in the Asheville area. In fact, he completed the 2 year degree program and was still picking up classes as he had time to finish off the bachelor degree he had begun more than a decade before I met him. When I asked him about it, I mean clearly he was a successful business man having run Camp Adohi for so long without some college telling him he was qualified to do so, he responded with a simple phrase.

"Education is the key to the future Martin!"

David James valued education and believed that the pursuit of knowledge was never in vain or without purpose, even if the piece of paper stating you had learned something was not required for anything but proof to yourself that you had finished it. He also was a steadfast believer that as humans, when we choose to stop learning new things we are damning ourselves to stumble through our remaining days with only one eye open. We become constantly focused on the past rather than fully aware of where we are, and all the wondrous places we have the ability to go.

I never had such a high opinion about school myself, but I did see some of the wisdom in his belief. I just hoped to be able to do my life-long learning outside of a stuffy classroom with its requisite homework and tests.

Chapter 17

The following few weeks flew by feeling to me more like just a few short days. I had taken up residence in a cabin not far from the one David James would spend his summer in. The first week I was alone in the cabin acting as an extra set of hands for the man with two first names. We were getting things ready for the rest of the staff to arrive for pre-camp training and clearing trails and buildings from debris that had fallen over the winter. My work also included sorting paperwork into staff manuals, inventorying canoes, packs, and mattresses, and helping David James remove a few rogue critters from cabins. Most of them had fur and 4 little feet. The ones I really hated dealing with and hoped to never see again came with none of that and instead had scales and very sharp teeth I did not wish to experience. It was hard work some days, but it was honest work, outside, and I loved almost every minute of it.

Week two brought in 50 new faces, about half male and half female, and for more than half of us this was our first summer at Camp Adohi. My empty cabin quickly filled with fellow staff who were happy I had arrived early and done all the inside cleaning for them. We were one job ahead of the other staff who had to first clean the inside of their cabins, sweep them out, wipe down mattresses, and remove a few creepy crawly critters of the insect variety to make it feel like a space you would want to sleep at night.

I blended into the crowd as best I could and gradually began to feel comfortable with more and more of them as the week went on and things like lifeguard training were completed. It started with the other 9 guys I was sharing a cabin with for obvious reasons, but eventually I branched out trying to sit at tables for meals with people I was not sharing a cabin with. By the end of the second and final week of pre-camp we were mostly one big happy family ready to face new challenges and enjoy our summer together. Though I admit there were still a few people I had trouble recalling the names of and more than a few I felt like I knew very little about. It was in part because that family did have a few factions inside of it, similar to the high school cliques I hated so much, but unlike high school when we came together as a group we blended well and everyone seemed to get along.

On the second to last night of pre-camp, Friday evening, we were given our staff assignments for the summer. Since Camp Adohi served campers as young as 7 and as old as 16 the sessions ranged from 1 to 3 weeks and offered a variety of activities both in and outside of camp Adohi's gates. The older groups came for a minimum of 2 weeks and covered all six sessions (meaning they really only had 3 sessions) while some of the younger kids came for just one week sessions. As David James walked around handing out the paperwork telling each of us what we would be doing for the first two sessions I was nervous. I was not sure I was ready to work with kids, certainly not those who had never been away from home before and might get homesick. At the same time, I was not sure I wanted to just sit back and watch all the fun happen either and be some sort of maintenance hand.

"This is for you Martin –"

"– Marty."

Reaching for the paperwork in front of me the only reply I managed to speak with the lump in my throat, other than correcting him on my name for what felt like the thousandth time, was a simple, "Thanks."

Oh crap this is it. Kids, no kids? Can you really do this? Are you just insane for even being here?

"You'll be fine Martin. Come see me after this meeting we'll go for a walk. Talk it out. I know you are nervous but trust me. You can handle these kids better than most of my staff," David James said as if he could hear the thoughts in my head as I read over the unit assignment for the summer.

Chapter 18

"I know you doubt my wisdom here Martin –"

"– Marty. –"

"– but I believe in you. Not many of my staff here has the courage to step out on their own so young without a safety net. I don't know your full story but I know enough. I know you are out on your own, made your way from your hometown on your own two feet, found a place to stay for a while and a job here this summer. Those facts alone tell me all I need to know about your character, Son."

Those were the first words I heard from David James as we walked away from the main lodge where the rest of the staff were looking over their summer plans, who they would be working with, what trips if any they would be participating in. I was terrified plain and simple. I liked kids, at least on some level though I also knew how annoying they could be, especially pre-teen and teen age girls. I had lived that drama first hand with Kera and Kylee. Never the less, I was looking forward to my time with the kids and even being a Junior Counselor for the first two week session beginning in just a few days. It was the rest of the schedule that concerned me.

Leadership? Me IN CHARGE of a group of kids? I mean, I raised my sisters, but there were just two of them, and they had to listen to me I was their older brother! What about kids I have no history, no bond with at all?

"Junior counselor the first two weeks is cool. Lead counselor the rest of the summer is what I am, well, I guess afraid of Sir," I finally replied.

"I know Son. I have a plan B in my head in case you aren't ready but I really don't think I will need to use it. You need to spend a couple of weeks getting use to the routines, the traditions. After that I am very confident that you can run with it and help make this the best experience for those kids the rest of the summer."

"And then the lead on a three week trip to finish out the summer?" I questioned.

"Absolutely! I need staff I can trust, staff that knows the traditions, the goals, and the rules but also staff that can think on their feet when nature throws them a curve ball. You have already proven to me you can handle that part. You are perfect for that trip Martin. Is there any better way to show kids nature than out on the trail carrying all the requirements of life on their backs in those beautiful mountains?"

"No Sir, I guess there really isn't."

"And who better to lead them back here to camp than someone who had the courage to know that what was best for him was to leave behind everything he knew, everyone he knew, and set off on his own in life?"

"Well ... "

"Well nothing Martin. You may not see it yet but in time you will. Like I said, I don't know your full story, but I know enough. Sometimes in life the right choice is the hard choice to leave it all behind you and move forward. Few have the courage to even see that as an option let alone make that decision. You are among them and that tells me you are a born leader, confident enough in himself to take charge when you need to and get those kids through whatever troubles you might find out there in those mountains."

I was still a nervous wreck and I am sure David James knew that but I did feel a little better about the plan for my summer after our talk. I would be learning the ropes the first two weeks, stepping into a lead 'trial' role the third for a one week session of younger boys. Then I would close out my summer on a mixed boy and girl trip for 9th graders along the Mountains to Sea Trail (MST) and Appalachian Trail (AT) covering nearly 150 miles. We would begin north of Camp Adohi deep in the Pisgah National Forest along the MST, connecting to the AT on day two or three, and then completing the adventure as we entered the camp property from a spur trail that lead into the southern boundaries of the Adohi property. All of this on foot. That was a trip I was looking forward to for certain, though I was not certain how we would effectively mix the group of boys with girls. They would be entering the tenth grade the following fall making them all between the ages of 14 and 16. I was not that much older than them and remembered well the challenges that the age brings, not to mention the challenges of anything co-ed.

"I am honored you see that in me Sir. I hope you are right. This summer is certain to be a challenge," I finally admitted.

"Those are the best kinds of summers Son. You will be fine. I am here any time you run into issues, the rest of the senior staff will be more than willing to help you as you get a feel for how we do things. But in the end, this is your summer to prove to yourself you are as strong as I can already see you are. Now is the time to learn and grow, but don't forget to enjoy the ride Martin."

"It's Marty, Sir."

Chapter 19

As it turned out, the man with two first names, David James was right. In fact not only was he right about me being able to lead a group of kids into the wild on a backpacking adventure, he was right about so many things. Honestly, I am sure there were times he was wrong on something, but even now all these years later I cannot for the life of me recall a single instance of it. He was not a god or some 'all knowing genius' by any means. He just seemed to have the best intuition and sense of what choice to make of any person I have ever met. He was as reliable as any compass when you were choosing direction. Simply ask the man with two first names what he thought and listen to his guiding words. He also had a way of providing guidance without simply telling you what to do. A quality I loved most about him over the years and yet often made me the craziest too!

My summer flew by with entire weeks seeming to last mere days. Before I knew it, not only had I become a lead counselor for a group of eighth grade boys, some of whom had never been to camp before, but I was also saying good bye to them at the end of their session and actually looking forward to closing out my summer with the co-ed backpacking trip along the MST and AT. I had worked alongside my co-counselor Amy for the last week while she was the lead for a group of eighth grade girls. We worked well together, had become friends, and were ready for the challenges of older kids and a longer trip outside of camp. We would also be joined by Sean Jackson, a junior counselor from the area near Camp Adohi who had grown up in the program. Sean attended Adohi as a camper, then a counselor-in-training or CIT, and finally was old enough to work as a Junior Counselor. In fact he had just turned 18 during our first camp session in June and was preparing for his freshman year at UNC in the fall where he planned to be a dual major in music and social work. An odd choice to most but for Sean it was a perfect mix and would set him up well for a career helping others.

Sean and I had become friends during pre-camp, bonding over music initially since we had both shown up to staff training with a guitar in hand. I was self-taught with a second hand guitar given to me by Mr. Johnson one hot July afternoon. I had spent the day helping him clear things from storage in preparation for their annual yard sale and the guitar was found among the dusty boxes and furniture. It was missing a couple of strings, had a cracked fret or two, and needed some serious cleaning but it was a beautiful Gibson LG-1 circa 1950's. Even in that condition I knew it was worth money and initially accepted it thinking I would repair it in my ol' man's woodshop and sell it. As it turned out, I liked playing the guitar and though I could only play a few chords I decided to keep it for myself.

Unlike my guitar skills, Sean could play nearly anything he heard on the radio just by picking up the guitar and playing the notes he heard. It might not be the exact notes they used, but it was always close enough that I couldn't tell the difference most of the time. As we spent more time talking about music Sean and I discovered that we had many things in common and I can safely say he was my first true friend in a long time, maybe since my childhood camping days.

The first time we spoke on a personal level was the last day of pre-camp. I had wandered off during some free time to clear my head. I walked trail after trail before eventually finding myself at the end of the dock in the swimming area staring out across the water lost in thought. The lake was peaceful and silent. So silent that when I conjured thoughts of Mother, something I often did to calm my nerves and center myself spiritually, I could hear her voice. It was of course just a memory, something I had tucked away in my brain for later use when I heard her clearly say "Martin you are stronger than you think my son. You can do this. You can do anything you set your mind to!"

"Hey, everything okay out there man?"

Quickly shaken from my almost meditative state looking over the water I turned my head to see someone walking out on the dock toward me. Sill a bit dazed by the interruption it took another second or two for me to recognize Sean and answer back.

"Oh! Hey Sean. Yeah I'm cool. Just admiring the view."

"It is beautiful, but you're lying Marty. Homesick? Missing your girl maybe? Or just freaking out about kids showing up Sunday and contemplating running for them hills?"

I laughed. I laughed hard. I had found someone who was as observant of people as I was and willing to call them out on their half-truths. I liked this kid already and had known him for less than two weeks.

"Sean, you and I have a lot in common. But no, I am not home sick. No home to be sick for honestly. And no girl to miss. This is me, my life, my past present and future all right here. Just living for the day and maybe looking forward to going off to college in the fall."

"Everybody's got a past, and a place they came from man. But it's cool if you don't want to talk about it. If David James hired you to work with kids you must not be running from anything too big and scary. That makes you okay in my book. But hey, ya' know if you ever do want to talk about it, I got good ears and know how to keep that shit to myself. That's why I am going into social work, or psychology, in the fall. Well that and music don't pay the bills these days."

"Music? I saw the guitar case and assumed you play but you a writer, singer, or just play?"

"All of the above honestly. I write my own stuff, actually wrote the camp song lyrics back when I was a camper here. In fact it was here that I learned I could write. I had a counselor who played the guitar, was always picking at it when we had time. I started singing along about how cool camp was and all the fun stuff we got to do as kids here. By the end of those two weeks we had written a new camp song. He even taught me to play it so I could show my Mom when she came to pick me up. When I came back the next year, it was in the song book and the staff had learned it."

"That's the coolest story I've heard about this place yet. Is that why you are here?"

"Maybe a little. This place is special to me. But honestly I just want to maybe one day be the counselor that some kid remembers when he is my age and thinks 'hey that guy made a difference in my life' ya' know. I think all of us want that, we just won't admit it to anyone."

"Probably some truth there. You think that is why David James keeps this place going, so he can feel like he is making a difference in the world?" I asked aloud but more to myself than to Sean.

"Don't know man, but I think it is safe to say he has already made a big difference and every kid that comes through here leaves a better person when they go, even if just a little bit. You'll see soon enough. It is the coolest thing ever to see a shy kid come in on

Sunday, work hard the whole time they are here to make friends and fit in while acting like they couldn't care less, and then be in tears come Friday night closing ceremonies. Coolest thing for sure to see that kid grow up a little right in front of you!"

"And maybe that is why I found myself here this summer. Could have gone anywhere but the Universe landed me here. Guess I just need to ride it out and see where this road takes me huh?"

"Dude, it's going to be a good summer and the two of us are going to be great friends by the end. I can see that already! Going to get you to tell me your story at some point I think but for now we should head back to main camp. Dinner will be happening soon and then we get a day of freedom before the kids show up and this crazy ride really takes off!"

"You're very optimistic Sean. Maybe a little foolish too. I like you already!"

Chapter 20

Sean was not over exaggerating when he called what I would experience that summer a 'crazy ride'. My first day with kids seemed to last for well over 48 hours as we all adjusted to the schedule and settled into some sort of crazy rhythm. However, the rest of those two weeks felt like it was really only a day or two before we were helping them pack their bags, haul them to the unit luggage pick-up spot, and hug them good bye after dinner when their parents arrived. My next group was a little less hectic, and yet more stressful because I was now a co-lead and was in charge of making decisions a lot of the time. Even that week managed to smooth out after just a day or so spent finding a rhythm and again the remaining days felt like they just flew by. In fact, the first three weeks of my summer passed me by all too quickly and before I realized it, I was just a day away from leaving camp Adohi with a group of 8 boys and 7 girls for a 146 mile hike along the MST, AT, and some connecting spur trails back to camp.

The trip would take us a total of 12 days averaging 10 to 12 miles per day. We planned it to also have a short day of just 7 miles in the middle and a longer 15 mile day that would be mostly downhill in the final stretch. The group dynamics were a little rocky initially. From the first night they arrived it was clear we had a clique of campers, both boys and girls, who knew one another and were already friends while the remaining five kids were left trying to make new friends. There were minor conflicts among the group while in camp but nothing too major. Amy, Lisa her junior co-counselor, Sean, and I were all hopeful it would iron itself out along the trail as the kids were forced to work as a team and rely on one another for survival on the trail. For the most part we were right but, not entirely.

The first few days seemed to go without incident other than the expected complaints about feet hurting, being tired, and not having enough water in their bottles at the end of the long hot days on the trail. That all changed on day five. After hiking from just after sun up to nearly 8 o'clock that evening and only covering 9.5 miles, the group was tired, exhausted maybe, and nobody had the energy to go filter water from the nearby stream or cook dinner. Still, things needed to be done. We needed shelter, food, and water.

In an effort to break up the work and help get things done more quickly before the sun set behind the ridge line, Sean and Amy took half of the group to set up tents while Lisa and I took the other half to get water. Pumping water through the filters and into 36 water bottles plus a pan to make dinner was a daunting task. We tried to alternate the groups between tent and water duty nightly to give their arms a break. Even with four water filters and both counselors taking turns filling bottles, it still took nearly an hour to finish the job, clean the filters, and get back to camp.

That night, because the campsite was so close to the stream we were filtering from, and because we were hoping to get a jump on making dinner for the crew, Lisa and I allowed the first group of kids to take a load of filled bottles and the pan for dinner back to the campsite while the rest of us worked to fill the remaining bottles. With only eight bottles left to fill I stood up to pass the filter off to one of the kids who had not yet filled any bottles. It was then that I realized there were only two girls plus Amy and I standing along the shore of the stream. Apparently the rest of the group had decided to head back to camp without taking their turn in sharing the work. Before I even had a chance to get mad I heard yelling coming from camp and a growing chant of "fight, fight, fight!"

I dropped the filter and bottle I was holding and ran toward camp yelling to Lisa and the two campers to "stay here!"

When I arrived at the campsite there were empty water bottles all over the ground. The pan for dinner was being swung as a weapon at the head of another camper by one of my boys who had blood streaking the side of his face. Two more campers were trying to step in to separate the boys but were no match for the older, bigger boys and were easily pushed aside as the one wielding the dinner pan made another attempt to swing it at the other boy. I could see Sean bolting up the trail from the opposite direction and without exchanging a single word we both lunged for a different boy just before the pot made contact.

After administering first-aid to both boys who surprisingly had escaped with only minor cuts and a few bruises it was time to find out what the heck had happened. We separated the group, interrogated everyone who was in camp when the fight broke out, and still came up empty. When we asked the two involved in the fight, the only answer we got were 'he started it' from each of them. These were two boys who had never been violent or friendly to each other and also claimed to not know the other from outside of camp.

I was at a loss for what caused the disagreement and how to best handle the entire situation. If we had not been in the middle of nowhere, I would have made a phone call and sent both of the boys home immediately. That was not an option here however, so I decided to pull a trick from the standard play book for kids who can't get along. Sean and I went through their bags to ensure that neither had anything that could be turned into a weapon and they became tent buddies. They were also paired up for chores and the two of them worked together, under careful supervision, to refill every dumped water bottle while the remainder of the group went back to work on setting up tents and preparing dinner.

Sean, who had apparently sprained his ankle while helping to break up the fight was icing his ankle in the cold running water of the creek and only helped the two boys by taking off and putting on water bottle lids. Everything else was up to them including making multiple trips back to main camp carrying the filled water bottles. I kept my distance, but I also kept my eye on the two of them as much as possible. I knew that with Sean injured it would need to be me that separated the two should they get into it again filling the bottles.

The next morning when it came time to pack up camp and move on down the trail, Sean quickly discovered that while he could walk normally with little pain in his ankle without his pack, the added weight was an issue. Before I even made a decision in my head about how to handle the situation Jason, the boy who had been swinging the dinner pot the night before, stepped up and asked if he could take some of the heavier items from Sean's bag and add them to his own. Not to be outdone, he was quickly joined by Kyle, his new tent buddy, and two others plus one of the girls who offered to help lighten Sean's pack so he could take it easy on his ankle.

Lucky for Sean, day six of our trip was the pre-planned light day and we had only 7 miles to go over fairly level terrain. Because of Sean's ankle we took it slower than normal, stopped for more breaks than usual, and what should have only taken a few hours to hike wound up taking most of the day. We finally arrived at our next campsite about 4 o'clock. When I went to help Sean take his pack off, I discovered that it was nearly empty. Unbeknownst to me, each time we stopped throughout the day for a rest one of the kids had taken more and more items from his bag leaving him with just a sleeping bag, his clothes, and a small bag of ramen noodles. I later discovered that much of it had been put into the bags of Jason and Kyle.

For the remainder of the trip Sean carried a mostly empty pack filled only with the lightest items we had between the group and his personal belongings while Jason and Kyle took the heaviest and split it between them. While the two of them were by no means best friends, at least not that they would let me see anyway, it was clear that my decision to make them inseparable tent buddies had worked in some way. They were finding a way to co-exist and work together for the benefit of the group. It was all I could ask of them and though I did have to step in to stop a verbal argument on our last night out on the trail, I never had to break up a fight between them even after we returned to camp.

I am not certain we were ready for all the troubles that mixing boys and girls of that age together could bring, and none of us was prepared to break up a fight between two of the boys or deal with an injured staff member because of it. Yet, once the dust settled I watched that segregated group of old friends and outsiders come together as a team with a common goal, finishing the trip together. They each stepped up and took on more responsibilities, often without being asked. They saw a need and fulfilled it, and they found a way to at least get along even if they didn't necessarily like the others they were forced to be with for three weeks.

When all was said and done the entire group made it back to camp safely, without further injury or incident, they were clearly joined in a unique way making them seem much more like family than a group of random mostly strangers who landed together on a backpacking trip. Witnessing that transformation was one of the most amazing things I was privileged to experience over that summer. I walked back into Camp Adohi on the final day of the trip with my head held high, my body tired and dirtier than I would have thought possible, and my heart filled with pride for myself, my co-staff, and most of all my group of 15 boys and girls who had overcome so many physical and emotional challenges in the last two and a half weeks to become better versions of themselves.

I knew that trip had changed them, and me as well, but I also knew that most wouldn't realize how deep those changes would run until well after they were back in their homes and classrooms. Perhaps some would not even realize it until years or even decades later, but regardless, it had changed them in profound ways. And, if I am being totally honest, it would take me a few years to fully understand just how much those days with them had changed me as well.

Chapter 21

With much of the Adohi staff that summer I managed to be open and friendly yet fairly reserved about my story. Almost nobody knew anything about my future, or lack of, and certainly nothing of my past. For the most part all anyone knew was that my home town was the other side of Asheville though in which direction I don't think I ever did mention, and my only living kin was my ol' man. However, to me it seemed that the man with two first names, David James always knew far more about me, and the past I was working so hard to hide from everyone whenever I talked to him one-on-one. He was very much a real life Yoda, the little green, all-knowing, all-seeing character from those galactic conflict movies who spoke his words out of order and yet made perfect sense to anyone who listened carefully to the message. David James did not speak his words out of order however.

Often times it did feel like David James had some sort of super power. He seemed to possess the ability to look into your eyes and read your deepest thoughts like a page from one of his dusty old cowboy novels. In fact, though I had told him I was headed for college at UNC in the fall to study English I am certain I never said a word about history at all. Yet, he somehow also knew I wanted to work on a minor in history though what those two subjects had in common or how useful it would be in the future made little sense to me. History and writing were the two things I loved most in life and to me it made sense to get a degree in both, what I would do with them down the line didn't matter. I knew that I could always get a teaching job someplace if I had to, though teaching wasn't really something that interested me as a recent high school graduate. In fact, more school on either side of the desk didn't interest me much lately but I already had a scholarship, and nothing else to do in the fall.

Without realizing it though, there was an exception to my silence that summer. I still never gave many details about my past, family, or home town but Sean and I talked about enough things over the summer that he knew me better than anyone else at Adohi for sure. The man with two first names may be an exception to this but his knowledge did not come from me telling him details. That super power he seemed to possess tipped the scale in his favor.

One evening late in our backpacking adventure along the Appalachian Trail, I even spilled the beans to Sean about Mother and the twins. It was not exactly intentional but it felt very natural to talk about them with Sean. That had never happened before in my life. I had always been immediately uncomfortable in the conversation whenever their names came up in the past. With Sean, it all just sort of fell out of my mouth. Before I realized what I was even telling him, I had described in vague detail how I lost Mother so young to a disease I now understood was Cancer and the twins last fall in a horrific car accident I still felt very responsible for.

Sean took it all in stride too, like any good friend would I suppose. He asked a few questions but tried not to pry too much. He was respectful and sounded sincere when he told me how sorry he was that I had to go through all of that. He also smacked me across the back of the head when I told him the car accident had been my fault because it was my car and I was too busy to drive the twins home after that football game.

"That is about the dumbest thing I have ever heard you say Marty!" Sean told me. "You didn't drive the car that hit them. You didn't pour the alcohol down the guy's throat. You likely would not have been able to avoid smacking into him even if you had been driving. How in the hell are you responsible for that accident?"

Because they were my little sisters and I was supposed to protect them. God knows my ol' man couldn't, wouldn't do it. It was my job and I failed!

I never answered him aloud that night, just nodded his direction signaling that I agreed he might be right.

Looking back on it now, this conversation sums up perfectly why that summer, that one three week backpacking trip to end our summer, forged a friendship that would stand the test of time and change my life forever. Sean and I became inseparable once we returned to camp and it didn't take long for us to find one another in life later that fall either. In fact Sean is still a man I consider a great friend even today, decades later!

Chapter 22

Befriending Sean was an important part of my first summer at Adohi, and we did return to work together for two more years there on our summer breaks from college. However, in many ways it was the connection I made with the man with two first names, David James that overshadowed everything else that happened to me on the magical grounds of Camp Adohi. It was he of course that put me in the position to meet Sean in the first place, and to begin to see myself as the person I had the potential of becoming. It was also David James who stepped in and talked some sense into my rebellious teen brain when I was contemplating not taking advantage of that scholarship to UNC.

That conversation began innocent enough, mostly just thinking aloud to myself while catching up on laundry after our Appalachian Trail trip. The night we got back to camp both lead counselors were given a night off while the kids cleaned and checked back in the gear we had taken with us and then had an evening to hang out in their cabins and put together a trip report. Those reports were filed with the camp paperwork and sent home with each camper as a memento of their adventures and a brief glimpse into how they saw the experience as a group. It was always fun to read through them and see what the kids picked up on as their 'highlights' and compare them to my own memories of the adventures. Often times we had shared memories of the events but, from time to time, things showed up in those reports that I never viewed as significant, or just plain forgot happened at all.

Anyway, since we had been out of camp for a little less than two weeks and the summer was rapidly coming to a close, I chose to spend my night off in the staff room taking care of laundry after a long warm shower. As I watched my summer adventures coming to an end I began to wonder, somewhat aloud what my fall plans should really be.

"Of course you should Martin!" I heard the booming voice of David James over my shoulder.

I had long since given up attempting to get him to call me Marty and allowed him to join the very short list of those allowed the use of my full, legal first name. A bit startled at the sound of his voice, I turned around to be sure he was really standing in the room behind me and that it hadn't been just inside my own head. That happened from time to time, hearing others tell me things as if they were standing in the room next to me when it was really all just inside my head. Most times it was the voice of Mother. I always assumed they were just memories from my earlier years that surfaced when I was searching for answers to challenges in my life. Now that I am older, and a little more 'seasoned' I have a different opinion. It's one that some could think makes me crazy. I don't talk about it much to avoid the inevitable stares, laughing, and potential calls to the psych ward that I assume will follow. But we'll get to all that later.

"I mean I know I have a scholarship and all, but there is so much that can't be taught in a classroom Sir," I answered back.

"This is true Martin, but there is also much to learn inside those walls. Talk to me, tell me what it is you think you will do with yourself if you pass on this chance for an education," David James said as he pulled out the bench across the table from me and took a seat.

While I folded the last of my clean laundry David James prodded for information about what was bothering me, why I thought school might not be the right choice in the coming months, and what I would do instead.

"Your future lies in education Son. You said you have a scholarship, so what's to think about?"

"College was always my ticket out of Thompson Station, er, um, my hometown. Now I don't really need it to be. I guess I am just wondering if the time and expense is really worth it."

Crap I said the name. Does he know anyone there? Does he even know where it is? Shit I hope not! Way to blow that cover Marty.

"Worth it? You are wondering if you should expand your knowledge, get skills that will last you a lifetime and provide for your future? You can't be serious. Of course college is worth it."

"I guess. I mean I just don't want to sit in a classroom learning things I will never really need to know."

Whew maybe he didn't hear me. Or doesn't know where it is so he let it slide.

"Martin, not everything they teach in those college classrooms will apply to your life. Not all of it will matter, or even make sense to you now. One thing is for certain. College is the ticket to your future Son. An education allows you to chart your own destiny not just be forced into a job that pays the bills always hoping for something more."

"That I know, Sir. I'm just not sure what I want to do and don't want to waste my time while I figure that out. I had a chance to get a scholarship for English and since I had no other way out of my home town I jumped at it. Now that I am here, on my own two feet away from that place, I am not certain if English is the right direction to take."

"I have seen the trip reports you write, and not one of your groups has turned in one with a single grammatical error I could find. Martin, English is perfect for you. Who knows one day maybe you can write a book about all this," he chuckled though he was most definitely serious.

"It is something I am good at for sure, but what do you do with an English degree?" I asked more of a rhetorical question than anything I expected a response to.

"Whatever you want Martin. Find that dream inside your heart and chase it down. Do it now while you are young enough to take those risks. When you get to my age you find that you have settled for too many things in life and wish you would have made other choices. It happens. Take those risks now and settle for nothing but the best you can be. That way you can look back and know that even if it doesn't all work out in the end, you made the choices you knew were right."

"How did you get to be such a wise man David James?"

"Years of practice Martin. More years than I care to admit."

With that he stood, slapped me on the shoulder in that good job, fatherly way of his and finished this part conversation part pep talk with "Your future might not be in English Martin, but you will find it someplace along the way in your studies that I am certain of. Follow that path with your eyes open wide and soon enough your heart will lead you in the right direction. But keep your summers free for as long as you can. There are many more kids whose lives you can affect one week at a time up here."

I was speechless processing all of what he had just said. I knew he was right, that going off to college was the right choice. I was mostly just afraid to fail with not much of a safety net to fall back on. Before I realized it David James had crossed the room toward the door and paused for one last statement before leaving me alone with my thoughts.

"Martin, Thompson Station is a nice little town but I can see why you would feel smothered there. UNC will let you spread those wings and find out for yourself just how talented and amazing you can be. Don't give up on yourself before you even take your first flight Son."

With that he was gone, out of sight, and I was alone with my thoughts and a pile of folded laundry again. He was right. It was something I had come to understand happened a lot with him.

Chapter 23

Heeding the advice of the man with two first names, someone who had quickly become a friend, mentor, and father figure to me over the summer I did indeed begin my college journey not long after sessions wrapped at Camp Adohi in August of 1996. For the first time in my life, I became a very small fish in a sea of unfamiliar faces, many of whom were just as lost as I was those first few weeks. Together we managed to find our way around, get comfortable with the pace of college life, and begin a path that would take each of us to new and different places. Some, like my first semester roommate whose name I can no longer recall, would spend less time in college than they planned. They would instead move on to life's harder lessons far sooner than they should have. In my case, I kept my grades up, head in my textbooks, and my little bits of free time filled with activities that did not involve overindulging in 'fun'.

Though I had saved nearly every penny I earned working at Camp Adohi over the summer, I still sought and took a position on campus at the library. It allowed me to earn money for incidentals and often when things were slow at night, I was able to get a little homework done while being paid to do it. I also worked many weekends and holiday breaks with David James up at Camp Adohi. He occasionally had groups that came out for weekends and needed a hand as a group leader as well as some general maintenance things in the off season. For the Christmas and Spring break weeks when I was forced to vacate my dorm due to college policies, Camp Adohi was where I went. David James lived on the property nearly year round and welcomed me into his home in exchange for some hours spent on whatever project he had going at the time. I loved every minute of it though I pretended not to most of the time. I mean how much fun can you admit to having when you are painting little canoes and row boats on the small craft buddy board New Year's Eve?

As time permitted during classes I also managed to spend time with Sean. It took a few weeks for us to bump into one another on campus but once we both began to settle into a routine, we also managed to make time to hang out together for a bite to eat at the very least. Often times we simply talked about summer memories or wondered aloud why on Earth we were forced to learn facts and figures that seemed so pointless in the grand scheme of things. Sometime around Thanksgiving we finally managed to get together off campus at a local bar for a meal and a little time to let off some steam. Lucky for us, they also happened to have a stage, a couple tunable guitars, and an open mic night!

Sean took the stage first figuring it would be fun to play again even if just for one song to a crowd who could care less. By the middle of the 2nd chorus he had the entire bar singing along with him "Don't stop beleeeevin'! Hold on to that feeeelin! ..." Before he could put the guitar down after the song was done they were chanting "One more song! One more song!" Sean agreed and ended up playing an entire 15 song set while I sat back and admired his courage from my seat at the bar.

By the middle of January I was joining him on stage for his regular Thursday night gig down at that student bar just a block off campus. The crowds were growing each week as word got out that they had scored some local talent to entertain, and it was fun. It also paid decent so even after we split it up both Sean and I walked out with a little extra money in our pockets to help with growing college expenses. I never figured myself as someone who could play in front of a crowd, or really play more than a couple chords to some old country songs on the radio honestly. Sitting next to Sean on that stage gave me the courage to tap into some musical abilities even I didn't know were there.

I never had dreams of making it big, getting a record deal, or becoming famous for sure, but music made me feel good and playing it with Sean on that stage was likely some of the best times in my college years not spent under the summer sun. We had a regular following who came nearly every week to see us, or maybe to drink and we happened to be there, but I like to think they were there for us. The bar owner even asked Sean to fill in solo on Tuesdays a few times so at least half of our duo must have been good for business. In any case there were a lot of good times in that bar on stage, and off. It also helped Sean and me to become even more inseparable as friends, something that would both open and close doors for us down the road of life.

The following summer I returned to Camp Adohi as a Lead Counselor and took on two of the three week adventure based trips. Sean joined me as a Lead Counselor at Adohi but due to us both being leads we spent little time together unless our days off happened to coincide. My summer was spent with kids ranging in age from 14 to 16 hiking trails, rafting rapids, and sleeping outside in nature. I was back in my element and loved every moment of it even on those days when it poured buckets of water from the sky and we found ourselves eating the emergency peanut butter and crackers for dinner for lack of anything dry enough to spark a fire.

I again watched in amazement as groups of strangers arrived from all walks of life and gradually became a cohesive team in the first week and felt an awful lot more like family by the end of the third. The people, more so than the adventures, had a very profound impact on me and the direction my life would take from that first summer but it was more than halfway through the second summer before I realized it. Maybe it was just maturity catching up with me, maybe it was the kids or staff there the second summer, but it was during a final campfire speech by the man with two first names, David James that reality hit me smack in the face and left its mark deep in my soul. His words of "The memories you made here this summer will be with you always. Your friendships may fade, distance and time will take its toll, but the lessons you gained from them will be with you forever," still ring true with me today, maybe more now than it did even that day.

Chapter 24

The following fall both Sean and I returned to UNC. This time it was as roommates sharing a small dorm room in the cheapest dorm on campus. I returned to my work study job at the library on campus and we resumed our regular Thursday night sessions at the bar. Sean had a lighter class load than I did this time around and was able to pick up a Tuesday and Wednesday night slot playing solo while I needed the time to study for my 16 credits. Occasionally on weeks when the work load was less I would take myself down to that bar and watch Sean perform. He was a natural playing covers from all the current hits and many classics from the 70's and 80's in both rock and country music. I barely knew the words to all the songs he had in his catalog but Sean not only knew the words, he could play the chords on guitar as well as piano for many of them.

At one point in mid-December I went out on a Tuesday night to see Sean play and found myself sitting next to a girl who looked familiar but whose name I could not recall. I knew I had seen her before but when or where was a mystery and her name I was certain I never knew. Sean put down the guitar after completing his first set of the evening and announced he would be taking a 30 minute break for dinner. To my absolute shock he walked off the stage and right up to the girl seated next to me at the bar.

"Anneliese! So good to see you. When did you get in?"

Anneliese? Wait Sean knows this girl? Is that where I have seen her before, with Sean someplace? He didn't mention a girlfriend, and she is certainly not a sister. How does he get so lucky to know all the beautiful women in this town?

"Hey Marty c'mere man I want to introduce you to someone. This is Anneliese. I've known her since we were kids playing in the sandbox together. She's thinking of transferring here to UNC next semester. Help me talk her into it will ya'? You two will hit it off I know and then we can go from this odd 'couple a dudes' to a threesome on campus!"

"Ah yeah, threesome, that is exactly what we need to be seen as Sean," I said laughing aloud at his strange sense of humor. "UNC is a great school though, and you would probably fit in just fine with people far less odd than Sean and me here. What are you studying? By the way, I'm Martin, friends just call me Marty. Pleased to meet you Anneliese," I said extending my hand in friendship.

"Martin, I think I like that better but I can call you Marty if you prefer. Nice to meet you too. Sean has told me a little bit about you but I would love to hear it from you instead. You free for dinner sometime?"

WHAT?!? Did she just ask me out on a date? Um yeah I

think she did. Holy crap ... I like her style!

"D-dd-dinner ... yes of course dinner would be good. Maybe Saturday? Will you be around the whole weekend?" I stammered.

"Actually, Saturday I do have plans to see an apartment. Can we do something after say 8? I should be done by then."

"Absolutely! Pizza at your new apartment at 8!" I joked.

"Pizza would be okay, I mean this isn't an official need to be all fancy sort of date. But we'd better plan to eat someplace else. I don't have the apartment yet Marty."

Oh and she thinks on her feet with whit and sarcasm. She is definitely my style!

"Oh all right but if the apartment isn't yours by the time you walk back out the door it will be because you didn't want it bad enough. Who would turn you down? But I guess we could meet here and then maybe walk over a block or two to Tony's. Their food is great, pizza included. Sound good?"

"Looking forward to it Marty," she said working hard to hide her smile. Her eyes gave her away instantly though.

Chapter 25

Anneliese did in fact get the apartment she looked at and she did make the move to UNC the following semester. Our date Saturday turned into a date every Saturday evening for much of the rest of that school year and the one that followed. She returned home for the summer of '98 but when I heard she was looking for summer employment that following year, I of course got her an application for Adohi and offered myself as a personal reference.

I would spend two more summers working at Camp Adohi while in college and one of them included a summer spent working alongside Anneliese. Aware that we were dating in the off season David James was wise enough not to place us on any trips together, in fact while I was off on two more three week adventures in the wild, she remained at camp working one week sessions with the younger campers. From what I heard from parents and other staff, she was very much in her element and well suited for the youngest kids in camp. She had the gift of patience to deal with their homesickness, tantrums, and inexperience. That was a quality I lacked often and very much admired in her for sure.

I can remember, even now a decade later how it felt to walk out of Camp Adohi on the last day of my final summer. It was August 1999. I was entering my final semester of college, preparing to start a paid internship with a local media outlet as a copy writer, and engaged to Anneliese. I was filled with anticipation about my future, the uncertainty that it held, and the excitement of making permanent changes in my life like marriage and life beyond college. I was also filled with a sense of loss, sadness that perhaps my youth was in fact coming to an end. I no longer could afford to spend summers paid to play in the sun and educate kids about nature. I needed to secure full time work, something that would pay the rent on an apartment while Anneliese completed her last year of college and an internship that would follow. I needed to begin to live less like a college kid and more like an adult. It was very bitter sweet to say those last good byes and pull out the gate one last time as a member of the staff.

Chapter 26

As much as I can recall the memories of my last days on staff at Camp Adohi, I can also recall the pain of losing my good friend and mentor David James just five short years later. By then I was a full time copy writer working my way into the editing portion of a local publishing company. I was working alongside writers and editors who often told me I should turn my stories of camp into a book someday. It wasn't until I got the call from Hank, the maintenance man David James had hired to help him after I was no longer able to in the off season that I began to actually write them down.

I had used journals as a means of therapy all my life and had accrued boxes of them over the years. It was actually much of what filled my pack the day I walked out of Thompson Station to be honest. Those journals were important enough to me that they took the place of a few extra pairs of clothes and dry socks. I knew I could never replace them and they contained memories from my childhood, my sisters, and Mother. Those were priceless in my eyes. Now, as the news of David James' passing slowly sunk in, I began to regret not spending more time documenting my years working at Camp Adohi or the conversations we had both while he was my boss and just man-to-man.

The days that followed hearing the news were as much of a blur then as they remain to me now. I know I went out to Adohi to meet with Hank. I know I spoke with his lawyers who informed me that I was named in the will. David James had no next of kin, no family that claimed him. What he did have were friends and a family he had built through people like me, kids he hired to work a summer job and stuck around year after year because they grew to feel a part of his family. Because of that I was named as the caretaker for his remains, a task I was more than honored to accept. The remains of his estate were gifted to the community Camp Adohi sat in to help in the care and eventual transformation of the camp into public land. With his passing, Camp Adohi had passed as well.

I also know that there was a wake, one which both Anneliese and I attended but that as well is a blur of conversations with names I knew, but faces I could not place and faces I recognized, but whose names I could not recall then, or now. David James was not a fan of funerals or memorial services. He said that death was a natural part of life and being remembered in sadness was never how he wanted his life to end. Hank and I didn't give him much choice and held a staff reunion/wake in his honor anyway under the guise that it was a farewell to Camp Adohi party for staff and former campers. I don't remember now who was there, or even when it was to be perfectly honest. I do know the turnout was more than we anticipated and it lasted long into the night with story after story shared by those who shared a moment, or a decade of their life with Camp Adohi and the man with two first names. A few tears were shed, maybe even a few by me, but all in all I remember it as being more happy than sad. Exactly how David James would have wanted to be remembered.

Unfortunately, that was where the positive side of his passing ended for me. I had spent much of my childhood and early adult life dealing with death and the fallout it creates when the light of someone you have come to rely upon is extinguished. Over the last few years since leaving Thompson Station, I thought I had finally put that pain behind me and moved forward in life without the baggage of guilt and death. Maybe I had, for a while at least. The moment I heard Hank on the other end of the phone explaining that David James, a man I had thought of as so much more than an employer or mentor had passed, it felt like the world had been tipped on its head and I was right back in that hospital hallway the day Mother left me.

That was when the nightmares started back up and sleep became something I feared most nights.

Chapter 27

Smoke hung in the air like dense fog. All around me I could smell the stench of burning rubber and plastic, feel the heat of the fire, the sting of open wounds on my body. Every inch of me hurt. From head to toe I was covered in debris, dirt, and blood.

Rolling to my side on the pavement the pain was so intense my vision went pure white. Some say you see stars when your body can't take the pain. Maybe pure white light is what stars are made of. The fog in my head was beginning to clear. I remembered being in a car, with someone.

"Hey! Is anybody there? Are you okay?" I shouted into the murky night.

No response. No sound at all actually. The night was eerily silent. I could see the flames of the fire burning. I could see figures in the distance, lights flashing maybe. Yet, I could hear nothing. Had I gone deaf?

Struggling to my feet I dragged my badly torn leg behind me in a limp as I slowly made my way toward the overturned car. I had to see, to find out if whomever I was with in that car was okay. Still the world was silent.

As I neared the car, heat from the fire increasing,

prevented me from getting too close. I did not recognize the car. It was a brown late model something. It was not my car. Where was my car? I remembered driving my car, and they were with me.

"Oh God! They were with me. Where are they? Where is my car?" I shouted again.

No response, no sound. Not even of my own words though I was certain I had screamed them.

Turning as quickly as my damaged body would allow, I surveyed the scene. Smoke still hung low to the ground obscuring things from my field of view. I could see something large behind me, very near to where I had just been laying on the cold wet pavement. Again, dragging my injured limb behind, I worked my way toward the object. It had to be the car. It was too large to be anything else.

"Kera! Kylee! Are you there? Can you hear me?" I shouted again feeling the words leave my body but never hearing them in the suffocating darkness.

"Anybody? Can anybody hear me?"

Still alone, injured, and unable to hear I felt a chill begin to creep up my body. It began in my injured limbs, both arm and leg, slowly working its way toward my core. Something was very wrong. I had been injured in some way. There had clearly been an accident here. Yet, no one was here but me. No bystanders to call it in. No responders to help the victims.

"This is wrong, all wrong," I told myself. "People should be here helping. Someone should be here demanding I sit my ass down while they get help. Someone should be here damn it! Where is everybody?"

Finally reaching the large dark object I looked down to see it was not my car after all. Leaning in for a closer look I lost my balance and felt myself begin to fall forward. Instinct thrust my hands in front of me but rather than hitting the object to break my fall, they pushed through it and I continued downward toward two tattered bodies below me.

"Kera? Kylee!" --

-- "Marty! Marty wake up baby," A familiar voice spoke. Female. Not Mother.

"No Martin it's not your mother, but listen to her anyway. She keeps you grounded in this life, never forget that," another voice, a male voice I recognized immediately spoke. It was that of a very good friend and I often heard him here in this space between dreams and the waking world. Sometimes when I am wide awake too, but those always make me feel like I am just daydreaming anyway.

"Marty! Wake up Marty, you're screaming again. All soaked in sweat. What the heck were you dreaming about?"

"Dreaming?" I asked as I rubbed my eyes and looked around the room. I was home, safe in my bed next to my wife Anneliese. I had been dreaming. A dream that felt all too familiar!

Chapter 28

"Marty? Hey man I haven't seen you in here on a week night in, well in a really long time. Let me buy you a beer man. I have about 10 minutes left before my next set starts"

"Sean, yeah I have been pretty busy with the family since Beth came along. Never seem to have the time to get down here and see you play like I used to."

"Or to get your butt back up there with me where it belongs. Man you going to be here long? I have an extra guitar, you know I always have a spare up there. You want to join me for a song or two?" he asked clearly hoping I would jump at the chance.

"Nah, not tonight. I came to see you play Sean. Maybe some other night though," I said taking a sip from the frosty mug the bartender slid in front of me.

I didn't drink beer anymore, something I left behind in my college days I guess. But that night, oh that night not only did I drink the beer Sean bought for me but also three or four more I bought for myself. And I enjoyed every last one from that first sip to the last drop in each glass. Luckily I had already eaten dinner and still had enough body mass to handle that much alcohol. Just to be careful I walked home from the bar at the end of the night anyway. After all, the house was only about a mile away down mostly residential suburban streets lined with concrete sidewalks.

I remember it being very late when I finally stepped up on the front porch and thought the wind was responsible for the creaking of the tattered white swing gently moving back and forth. Then I looked closer and saw Anneliese sitting there slowly rocking it.

"Hey babe, sorry I didn't call, Sean was great tonight!" I slurred

"Sounds like the beer was too," she said with an obviously measured tone.

"Yeah I had a couple. Left the car up there just in case. But I'm not drunk! Just felt like walking."

"You might be drunk Marty. I know things have been rough the last few weeks. Are you okay?" she asked her voice so soft and gentle the night crickets nearly drown it out.

"I'm fine. I'll be fine. I'm going to bed," I said trying to convince myself far more than my wife before turning on my heels and staggering into the house.

I never made it up the stairs. That night was the first of many over the next month that I would spend on the couch. Some were my choice, some were not. All of them started the same way, with a trip down to the bar after work and many mugs of sweet amber liquid drowning out my senses, my memories, and most of all my fear that losing my friend David James was just the beginning of a new string of death and destruction.

In some ways it was exactly that, I mean I was doing a fine job of destroying my family, my life, and my career with my new love of bar nights. It was also the catalyst of a trip back to Thompson Station that would complete the destruction of the life I had worked so hard to build since leaving that place more than a decade ago. It would take a long conversation with Anneliese, then Sean, and then David James of all people (yes I know he is dead stay with me on this one) to finish kicking that ball in motion, but I was already starting down that path and though I believe in free will, I also believe I was meant to follow it.

Chapter 29

The conversation with Anneliese happened on a Thursday evening about three weeks into my new routine of working long days, heading to the bar on my way home, and sleeping on the couch after staggering in a little buzzed from the evening's activities. My new schedule was catching up with my no-longer-25 body and instead of following my new routine, I was home sound asleep on the couch by 4:30 that afternoon. I had left the office early for a change and it was to go home and take a nap before heading out to see Sean play that night, of course at the bar. I mean it made perfect sense to me at the time.

I don't think Anneliese was home when I crawled onto the couch for my nap, and I could have just as easily gone upstairs to bed but chose not to make the effort. The couch had been my bed more times than not, it seemed like the perfect nap spot. Turns out it was the first good decision I had made recently and was only the beginning of my climb from the bottom of the hole I had dug myself into recently.

The clock read 4:25 when I last looked in its direction before nodding off. It read 7:15 when I was jarred awake laying in the middle of the living room floor by Anneliese who was holding a screaming, and clearly terrified Beth in her arms.

"Marty! Wake up honey! It's a dream. Wake Up you are scaring Beth!" she was yelling at me.

Those are the words that brought me back to the waking world and they were in stereo. One version was clearly Anneliese. The other I did not immediately recognize but it too was female in origin. I bolted up to a sitting position wiping my eyes with my right hand and steading myself with the other on the edge of the couch.

"Marty are you okay? You were screaming so loud you scared Beth," Anneliese asked her voice trembling a bit.

"Daddy you fell off the couch. Did you get hurt?" Beth asked wiping away her tears and sniffling a bit to catch her breath.

"No baby. Daddy is okay now."

"Then why you scream so loud?" her innocent voice asked.

"I guess it must have been a bad dream. I'm okay, but I could use a hug. Can I get a hug from my little girl to make me feel better?"

"Yes! Mommy down please. Daddy needs a hug."

Her feet no sooner hit the floor and she was in my lap arms wrapped as tight as she could get them around my neck. I gently hugged her back telling her how much I loved her and that her hug made me feel so much better. She eventually let go and scampered off to go play in her room again telling both Anneliese and me that she was the best hugger ever. All I could do was smile and think to myself that she was likely the most perfect thing in my life.

"So you heading out again or planning to spend time with your family for once Marty?" Anneliese asked as soon as Beth was out of earshot.

"Sean is playing tonight"

"Yeah, I know he is. But he didn't miss you for nearly five years of Thursday nights at that bar. I think he could manage one more without you."

"Maybe."

It was not an argument I wanted to have. It was not a conversation I wanted to have. All I wanted was to escape again. That is what the nights at the bar were honestly, an escape from my terrified moments at home. A way to forget how much my life was out of my control and how bad it could get.

"Maybe. Maybe he won't miss you. Maybe we do. Marty I don't know much about your childhood but I do remember you telling me about how after your mom died your dad more or less just walked away from the family he had left. What do you think you are doing? Are you trying to give Beth the childhood you had? You leave for work before she gets up. You stay out till all hours of the night working, or drinking, or whatever it is you have been doing. When is the last time you sat at that table over there and ate a meal with us?"

"She is right Martin. You know she is. Look at what you are doing. You are repeating his patterns. And for what, to avoid getting hurt again?"

Who said that? David James? You're dead. I don't believe in ghosts and you are dead. What the hell! Am I going crazy already?

"Marty? Don't you have anything to say?"

"No. I mean you are right I have been gone a lot. And I do spend a lot of nights out. But I need to go tonight. I'll cut back after this I swear but I need to go tonight. I can't explain it I just need to be there."

To be there and drink this crazy notion of a ghost talking to me away for sure. I just can't be here. Night mares and ghosts talking to me. This house is making me crazy!

"To be there, or to not be here Marty? Go, just go leave your family behind and do whatever you want. But remember how it felt when your dad did the same thing to you and realize that eventually Beth will feel about her dad the exact same way you feel about yours!"

Those words stung, no much more than stung. They tore into my heart and hurt like hell. I knew she was right and yet I stood beside her, silent, and could not think of anything else but getting out of that house as quickly and I could. Exactly what my ol' man did for most of my childhood. I was no better than him.

Chapter 30

Sometime between my first and second beer the words my wife had said played over in my head. This time I listened to them. I was in a place I almost felt safe, almost felt like those moments of hearing the voice of a ghost was nothing more than a dream. I allowed the words to replay over and over again and actually hear what she had to say. It was a painful thing to hear, to realize I was becoming my ol' man. And it was interrupted by that same voice from beyond.

"Martin what the hell are you doing? You are turning into your worst fear and all because I died? Snap out of this before it is too late!"

Damn it! I'm not even safe in here anymore. His voice is haunting me from this damn stool. How can I go on with life if he won't leave me alone?

"Start living your life again instead of running away from it in fear and perhaps I could rest in peace Martin. For now I would settle for not running away from your family. Anneliese and Beth need you just like you needed your father as a child. You have the chance to be there for them. All you have to do is let go of some of this unhealthy fear you are clinging to and get back to living your life," he spoke again.

"Life's a dance you learn as you go. Sometimes you lead. Sometimes you follow. Don't worry 'bout what you don't know. Life's a dance you learn as you go."

I know this song. Sean and I use to play it that first summer we worked together up at Adohi. I think it was the only song I knew all the chords to that summer to be honest. Wow. It's been ages since I heard it.

As I turned on my bar stool toward the stage I swear I actually saw David James standing next to Sean up on the stage while he played *Life's a Dance*, a single made famous back in 1992 by John Michael Montgomery. Of course it couldn't have been true, but I'd only had one mug of beer so far, so it couldn't be blamed on the alcohol either. In any case, I sat there listening and singing along with my eyes closed picturing the two of us serenading the dining hall with it at the end of our last session back in '96. It turned out to be one of those moments in time that stuck with me over the years and I would think of it often whenever I dug back through my mental file of Camp Adohi memories. It was also one of those songs Sean and I did every Thursday night when we would sit up on that stage and play together. In fact, it closed the last set every single night.

By the end of the last verse I was singing right alongside him, standing next to him on the stage. I picked up his spare guitar, fumbling only momentarily as I searched for the right chord and began to play along.

> "Life's a dance you learn as you go
> Sometimes you lead, sometimes you follow
> Don't worry about what you don't know
> Life's a dance you learn as you go
>
> Life's a dance
> Life's a dance
> Life's a dance
>
> Take a chance on love
> Life's a dance
> You learn as you go"

Sean and I spent the next hour taking requests and playing the few songs I could remember from our years together up on that stage. The longer I sat there next to him, the more I felt the weight slowly begin to lift from my heart. I didn't realize just how heavy it had become since losing what I thought was my only real friend when David James died. It took another week or two to fully sink in, but that night I was reminded that I was certainly not alone. I had another friend, one that had felt like a brother to me a few years ago, and a wife and daughter who still loved me and needed me in their lives.

I later found out that Sean had called Anneliese when I arrived at the bar, before he took the stage, to let her know I was there. He called her again while I was in the bathroom after we finally took a break from playing together to let her know his plan had worked.

In his day job Sean was a music therapist. Don't scoff, it is a real job and there is some science behind it apparently. In any case, Sean is trained to use music to help people deal with things they are struggling with. Much of his work is with children who are hospitalized for cancer treatments and a few who are on the autistic spectrum. He uses music as a way to make a connection with them, to bring them out of their shell a little and give them a constructive way to express their feelings. Many of the kids he works with don't know how to get out all the fear and frustration from their situation in a way that does not involve violence. Music therapy lets them put those aggressive feelings to work banging on a drum, or keys of a keyboard, or just shaking a tambourine.

In my case, Sean used that extra guitar, and a song he knew would strike a chord deep in my soul to reach through my stubborn, terrified shell. I did not know it at the time, but it was something he had talked to Anneliese about a week or two before that night. To be honest I didn't know that Anneliese and Sean still talked at all. We use to be great friends, spent time together when we could, even went on double dates with Sean and whoever his latest girl was. That stopped not long before Beth was born and though Sean was always invited, and I think arrived, for all the major events in Beth's life, things were different now. I had a little girl to raise, and a wife with whom I got less and less free time with. What little we did have we spent alone by choice. I know that is common for couples after the birth of a child, and there is not a single moment I would want to change, but it was pretty obvious to me that I needed more than just family to get through this and I was happy that Sean cared enough to do what he could.

Chapter 31

That night at the bar with Sean, and some form of David James even if it was just my grief and imagination playing with my mind, was a wake up call to me for sure. Sure the words of Anneliese had something to do with it. I mean she did point out that I had nearly turned into my ol' man, something I refused to ever become. However, it was more than just realizing the road I was heading down that finally managed to put me on the path to healing the giant hole the loss of David James had created in my life.

It was not the end of my nights at the bar or working late though. I mean, I am human and can only handle so much change at a time right? I was more conscious about the number of late nights I worked and, as promised to Anneliese right after I wandered home from the bar that night, I cut down to only one night a week. I had played that stage all through college with Sean on Thursday nights. It was the place that I could be myself, spend time with my friend, and even where I first met Anneliese. I didn't know it at the time but that stage had helped me put aside the anger and betrayal I carried with me from Thompson Station. Now it would be the place where I used music again to heal my soul from the loss of the man with two first names. He even occasionally came for a visit, well his voice did at least.

By August of 2008, nearly a full five months after the loss of David James I was finally getting back to a healthy groove of life. I was still struggling with those irrational fears that his death was only the beginning of something but it no longer felt like the next shoe would drop at any second. I had been in possession of his cremains, he was cremated, for most of those five months and aware of his final wishes for them for years before that. But I was not ready to carry them out. Not yet.

I carried the green plastic urn containing the ashes of David James with me almost four full months, which I often just left in the car. The urn was inside a cardboard box tucked securely into my back pack, not actually in my hands. That would have made me crazy for sure! One Thursday night when I was playing down at Grady's Pub with Sean, for some reason I was compelled to take them with me both inside and up onto the stage. I sat the box down on the edge of the stage between the stools Sean and I spent the night singing from. He never asked but I am certain he knew exactly what was in that box. Our play list that night was proof enough.

We covered old favorites from camp like *Every Long Journey* and *On the Loose*. We did some 80's hair bands ballads, some pop, and of course a little country. The last two songs of the night were not talked about or pre planned, they simply happened. One after the other Sean and I looked at each other and began playing that John Michael Montgomery song *Life's a Dance* followed by Garth Brooks *The Dance*.

During the first chorus of "And now I'm glad I didn't know, The way it all would end, The way it all would go, Our lives, Are better left to chance, I could have missed the pain, But I'd have had to miss, The dance" I was in tears. By the end of the song I was not. I felt like it was time to finally let go of all the pain and loss I had been holding onto the last few months. It was time to let David James rest in peace and move forward with my life.

The following Saturday I took my pack, with the box of cremains inside, and headed out to Camp Adohi to carry out the final wishes of my lost but never to be forgotten friend.

"So long my friend! Until we met again, I'll remember you and all the times we use to sit right here, on the edge of this cliff and talk about the world below us. The good, the bad, the things nobody else could see percolating not far below the surface. Scars from my past, challenges I faced, heck even questions about where I should take Anneliese to 'pop the question'. You know, to be honest I guess in a way you were more of a shrink than a mentor much of the time. A shrink I trusted at least, not like those I had to see after Mother died. But more than that, you were my friend and filled a void in my life I never really knew was there until the day I first met you.

"I have always believed that people come into our lives

for a reason. That there is a greater plan somewhere driving us to do the things we do, go the places we go, and talk to the strangers that we meet along the way. You, my friend, are proof of that in my life. As much as the kids you worked with at Adohi are your legacy, so am I."

"And I couldn't have asked for a better one Martin!"

I figured you would pay me another visit. Seems fitting that it would be now. You know this makes me feel crazy sill right?

"Always so logical Martin. Sometimes you need to just have some faith in yourself. You are not crazy Martin. Someday you will understand that."

If you say so. Not that I mind hearing your voice from time to time, but I know you are dead and that most people don't talk to the dead. That makes me 'special' for sure.

"Oh you are special. More people than you think hear the voices of ghosts in their head, they just ignore them or call them a memory. Remind you of someone?"

"Maybe it is you who is special old friend. Nobody else has talked to me after they died but you. Well, except for Mother," I said to what I hoped was nobody. I checked over my shoulder to be sure I was alone just in case though.

Opening the container I slowly began to pour the

contents over the edge of the cliff and watch them quickly swept along on the current created by the gentle breeze. I had refused this task for months, refused to let his memory or cremains go. Today it was time to release him completely and allow myself to move forward on my own.

"It is with the heaviest of hearts that I hike along this trail today on a journey you asked me to make long ago. When I agreed to carry out your last wishes I never dreamed it would be so soon dear friend. You will be missed by many but likely none more than me. This trail seems far too empty, the sky less than blue, the grass not quite green. And yet, I know you are near even if just out of reach.

"I know in time this pain in my heart will fade and your lessons will live on inside me forever. I hold my head up high, my eyes toward the future and stumble toward tomorrow. I speak to you from the heart when I say you were far more than a friend, mentor, or employer to me. You were the father I had longed for much of my life and I will mourn your passing in a way I never can for my ol' man.

"Be well dear friend, I set you free today. Free to scatter on the wind, to return to the Earth in your truest form. To become one with all that surrounds me."

PART 2

SEPTEMBER 2011

So let the light guide your way
Hold every moment as you go
And every breath you take
Will always lead you home

> Charlie Puth
> *See You Again*

We have got scars from
Battles nobody won
We can start over, better
Both of us know
If we just let the broken pieces
Let the broken pieces go.

> SMASH
> *Heart Shaped Wreckage*

Chapter 32

The leaves blew swiftly across the pavement as I turned off the main road into the cemetery on the outer boundary of Thompson Station, NC. I hadn't been here in nearly fifteen years, not since the day after the last argument with my ol' man. The day I packed a backpack with all that I could carry, and couldn't live without, and headed off to begin a new life on my own. Just one of the many decisions I occasionally wondered about over the years but knew, both then and now, was what I needed to do.

As I slowly pulled the car through the old iron gate at the entrance to the cemetery I bit down on my lower lip to keep the emotions from overwhelming me. Winding my way down the sand and gravel road of the cemetery, I was taking it all in. Every blooming flower, moss covered stone, and waving blade of grass I could see. Every bird and chattering squirrel I could hear. I wanted to remember them all with absolute clarity in case this was also the last time I was here. I had thought about returning a few times over the years but daily life, and a little bit of fear of being recognized by someone in town always kept me away.

Today, the fifteen year anniversary of Kera and Kylee's deaths I decided was the right time to face my fears. Having spent months reeling from the death of the man with two first names, David James and all the memories and old feelings it brought up again from my childhood I knew it was time to return. The constant reoccurring dream of the car accident, one I had nightly beginning the day the twins were killed and lasting until the day I walked out of Thompson Station was also a clue. Yet, I had managed to put off this day for a few more years.

I'd spent nearly all of the last three years pretending things were fine, ignoring the obvious sign of the reoccurring nightmare that began after the loss of David James, subsided for a while after I finally came to terms with that loss, and then began again a few months ago. Initially it was once in a while, every few weeks or so. Lately it had become weekly, sometimes nightly. I could no longer ignore my guilt. I had left things unresolved, just buried them under a pile of proverbial baggage and run from it as a teen. Now I needed to finally deal with it, to put it behind me once and for all. I needed to be here to take that first step.

I knew I had been away too long by now and felt I owed it to them, and to myself I suppose, to stop by for a visit. It was time to spend a few moments remembering why they had been taken from me so soon. I still had not managed to forgive myself for allowing it to happen and the constant nightmares lately were proof of that. I knew my sisters had forgiven me long ago, yes I do believe that ghosts can and do forgive those of us still here trying to carry on without them. Mother has been with me for more of my life in spirit than she was living by now. The twins were closing in on that midway point now too, though they never felt the need to talk to me from the grave. Thank goodness for small miracles I guess.

Even with the belief that they had forgiven me, I just couldn't shake the feeling that I could have done something different. Maybe it was just hindsight, or wishful thinking, heck it might just be guilt but I felt like I could have somehow prevented their deaths. Hell I had raised them mostly, taught both of them to drive, in that car no less!

Stop it Marty! Get a freaking grip. Even if you could have, you didn't. Accept it and move on already!

As I slowly coasted around the last corner the large shade tree came into view. It was the largest maple tree in the cemetery and sat just behind the place where we had laid Mother to rest so many years ago. It was her favorite place to sit, under the shade of large tree, on hot summer days. I was abruptly pulled from daydreams of lying on a red and white checked picnic blanket reading books to Mother and the twins by an unexpected sight. Just past the tree I could now see a man sitting on Mother's marble bench. I stopped the car immediately.

"What the --? Who the heck is that?" I asked the empty seat next to me.

My stomach began to spin cartwheels and my mouth

immediately began to water as I peered through the windshield of my worn out Chevy Blazer at the stranger who was resting on Mother's bench. I knew instantly who it was without ever seeing his face. He was clearly there to visit my family. He sat facing their grave markers rather than with his back to them looking over the fence row still green in the early fall sun.

"But it can't be him! He would never step a living foot in this place, he wouldn't even come to their funerals. What the ...? It has to be someone else"

After slamming the car into park and grabbing the keys from the ignition I took one deep breath and exited the blazer in hopes of finding some passerby who needed a rest and decided to use Mother's memorial bench for a bit. That was its intent after all, to be a grave marker that could serve a useful purpose rather than simply stand vigil over a patch of ground covering her remains. Having a stranger put it to good use was far more preferable than seeing HIM anywhere near it as far as I was concerned.

Approaching softly in an attempt to not disturb the stranger my hopes were dashed. The disheveled man sitting on the bench was too familiar to be some random stranger taking a break on his walk through the cemetery. No, it was definitely HIM!

What the HELL is he doing here? Now? Of all the times for him to grow a heart and pay his respects he had to choose now? Maybe I should just go. I could cruise around town for a little while, come back when he is gone. Yes that seems like the best idea, though I'll have to make a few laps if I want it to take more than five minutes. Maybe head for the park along the reservoir. I could hang out there for a bit. Always did like walking in the sand along the shoreline. Chucking a few rocks into that lake might do me some good too.

I had agreed to leave, to turn away from him again and come back later. I had talked myself into retreat rather than confrontation with the man I walked away from years ago vowing to never lay eyes on him again. I couldn't, no I wouldn't speak to him now. Not here of all places!

"Martin, perhaps he has grown these last few years. Perhaps he has finally forgiven his transgressions enough to grieve for them. Isn't that what you had hoped for all along, for him to pay his respects to his lost family?"

The voice in my head had returned. It was the voice of the man with two first names, David James.

After his passing I had heard his voice a few times. Each one I convinced myself was simply a well-timed memory. That is until I no longer could. For now, I have decided to simply believe that spirits or ghosts do exist on some level and that I have the ability to hear both Mother and David James when I need to. Maybe I'm just more observant or have better hearing.

Truth is, it doesn't matter the reason. I might just be crazy, but so far listening to what they have to say has worked out well for me. So, for now at least, I'm going with it.

Everyone has a little voice in their head, their subconscious that places thoughts into our conscious brain to guide our path when we are faced with choices. Perhaps this is just my subconscious speaking to me and simply choosing a voice it thought I would listen to. What it is never really seems to matter, they are right every time and I know the man with two first names, David James is right again now. I need to find out why my ol' man is here, if he has in fact changed since we last spoke some 15 years ago.

Rather than turning back to my car I began to slowly continue toward my lost family, those deceased and living.

Chapter 33

"Ya' walked away in silence, walked away to breathe I reckon. You never stopped to say goodbye to me."

"I couldn't –"

"– Just listen dagummit! Let me say this here, get off my chest fer once."

"All right, speak. I'm listening."

"You left me here with no word, not one inklin' of where you was. No note, no call even saying you was all right. I lost ever thing I had left that day Son. Took some time fer me to heal up from that. To get right in my own head and heart. But I done made peace with it eventually and found myself here. I slowly picked up them pieces, seen the pain I caused ever one. –"

"– Yeah RIGHT! You see the pain you caused me, Mother, the twins? You really understand what it was like for us when we lost both of you that day? I doubt it!"

"Now, I know it's hard to believe someone you thought was lost. But don't go givin' up on this, don't give up on us. I know what I done back then was wrong. Leavin' you to raise them girls by yerself. I understand what I done put you through son, I do. An, I'm right sorry for that. I truly is."

"I bet you are. Sorry I left you here and went out to have my own life. Sorry I made something of myself away from this place. Not sorry for why I left, or how you treated me for years. That's impossible!" I said as I turned on my heels and headed back to my waiting car.

"Don't you walk away in silence! I ain't the man I used to be!" he screamed from behind me.

I stopped walking.

"It ain't impossible dagummit! I is a changed man Son. An, I'd like another chance with you. Chance to get to know the man you've become without me in yer way. That's all I'm asking fer, just give me one last chance!"

"Some things haven't changed, still got a short fuse on that temper Ol' Man," I said as I slowly turned around to see him standing in front of Mother's bench, hands shaking at his sides.

"And you still drop that thick drawl when you get really angry," I chuckled.

"I ain't angry, just trying to get through to you, Martin —"

"— Don't call me Martin! You never did before, don't start that now," I interrupted.

"All right, Marty. That's what I always done called you. You right about that. Marty it is," he spoke slowly working hard to not sound like an Appalachian Hillbilly.

Maybe he has changed! I knew when I walked out of his house, out of his life it was the end of the road for us. I made my peace with that knowledge a long time ago. At least I thought I did. But he's so upset, begging for me just to listen. Maybe it's possible to at least see, if not actually understand his side. Maybe it's true that time can change a man after all.

My ol' man was a strong willed, proud, southern man who never forgave a man who showed him disrespect. Leaving like I did, after the fight we had and all that was said was the greatest disrespect I could ever give him. That's exactly why I did it back then. It was something I have occasionally regretted but never once wished I had done it differently for more than a fleeting moment or two. I knew deep down it was the only way to leave my old life and start with a clean slate on a new one. As the man who now stood face to face with my ol' man again, I knew, for the first time beyond the shadow of a doubt that I had done the right thing. Funny thing was, so did he.

"All right Ol' Man, I'm listening to you now. Tell me how much you have changed and why I shouldn't just walk away again. Leave Mother and the Twins out of this, I've heard enough excuses to last me a lifetime!" I replied with even tone and carefully placed pauses.

I was thinking about each word as it exited my mouth making certain to get my exact point across. If I was going to take this first step, it was certainly going to be on my terms and with all my guards firmly in place. I had been hurt enough by my ol' man growing up, I was not about to let him get too close too fast.

"I is right sorry Son! That's 'bout all I got to say, all I kin say. No words can ever set right things I done, or maybe things I shoulda' done. When we done lost her, I done lost it. Spiraled down to a place that took you leavin' like ya' did to shake me from. For that, I thank you. You was strong enough to walk away, leave behind ever thing you knew and go out on yer own. To leave behind the sorry excuse for a father I was. Fer that I am grateful."

"Sorry, thank you, and grateful. You know all my life I never thought you knew the meaning to those words. Perhaps I was wrong. So what now? You expect us to hug it out, pretend things never happened and be a happy family of two again?" I asked partly curious and entirely still bitter at my ol' man.

"Maybe a meal some time? Chance to catch up on yer adventures. Hear how ya' ended up?"

"Okay, I guess lunch couldn't hurt that much. Maybe next Saturday? The diner in town still have good burgers?" I asked partly hoping he would say he was busy.

"Sure do. I'll talk at Maybelle and git us a corner booth in back," he replied enthusiastically.

"Don't tell her why. Please. I mean I agreed to lunch and whatever happens, happens with, um, this," I said gesturing to the obvious physical and emotional space between us.

I was skeptical that this was even a good idea let alone would be more than a one-time deal. It was a way to rid myself of some guilt I had buried deep and watched resurface moments ago.

"But it is just lunch and nobody in town needs to know our business. Save the 'Welcome Home' party for somebody else ya' know?" I continued.

"Sure thing. Reckon I'll be on my way, let you have yer time with 'em," he said as he passed me by on his way to the dark blue sedan near the front gate."

Oh this could go so wrong!

"Hey, Saturday, say noon a good time?" I called to him

"Sure thing!" he shouted back before climbing into his car and driving off through the iron gate.

I was alone again, alone with my memories, my fears, my concerns that meeting with him was a bad idea. I managed to push that aside for a bit while I returned to the grave sites of Mother, Kera, and Kylee. I was here for them, to lay to rest my guilt for staying away so many years. Now it felt like I hadn't stayed away quite long enough.

Chapter 34

"I can't believe I let him talk me, no GUILT me into this!" I exclaimed to the face in the rear view mirror.

It was during my Monday morning commute to the office just two days after running into my ol' man again. I had spent less than 30 minutes with him and here I was right back under his thumb again. Well, maybe not under his thumb, but certainly feeling guilty enough about the physical and emotional distance between us, and maybe a little bit about walking away with no goodbye or contact since, that I agreed to a meal with him next Saturday.

"Marty you are crazy for this!" I told myself as I grabbed the keys from the ignition and prepared for a day of keeping my brain otherwise occupied. Something that proved to be far more difficult than I anticipated.

Hours passed as I sat at my desk staring blankly at my computer monitor wondering how I would tell my wife Anneliese about the meeting. I had not told her I ran into my ol' man last weekend on my trip to Thompson Station. In fact I hadn't told her that is where I went last weekend either. It's not like I lied to her about it. I just said there was something I had to go take care of and would be gone for a few hours. She never asked where I was going, and I never volunteered the destination.

When it came to telling her about seeing my ol' man, I wasn't certain how, or if I even should tell her. Our marriage was built on trust, and I felt a little guilty for not spilling the news as soon as I walked back in the house Saturday evening after it happened. However, I knew my ol' man well enough to not want him anywhere near my family. He was poison to everything he got near and I didn't want that to infect my wife or daughter. It was a big enough risk for me to deal with him, it was better this way for sure.

So how am I even going to get out of the house Saturday for this lunch meeting? Saturdays we both have off and almost always spend them together as a family. I need a reason to not be there. That means I have to lie to her. Not just a simple lie of omission this time either. No this will have to be a real, look her in the face, and not tell the truth kind of lie. Ugh! Another reason not to even go Marty!

Between my two morning meetings, lunch, and afternoon meeting with an up and coming author I attempted to get some actual work done. I had managed to complete a first pass on the manuscript we were meeting about this afternoon. Unfortunately, I had not taken many notes on areas of improvement or ideas for marketing it at the upcoming book fair in New York. I knew I had about two hours to skim back over it and generate some talking points for the meeting when I finished it last Friday. That was my plan for today. Trouble is, I was having concentration issues and by noon had not even bothered to go to lunch let alone make any progress on the manuscript in preparation for my 1:30 meeting.

I checked my watch one last time as I put on headphones hoping to drown out the storm of thoughts in my head while I got to work reviewing the manuscript. It was a well written second draft by an author the agency had recently signed after reviewing his two very successful self-published mystery novels. The third in the series was my first solo project for the agency and I was determined to make it a success for all of us.

The book had less of a 'cop mystery' feel and read more like general fiction with a mystery twist. The main character of the first two books was now working to help a friend find his birth parents rather than catch a serial killer. I always preferred stories that felt more realistic than the typical mystery novels on the shelves of all the book stores these days. This manuscript had that quality, and a feel good story line that would appeal to a wider audience for sure.

Just as I finally felt I was beginning to make progress, a chat window popped up on my screen asking

```
Hey   Marty,   client   waiting.   You
available?
```

I checked my watch and panicked when I saw the time read 1:45. I immediately typed back

```
Yes!  So  sorry  was  sucked  into  the
```

> story and lost track of time. Be there in a minute.

My colleague John may have believed the excuse that I was so engrossed in reading the story that I had lost track of time if I had not also been clearly distracted during the meeting after joining more than fifteen minutes late. Thankfully it was not a face to face client meeting but instead a conference call with the client, marketing, legal, and a representative from the upcoming event. We were supposed to be discussing plans for the NYC Book Fair where the agency was showcasing the author's previous two novels, a teaser video, and few chapters of the upcoming project. I should have been alert and helping to plan for what would be on display, how it would be set up, what the script of the teaser video would be, and especially what chapters we would offer as part of the media print package. Instead I was off in my own little world thinking about my ol' man.

"Marty? Did you get that? Marty?"

Shaken from my memories I looked blankly across the table at John, the advertising manager in charge of this account.

"Oh, sorry. I was multitasking. What did I just miss John?" I replied shaking the fog from my brain in a new attempt to focus on work.

"We need the author approval of this marketing copy by end of day Thursday. Can we make that work?"

John repeated.

"Sure thing. I'll get it over to legal today. Once we have their approvals we can get it reviewed by the client and approved. Shouldn't take more than a day or two. Thursday will be just fine."

"Great. I think we're done here then ladies and gentlemen. Thanks to those on the phone. Sounds like Marty will be in touch with a few of you today to close the loop on this."

John punched the 'end call' button and made sure it cleanly disconnected before asking "What the hell is with you today Marty? You were late, not paying attention, clearly something is up. Everything okay at home?"

"Yeah everything at home is fine. Just had a long weekend I guess. Feeling a little out of it today. Sorry I was late John, and not paying close enough attention. I'm on top of it though. Won't happen again."

"Just not like you Marty. You are always early to meetings and the one taking notes the whole time smacking me back into paying attention. Let me know if you need anything here. I've been through this a few dozen times. Stress can get to you if you let it but you got this. This work will sell itself once we get it to the public and the author seems like a good guy to work with. I've had some that are a real pain. This guy is not."

"Yeah. Stress might be part of it. Thanks for the offer of help. I think I have it under control. I'll keep you in mind though."

Chapter 35

Managing to concentrate enough to make it through the workday, I returned home still struggling with how to keep my upcoming meeting with the ol' man from my family. I was still distracted, maybe even withdrawn during dinner and evening play time with Beth. It was such a nice night out we decided to take a walk at the nearby park but, rather than carrying on a full conversation I chose to mostly listen while Anneliese told me all about her day. When she asked about my day I mumbled something about it being 'fine' and 'typical' but nothing else of substance. That was not like me at all but I had been so distracted all day that I had trouble even remembering what I had done besides think about my past, my ol' man, and next Saturday.

I am certain it was obvious something was bothering me, Anneliese could read me like a book most days, but she never questioned, not even with her signature raised eyebrow look.

By Tuesday evening I had decided I shouldn't go, that I would just skip the meeting all together and avoid lying to my family. To me it seemed like a much better option to skip out on my ol' man than to lie to my wife. Wednesday evening brought another change of heart and I was back to searching for a way to make it work and lose the guilt of not telling Anneliese. After another very distracted day at work Thursday, I had once again decided it was best to not go and never mention that I had run into my ol' man at all.

Anneliese had taken Beth to her Thursday evening swim class at the local YMCA so I was on my own for a few hours after work, including for dinner. I chose an old college favorite as a quick meal, the same thing I ate for dinner most every Thursday night. As I grabbed some pizza rolls from the freezer and began to spread them out on the plate for reheating, I was running through the very short list of choices I had in my head again.

Marty, how the hell did you get here? Choosing to lie to your wife and see the ol' man again, or to just walk away from him when he might be sincerely a different person than you remember. You were a kid when you last saw him. A kid full of grief and rage no less. Was it really all his fault? You know you've wondered that more than once over the years. You have to go see him. You know that too.

"Oh David James I wish you were here right now. You would surely have some advice for this one," I whispered into the darkened kitchen longing for some time with my friend.

"Go Martin. You'll regret it if you don't," a voice inside my head spoke. It was his voice, the man with two first names. Clear as a bell I heard him, in his own voice, passing on advice.

"Whoa. I know it's been a long week and I'm exhausted. Now I'm hearing voices again. This never ends well," I told myself aloud.

It was not the first time since his passing I had heard the echo of David James in my head. It was however the first time in months, the first time since I carried out his final wishes and disbursed his ashes into the wind along the High Ridge Trail at Adohi. I missed hearing his voice for sure, but I was also hoping I had put it behind me. It's one of those things that always makes you uneasy, question you sanity a bit I guess.

"You are not crazy. Well, not crazier than most. You owe it to yourself to do this Martin. Anneliese will understand. Go," he spoke again.

I am crazy that is for sure, most adults do not have conversations with dead people! He might have a point though. If I bail I will always wonder 'what if'. I owe myself the closure of this meeting. Let him apologize if he wants. Let him say his piece, maybe share some of mine, and then close the door on my past once and for all.

"Go and keep an open mind. Maybe he really has repented. Give him the chance to explain. See what becomes of it."

"I'll try old friend. I wish you were here right now to hug but thanks for dropping in anyway. No matter how crazy this makes me feel."

With that I quietly ate my dinner, cleaned up the mess in the kitchen, and headed off to bed. It was only about 8 o'clock but I really was exhausted, and sound asleep by the time Anneliese and Beth returned home. The last time I looked at the clock on my night stand before Anneliese softly walked across the floor of our bedroom it read 8:29. I hadn't even changed from my work clothes into pajamas or crawled under the covers.

My dreams that night were vivid memories of times spent with David James over the years mixed with what I think were happy memories from my childhood. I didn't have many of them that included my ol' man I could recall while awake, but that night they seemed endless in my dreams. Trouble is, I'll never know how many of them were real memories or just fabrications of times I wish we had spent together.

Chapter 36

The drive back to Thompson Station felt very different today. Last time I made this drive I was filled with a little apprehension and a growing sense of guilt for staying away for so long. Today, it was not guilt but full blown dread from the moment I kissed Anneliese and Beth on my way out of the house. I'd used the excuse of a work deadline for my early Saturday morning escape from the usual family weekend activities of play, chores, and groceries. I knew eventually I would come clean with Anneliese about where I really went, but for both of our sanity that would not happen today. I was not yet ready to even mention that I had run into the ol' man again the previous weekend. No way was I ready to admit I had agreed to see him again and was blowing off precious family time to do just that.

He asked for this meeting. Begged me for it in his own way. I hate that I agreed to it in the first place, that I am sneaking out to meet with him again. I hate him! I guess I just need to meet with him and close that chapter of my life for good. Anneliese and Beth don't need to be infected with his poison. I might even have a few things to get off my chest today too.

As I neared the edge of town I noticed a few things I had missed when I was here last weekend. The hardware store where I worked as a high school student was gone. In its place was a park with swings, a slide, and one of those spring-loaded bounce animals Beth loved to play on so much. It was nice to see the green space in town. It helped to break up all the pavement and buildings in a town that once was just a couple blocks long start to finish.

Thompson Station had now grown to about double the size I remembered it being as a kid with a big box hardware store just outside of town near the highway. Progress I guess. It was still a small town. No other way to think of it. However, it was a small town that had managed to grow a little since I'd been gone. Far too many of these little towns just crumble away to nothing and become just a group of houses with a school and almost no business or industry to speak of. Maybe it was the proximity to the highway, or the mill that kept it going and growing. Maybe it was just close enough to Asheville that some people were willing to make that commute out to the country just to keep from living in the more urban areas near their jobs.

In any case, Thompson Station still resembled the town I grew up in, and left behind after high school, but it was definitely not the same place. The air felt lighter, smelled sweeter than I remember. The streets were wider, better taken care of, cleaner even than what I remembered on my last day here. It felt less like some hole in the map and more like a nice small town suitable for raising children and living a peaceful existence.

Has the town changed that much or is my memory of it so tainted by my hatred for the ol' man it just felt more oppressive to me back then? Did he really have that much power over how I viewed the world around me?

My thoughts were interrupted by a horn blaring from behind me. Apparently I had become lost in thought as I paused at a stop sign. Clearly the driver behind was tired of waiting for me to return to reality and drive my car through the empty intersection. I cordially waved in the rearview mirror as an apology and continued on my way to the diner where I agreed to meet the ol' man today.

Our reunion began peacefully enough, uncomfortable for certain, but as peaceful as two men who held back anger and hurt feelings could be I suppose. As promised Maybelle, a woman I remembered from as far back as days before Mother got sick, had set aside a corner booth for us in the back of the diner. She smiled warmly at me as she directed me to the booth where my ol' man was already sitting. Though she did not say anything aloud, her smile and simple nod let me know she knew who I was. I could only hope that her memories of me were as fond as mine were of her.

I remembered Miss Maybelle as a kind lady who used to babysit the twins and me from time to time. Since she also owned and ran the diner, that often meant we would spend time in the office located in the back of the kitchen next to the ice cream machine. The staff would often sneak us small snacks of that yummy treat too!

As Mother began to spend more and more time at appointments, we in turn spent more and more time with Miss Maybelle. In fact, it was her hand on my shoulder providing comfort at Mother's viewing, funeral, and burial service. It was Miss Maybelle who saw to it we got home after my ol' man left us that day, and it would be Miss Maybelle who made sure we had dinner every night for the next few months.

It was also Miss Maybelle that taught me to cook and do laundry. Things Mother, or my ol' man should have done. Mother was too weak to teach me much in our last few months together, though she did try. My ol' man however, had no valid excuse as far as I was concerned.

No tables around us had been seated at all, in fact no tables anywhere near us had been seated with customers. As I fondly smiled back at Miss Maybelle and took a seat across the table from my ol' man, I realized that we were as alone as we could get in a public restaurant.

"So Joe, is you having yer Thursday night usual or picking something new from that there menu this time 'round?" Maybelle asked.

"Well, it's not Thursday. I reckon I could order somethin' new today. Let me take a look see."

"All righty then. Be back in a few to check in on you," Miss Maybelle said with a smile as she walked toward the front counter.

After a few moments of silence between us I awkwardly asked "So, you come here a lot huh?"

"Once a week or so. Usually on Thursday nights when Steak-N-Eggs is on special. Nobody makes Steak-N-Eggs like ol' Jimmy. He still works here ya' know."

Mr. Jimmy was the nephew of Miss Maybelle and had been working as her short order cook since I was in the eighth grade. I knew that because Mr. Jimmy was actually Jimmy Johnson, a kid I had gone to school with until he decided it wasn't for him and stopped showing up halfway through our eighth grade year. When Miss Maybelle found out, she put him to work as a dishwasher right away hoping he would decide school was more fun. Mr. Jimmy thought anything was more enjoyable than being in school. He worked his way from dishwasher to part time line cook and figured out he was actually really good at it. He's been a short-order cook for Miss Maybelle ever since.

Luckily before the silence became too awkward between us, Miss Maybelle returned to take our orders. Turned out that my ol' man was a creature of habit and ordered his usual Steak-N-Eggs even though it was Saturday afternoon. I on the other hand, went for a childhood favorite and ordered the breakfast special. It came with a stack of 3 hot cakes, bacon, sausage, toast, and eggs. There was no way I would eat it all, but it had been so long since I had even tried I couldn't resist.

I had missed the taste of those hotcakes over the years, nobody could make them like Mr. Jimmy. Not even my other favorite short-order cook Thomas who worked at the diner out on Hwy 80. That same diner a trucker named Bob took me to the day I left Thompson Station. Thomas' hotcakes were good, but Mr. Jimmy could make hotcakes so silky smooth that they almost melt in your mouth. His never needed syrup to add flavor. All they needed was just a good coating of melted butter, and slow bites to savor them for as long as possible.

Throughout the meal my ol' man and I managed to ask and answer simple questions about how the other had been keeping themselves busy. I learned that my ol' man was still living in the house I grew up in but had gotten a few offers from people interested in buying it. He had his eye on a cabin further out of town. It was up the mountain a few miles and he thought he might try to buy it if another offer came through on the house. He had long since retired and was living off his pension, savings, and a little extra from VA benefits he earned from his service in Vietnam. According to him it wasn't much, but it got him by well enough.

Thompson Station was not an expensive place to live by any means and for my ol' man it likely meant he was clearing about $2000 a month between all of it. That was more than enough for him to live comfortably and not have to worry about monthly expenses. It might even be enough for him to tuck a little away in case of emergencies.

I managed to keep the conversation focused on him mostly. I was not yet ready to let him into my life or how I managed to survive after I left. My guard was still firmly in place, refusing to allow him in too close or to give away information that I may later regret sharing. Toward the end of the meal the conversation took a more hostile turn and I was very thankful I had made the decision to keep him at a distance.

I'm not certain what set it off, maybe it was nothing at all and he just finally got up the nerve to blurt out something he had wanted an answer to for years.

"All right Marty, come clean wit' me Son. Why you had a bug up yer butt with me since yer mother passed? Wasn't my fault she done left us ya' know!" He blurted at me after a few moments of silence between us.

"You walked out on her burial! Couldn't even bother to show for the visitation or funeral of the twins! Heck why should you, it's not like you did much to raise em!" I shouted back at him. He had lit the fuse on my temper and this conversation was certainly not going to end well.

So much for a peaceful meal together! Peaceful, is that really what I was expecting? I knew that was impossible.

He honestly thinks my anger toward him is unwarranted? He is crazy if he thinks that is how kids should be raised. I can't imagine ever doing that to Beth if something should happen to Anneliese, God forbid. I mean I would do everything I could to keep her closer, not push her away!

"That ain't exactly true," he defended.

"Yeah, how so? Mother took care of us while you were working. She fed, bathed, and played with us. She took us to school and all that cultural stuff you hated. She took us to church on Sundays and out to ice cream and the park after if we behaved enough. Where were you Ol' Man?

"Were you ever there while she was alive 'cause I know you weren't after she died. You walked out on more than her funeral. You walked out on us that day too! Left me to raise the twins, to step in and fill her shoes while you worked longer hours, found other places to be without us.

"Hell if it weren't for Miss Maybelle over there the three of us probably woulda' starved to death without you even noticing!" I shouted back gesturing toward the front counter of the diner where Miss Maybelle stood trying to ignore the heated words that could be clearly heard throughout the diner.

"That is true. I wish it weren't. I got shame fer how I was after losing her. Spent years wishin' it was me the Lord done took that day. God knows she was what y'all needed for a parent, not me.

"I put food on the table, roof over yer heads, clothes on yer backs. But it ended there. I walked out on what it really meant to be a parent the day we found out she was so sick. I'm not proud of that Son," he paused, collecting his breaking voice before nearly whispering the words "But I can't change it none neither."

Did he just admit to not being a parent? No protest, no defense, just admitted that how I saw him was correct? This might be the first time in my life he has admitted I am right about anything. And that face, this is no act. Guilt is written all over his face, in his voice. I never thought I would see this day.

"I'm sorry, did you just agree with my angry view of my childhood?" I asked making certain to pay close attention to his face as he heard my words and formed his reply. His face always gave away when he was lying. He never could have been a poker player.

"I did son. I was a terrible father. Hell I wasn't even a father. I provided what I thought you needed but missed out on the point of being a father. To raise yer kids with respect and love. To show them how to grow into responsible, hardworking, honest adults. I was just going through the motions of what was required to do so y'all didn't starve or wear out clothes. I done missed out on all the good stuff when you was a kid. And I done missed out on everything with the twins. God, they was so young when she left us. All I could think 'bout was pushing away everything that I shoulda' been pulling closer. All goes back to that damn war! Not that it's a good excuse, but is the truth."

"Wow," I whispered.

It was all I could come up with for a response. He and I were on the same page for the first time in my life as far as I could tell. He agreed that he was not a very good father outside of providing essentials for his children. He agreed that he had walked out on us emotionally.

Now what? He admitted it. He apologized for it. But now what? Wait, he blamed the war? Vietnam? Okay I took some psychology classes, and I know Sean has worked with a few veterans lately who show PTSD signs. Could he have PTSD? So what if he does, it doesn't change anything. He still did what he did, he still abandoned us!

Chapter 37

The remainder of that first meeting went as expected. We talked a bit more, discussed staying in touch possibly with lunch once a month or so, and then parted ways. I walked out of that diner with a lot to think about, both from my past and for my future.

Returning home I stepped back into my life, my family, my world away from the ol' man and the childhood that I lost so many years ago. Eventually the effects of that conversation in the diner, and of me keeping it from my wife, began to eat their way inside my little cocoon. Before long, I was struggling to keep those thoughts out of my head and wondering if it had been real or just a dream.

I just don't trust him! How do I know if he is for real, that he really has changed? This isn't the first time he has tried to apologize before pulling me in for another blow. It's how he works. He messes up, apologizes, messes up worse the next time until you refuse to let him in for the next apology.

But what if? Oh this is crazy! He's my ol'man he hasn't changed, he'll never change. Once a backstabbing, lying bastard always one. Right?

"Hey there Marty, you look lost in thought. Is there

something wrong?"

"Oh. Um, I'm just running through some ideas for this new book project at work. Nothing wrong. Just lost in thought, Babe. Sorry," I lied to my wife looking back at her over the dinner table.

I was not ready to tell her what had been bothering me for weeks since returning from that meeting with the ol' man. It was not even the first time. More than once I had woken her up as I tossed and turned from a recurring nightmare. When she would ask me what it was about I always just claimed I couldn't remember. I was trying to protect her and Beth from him, just in case my fears were right. What she didn't know couldn't poison her. But all this lying was taking its toll on me for sure.

"You sure. You have been quite and a little preoccupied for the last week or so. Zoning out in the middle of a conversation. Retreating into that head of yours. And the nightmares ... Is everything okay at work? Seems you have been spending a lot of time lost in thoughts about it," she asked with carefully chosen words.

"Yep, just have a couple big projects I am trying to juggle for this new author. I'm sorry I have been so out of it. I will try a little harder to leave work at the office. Maybe go spend an evening with Sean playing music this week to unwind, or maybe for a hike tomorrow afternoon up at Adohi to clear my head. I haven't been up there since they got the new signs installed. Seems like it's about time to check out the old stomping grounds. My calendar is open starting about one o'clock tomorrow. How about yours?"

"Busy day tomorrow for me. But if you think it will help, why don't you go? I can wrap up early enough to get Beth from school. Maybe even meet you up at the park with a picnic dinner."

Clearing my plate from the table I crossed the room to kiss Anneliese on the forehead.

"That sounds perfect! A little time in nature to clear my head followed by my two best ladies joining me for a picnic dinner. Can't get much better than that!"

Chapter 38

It was nearly 2:30 in the afternoon as I pulled through the gates of Adohi Park, a place I was intimately familiar with having spent nearly four years of my life here as a college student. Of course at the time it was Camp Adohi, a resident camp for teens catering to both boys and girls who wanted to learn outdoor skills and participate in adventure trips including rafting, canoeing, backpacking, and rock climbing.

Those were some of the best summers of my life and my time spent there as a young man shaped my future more than I could have imagined at the time. It was where I found my mentor David James, the man with two first names, and honestly it was where I found myself again. I shed the baggage of a damaged teen that'd lost his entire family to death, or their lack of ability to deal with death in the case of my ol' man, and I learned to stand on my own out from under the shadow cast upon me in Thompson Station. I owed a lot to both this land and to its former owner David James.

I checked the zippers on my pack and the lid on the water bottles before slipping it over my shoulders. As I headed off down the High Ridge Trail I paused at a sign telling how the park came into existence and smiled at the photo of David James above the caption,

'This land donated by the estate of David James.'

I didn't need to read the sign to know the story, or its heartbreaking ending. I knew all too well that the camp attendance had dropped off significantly in the last few years of operation. David James and I had talked a few times about his possible retirement and if he thought anyone would be willing to take over the camp from him. I was willing, and made an offer at one point. Having just had a baby girl born, the man with two first names, David James quickly talked me out of it. He knew that the fate of the camp was too much of a burden to place on a new family and it would not support us for long, if at all.

The camp remained open with limited operation through the summer of 2007 but did not reopen for the 2008 season due entirely to the passing of David James in March of that year. It was his wish, and provided for in his estate, that the land be donated to the state and used for a park setting. He allocated funding to convert or remove the buildings, create signage, and maintain trail heads for the initial transfer of the property. His legacy would now live on as the gates were opened to the public to explore the land, river, and lake found along its trails. For me, his legacy would live on deep inside my heart but I often came here to feel closer to my lost friend.

The High Ridge trail was one of our favorite places on property and led to a clearing about 1,500 feet above the rest of the camp. From that clearing you could see the mountains to the north and west, the lake below nestled among the pines that provided its shoreline shade on hot summer days, and on the clearest of days you could see as far as the northern mountains of Georgia. It was this clearing I was headed to, to have a conversation with an old friend.

A little over a mile and a quarter after entering the trail near that memorial sign I arrived at the clearing and immediately felt just like seeing it for the first time as the green canopy below stretched out before me past the cliff edge. The rocks seemed to glisten in the warm afternoon sun as the taller grasses and leaves on the low brush swayed in the gentle breeze. Though the temperature was easily over 80 degrees today, it felt more like a cooler mid 70's afternoon this high up on the cliffs.

This place had become my new 'safe place' replacing the one I once snuck off to as a boy when I needed to be alone. It was where I would sneak off to on my time off during summers working at Camp Adohi, and often was a hike I would make with my groups in the first few days of each session. Not all of them had the same appreciation for it I did but it was rare for any of them to arrive at this spot on the trail and not stand in awe at the view that lay before them.

I shed my pack and took a seat on the rocks that hung out over the edge of the cliff. Instantly the weight on my shoulders, from the pack as well as the world, lifted and I could feel that sense of peace begin to creep back into my conscious mind. I was home again up here on this cliff looking out over the deep blues and greens of the forest and lake below.

I had come here to clear my head during some of the worst times of my life in the past. Today really was no different and I was secretly hoping that the magic of this spot and the view it offered would again help to restore my faith in myself, my choices, and life itself. It would help if it also restored a little faith in my ol' man too, but I doubted it contained a fraction of the 'magic' that would take.

Chapter 39

"Oh I wish you were still here old friend. I could certainly use some of that wisdom you shared with me so often up here on this cliff. It was you who told me to 'step into [my] future and not look back.' To 'walk away from the past and move to a brighter new day'. I listened to you then, though it took most of that first summer together to understand what you really meant. But I listened. I moved on, left him in the past, left that town in my past. I found a bright spot on the horizon, followed that dream and left behind the guilt of walking away from his poison. Well, most of it anyway."

I was talking aloud to no one. This place, this clearing high on the ridge overlooking much of what was once Camp Adohi was my most favorite place in the world to sit and talk with my friend, my mentor, my adopted father figure David James. We would spend hours up here over the years talking about all kinds of things, and often when I had something that was bothering me he would manage to find a reason for a hike up here and drag it out of me. He had a gift for understanding when things were bothering people, and without them realizing it, helping them to figure out what it was and what to do about making it better. He was my Yoda, but with proper grammar and syntax in his speech.

"I miss you old friend!" I said holding back the tears welling in my eyes.

It had been a little over 3 years since his sudden passing. He was a relatively young man in his mid-60's who had been in good physical condition. I was not prepared to lose him so early in my life. I was not prepared to say good bye to the only man who had filled my ideal father role for me. But I guess we are never really prepared to lose those we love, even if they are of an age that their best days are behind them.

Still, when David James was taken from this world in a car accident not too far from the front gates to what is now Adohi Park, I did not handle it well at all. I went first into shock followed by a deep depression lasting a few months. During that time, I reverted to my old college drinking days to handle the feelings of guilt and loss before eventually emerging back into life and the world that had begun to pass me by. Thankfully, my wife Anneliese, and my old camp and college buddy Sean were there by my side through it all. They both had known and loved David James too, and much of my grief was shared by them as well.

For Sean, he focused on his work with children helping them with what he called 'music therapy'. It was still a bit strange to me that he played music with or to children and it somehow helped them with whatever stuff they were dealing with like a regular therapist or psychologist would. I guess you could say

I was skeptical at best be he loved his job and swore he had made breakthroughs with kids that no regular psychologist could. Truth be told, his music therapy had benefited me in dealing with the loss of the man with two first names too, but I never admitted that to Sean. I wouldn't want him to get a big head about it or anything.

While Sean refocused himself and his grief toward his work, together Anneliese and I managed to focus on the bright light in our future, our daughter Beth, and find the resolve to move past the grief and back into the life we were meant to nurture. It was not easy, but each day I would tell myself that nurturing her to be a happy healthy child would eventually allow her to grow into a well-adjusted and respectful adult who could carry with her a little bit of David James into a new generation. In some respects it meant his legacy would survive well beyond even my own memories of our time together and the wisdom he shared with me over the years.

"Life always comes full circle Martin. Moving forward sometimes means returning to where you think you started only to do it all again, but better," a voice inside my head spoke to me.

It was the distant and faded memory of something David James had once said to me on this very spot. At the time he was talking about my relationship with Anneliese. We had split up, long before I asked her to marry me, and I had moved on to someone new.

However, each time I thought of Anneliese something inside told me she was the one I was meant to be with. I was afraid to act on it, afraid to get hurt again.

"Fear of getting hurt is the surest way to do just that. Follow your heart; let your brain take a rest for a while," the voice spoke again.

It was another excerpt from that same conversation about my then ex-girlfriend, now wife. Yet it seemed to apply to my current dilemma with my ol' man as well. Not surprising actually. The man with two first names, David James was good at providing well rounded general advice to many specific problems. His words and thoughts were just good common sense a lot of the time and if you gave it a chance to sink in you realized it applied not just to what you were struggling with at the time, but to so many hurdles you had already crossed and many you would later encounter.

"Follow my heart. Let my brain take a vacation," I repeated aloud.

Maybe that isn't such a bad idea here. What does my heart think is best with the ol' man? He sounded sincere. He doesn't seem much like the ogre I remember from my childhood. The monster I ran away from all those years ago is now just an old man who seems a lot less scary and overpowering now than he once did.

"Time can heal Martin. Time is the only thing that can

heal broken hearts and shattered dreams."

A new voice in my head spoke those words of wisdom and instantly produced a stream of tears down my face. It was the sweet voice of Mother and something she told me not long before she passed. Time had not healed that wound, any maybe it never would.

I had managed to move forward, to allow her to enter my thoughts again but each time it produced a longing to be near her, to feel her warmth as she wrapped me in those protective arms and placed a gentle kiss on my cheek. My memories of her had faded over the years, but often I could still remember the way she smelled when I would curl up in her arms as a boy. She was my security blanket, one that was torn away far too soon in my young life.

Now some 25 years later I still felt the sting of her loss somewhere deep within, but I had not allowed it to guide my life. I had managed to move forward to something new and look upon that loss with sad but open eyes. It had helped to shape my future.

"Oh what was it David James always used to tell me when I was struggling with the demons in my past? 'Today is what is important to you – move on in life – let go of those things in the past that drag you down. Human beings mess up all the time, it's the nature of the beast. Letting go and forgiving them is the real challenge we face.' Yeah, something like that. Can I let go of that demon and get to know the man who has taken his place?" I asked myself aloud.

Well I guess it's let go or condemn him for a mistake he made 25 years ago and become just as cold hearted to him as he felt to me that day. I have worked my whole life to not be that person.

I had a small lapse after David James died where I risked becoming as distant and cold to my family as my ol' man was to me. When I realized that was the path I was headed down, I worked hard to change directions, maintain a balance in my social time, and dedicate as much of my free time to my family uninterrupted as I could each week.

"Walking away from him now when he appears to be sincere and extending an olive branch just feels wrong. Though accepting he has changed will take a lot longer to fully sink in. Baby steps Marty, take it slow and easy but ya' got to give him a chance," I said to the distant valley below before shrugging back into my pack and heading down the High Ridge Trail toward the parking lot.

Chapter 40

I left the Adohi Park that afternoon resolved to do two important things. First, I had to talk to my wife Anneliese about running into my ol' man again, and about where I had really been the following weekend when I told her I was at work. I owed her that much for sure. Our relationship was based on trust and understanding and I knew that once I explained where I had been, she would understand why I had been initially dishonest. It would sting that I had lied to her, but we would move past it much more easily than I would begin to honestly trust my ol' man again for sure. That was the uphill battle I had resolved to face next.

I called Anneliese before leaving the park to let her know I was heading home and not to drive all the way up to Adohi. Instead, I suggested we meet at a little diner just outside of Asheville. It was the very same diner I had stopped in with a trucker named Bob not long after I left Thompson Station, where I first learned of a place called Camp Adohi and of its director David James, and it also happened to be where I took Anneliese on our second date. It was already an important place in my life by the time I met her my sophomore year at UNC Asheville. I decided that I might as well make it even more special by treating her to my favorite meal, at my favorite table, with my favorite waitress, in my favorite diner.

Meeting up with Anneliese and Beth in the parking lot of the diner I took a long slow deep breath to clear my head and leave the worry and doubt behind me in the car. I wanted to enjoy my dinner and let Anneliese see that my hike this afternoon had done a lot for clearing my head. I also wanted to enjoy time out with the two loves of my life, and forget the complications that lay ahead of me back in Thompson Station.

Over dinner we talked about our days, my hike up the High Ridge Trail, and why I had been so distant and distracted the last couple of weeks. As predicted, Anneliese was both surprised and concerned that I had run into my ol' man and waited this long to say something. She knew of our rocky past, that I had essentially run away from home after high school and refused to ever have contact with him again. She knew many of the reasons why, that my childhood after Mother's passing was not easy and my ol' man had mostly abandoned us. She never asked about inviting him to our wedding, or notifying him of our daughter's birth. She knew he was not a part of our lives and, until now, assumed it would always be this way.

"So are you planning to keep seeing him then? To establish some sort of relationship with your father again?"

"Yeah, I guess I am. I mean he has apologized, for

what it is worth. And maybe it's time to forgive a little of the past I thought I had put behind me. I don't ever want to be the cold hearted man I saw as a father growing up. Walking away from him now because of our history would make me that person. I think I owe it to myself, to you and Beth to give this a shot and see where it leads."

"I think you are as warm hearted as they come, and very wise. Your mother can't be solely to blame for that big heart of yours."

"Perhaps."

Chapter 41

I managed another Saturday morning brunch with the ol' man at the same corner booth in Thompson Station a few weeks after talking to Anneliese about being in touch with him again. It was a little more pleasant than the first meeting, less fireworks between us as we tiptoed around the basic questions of how we had spent the last 15 years of our lives. He never asked about family, school, or where I went to when I left. I suspect he knew those were likely not things I was ready to discuss with him yet. I never asked if he came looking for me, missed me, or even noticed I was gone from his life. All of those were questions that would come out far too bitter in both asking and answering. None of those answers really mattered to our current situation anyway, though I did wonder what his replies might be.

As fall gave way to winter and the year-end holidays approached, life was too busy both with work and family to allow any more weekend meetings with the ol' man. I had been traveling on business to NYC, LA, and Denver for various book fairs promoting a project for my first solo client. Though I was only gone for a few days with each trip, I still wanted to spend all of my free time with my family to make up for being gone those few days. Maybe I was overreacting, this was the first time I had been forced to travel on business since

Beth was born, but it just seemed like I owed it to her and Anneliese to be there as much as I could on the weekends.

I had given my ol' man my phone number, well my cell phone number anyway. I was not prepared to share the house number with him just yet for fear he might call while I was not home and find himself talking to a daughter-in-law I had not yet told him about. I wanted him to hear about Anneliese and Beth from me, not an uncomfortable phone conversation where he called expecting me to answer the phone. I guess I cared enough about his feelings that I felt obligated to be the one to share that news with him.

I was holding back until I could do it in person, maybe after the first of the year, and hopefully in a way that would hurt as little as possible. After all I had walked out of his life, made my way in the world. That news he could accept. Could he also accept that in doing so I had a wedding he was not invited to and a daughter he knew nothing of?

Sometime in mid-January I finally managed to pick up the phone and dial a number from my contact list that had never been used. Maybe it was the holidays, or the year end activities at work. Maybe it was just plain old guilt but I had lost all track of time and began to feel bad for also losing touch with the ol' man again after our brief reunion the previous fall.

His voice on the other end seemed to perk up a little

when he realized it was me calling and he sounded almost happy when I suggested we get together for a long overdue brunch meeting. Because of some conflicts in his schedule we planned it for early February and I found myself actually looking forward to hearing him ramble on about how good the coffee was, or how nice the winter had been.

Walking into the diner again on a sunny February morning felt good. It felt like I belonged here in this place for the first time in longer than I could recall. I hoped I would be welcome to come back after today, after this brunch meeting. Given the conversation I was about to have, I knew it was possible it would be the last time I was.

I was beginning to form a friendship of sorts with my ol' man, something I never thought could happen in this lifetime, and I knew that it was time to tell him about my family. Maybe I also figured it was a way to end this before it was too late. I mean I told myself I hoped that he would understand my decision to keep it from him but I guess it's possible I was just hoping that it would reopen a wound we had begun to close. Then it would be him walking out and not me.

Chapter 42

"Hey Ol' Man coffee still awful?" I asked in jest as I took a seat in what had become our corner of the diner when the last of the tables emptied moments ago.

"Wonderful. Hot. Black. Bitter. Exactly how I like it."

"Bitter eah?"

"Jus like the two a us!" he winked and smiled making sure I understood he was joking, in part at least.

"Not so much these days I admit. But you might feel differently after today."

"Oh? Well I guess we should eat first. Jus n case."

The next half hour was spent in cordial conversation avoiding anything to do with our past, or current strained relationship. In fact, all I can remember about it was how good the hotcakes were, and that it was nice to be sitting across the table from my ol' man in a pleasant conversation filled mostly with small talk. I recall thinking to myself that I wanted it to last, that I sincerely hoped he could understand why I had not reached out to him before my wedding or daughter's birth. I was sure it would reopen old wounds, but I hoped it was something we could get past together.

For the first time in my life, I was seeing my ol' man as a human who made mistakes but likely did the best he could at the time. I was almost ready to forgive and forget those mistakes.

"I love dis song. You know yer mother and me danced to it ever time was on. No matter where we was when we heard it? In fact dis song is how we met. Was at this here diner, sittin' up that counter there where the soda fountain used be. She was wit her girlfriends down yonder by that jukebox and I heard dis song start a playin'. Well I done got up my nerve and walked right over to dat table and asked her to dance wit me. An she did!"

"Really? I've never heard this story before. I know the song, Mother played it a lot. She used to put that turn table on and I swear she wore out the 45 more than once," I said trying to hide the tears welling up in my eyes.

"Sho did! I bought her new one fer Christmas ever couple years. Now you knows why.

"So what this news you need to tell with me Marty? You agreed to sit down to a meal with me, come back a few times now, and now you reckon you have something to tell might go change things. Got me curious Son."

Tell with me?

"Not sure it will change anything, but likely to reopen

some old wounds. No easy way to say this but I think before this goes much further between us you should know that I have been married for going on ten years now and in a couple months my daughter will be celebrating her fifth birthday. Though maybe this will help. That song, *Earth Angel*, Mothers favorite. It was the song we danced to for our first dance at the reception. It was a way for Mother to be there with us that day. Now that I know the whole story, I guess you were too in a way."

"Father-in-law and Grandpop huh?" he said aloud but more to himself.

"Guess I deserved to be last to know. Lord knows I wasn't part a yer life back when you was getting hitched. She nice? Course she is, you married her an she give you a baby girl. What's her name? Both em?"

"My wife's name is Anneliese. She is very nice, I mean she tolerates all my quirks and has helped make me a better person and father. Our daughter is Elizabeth Marie. It worked out that she is named for both of her grandmothers. Her maternal grandmother's first name is Marie. I chose it to honor the Twins though. We call her Beth."

The following pause was long and almost unbearable near the end while I watched the ol' man's face mull over the news and consider his reply. He had just been told of two new family members. Two people who were such an important part of my life and had become part of my family without his knowledge years ago. The newest member was a beautiful little girl who carried the namesake of his lost wife and daughters. I watched for minutes while he struggled with what to say, and I swear I saw a tear or two welling in his eyes while he pondered. It was not at all the emotion I expected to see on his face. There was no anger, or resentment. What I saw instead was a mix of joy and sadness.

Pulling out my wallet I retrieved a photo taken at the holidays of my wife and me with our little girl. It was meant to be the front of our holiday cards but time got away from us and they were neither printed nor sent. Sliding it across the table toward my ol' man I said "This was last December."

Those tears I thought I had seen earlier were now clearly visible and very near falling to his cheeks while he looked over the photo, but none were shed. My ol' man was too strong to cry and willed them not to fall though they seemed to fill the bottoms of his eyes before he managed to blink them away.

"Now that's a right beautiful family. Sho done well fer yourself. Always wondered if me being failure as a father would rub off n you. Nice to see it ain't. Cherish 'em all yer days an never walk out on 'em. Got to be strong fer 'em, but most all, you got to be there, in the flesh, and the heart."

"That I will do for sure. They are my world now."

"I know this might be asking a lot but you reckon we could go someplace Marty? Have somethin' I think time you see wit yer two eyes."

"Sure. Okay. I think we could do that. Where to?" I asked a bit skeptical of what would come next.

"Home. Well, my home anyways."

Chapter 43

As we climbed the rickety wooden staircase that led to the attic of the garage along the back wall, the dust was so thick in the air you could almost taste it. This space used to be off limits to us as kids, but I had still spent many hours in here digging through old boxes and finding treasures that had long since been packed away and forgotten about. They were treasures to me of course, to most they were just old clothes, broken toys, and scraps of fabric from dresses Mother once wore.

My ol' man placed the key into the lock at the top of the stairs and the door gave way on hinges so rusted and worn they made an awful whine when forced to rotate against the pin. Fishing his hand along the wall he managed to locate and flip a switch that illuminated two of the four overhead lights. Here the air was nearly clear. The layers of dust had not been disturbed in long enough that few particles floated in the air. The contents of the room however looked like it had gone untouched in more than a decade. Some boxes had a layer of dust nearly a quarter of an inch thick upon them.

"Haven't been up here in a very long time," I said aloud.

"Ain't been here myself nearly as long. After you done left, didn't need to hide it no more. Stopped coming up in here to look at 'em."

"To look at what?" I asked both confused and curious.

"These," he said moving a box aside to reveal a corner of the room covered in photos of Mother and the twins.

Some of the photos even had me in them. A wooden bench he had made for me to reach the sink in the bathroom and kitchen as a boy sat upright, leaned against the wall below them. I was at a loss for words.

Is this where he went all those nights after she died. Is this where he mourned her loss when he couldn't stand to be in the house? I always thought he must have been off at the bar or a buddy's house forgetting. Was he really right here not forgetting, but remembering?

"Was as close I could git to her back then Marty. I done worked all time when she were alive. I worked to stay busy 'cause when I sit too long was haunted by dagum voices an visions. Flashbacks they call 'em now. Were ghosts from that damn war. I kept 'em away working. Keepin' busy ya' know. I done worked so damn much, missed out on all yer growin' up. And last years she was with us.

"Never told nobody this for, but never understood why she agreed to marry me in first place. Then stuck wit me so long after I come back from that war. Was a right different man, less man when I git back. Place done changed me Son, not for good neither. Saw things, did things still haunting me today. Lost good men, gone to so many damn services. All of 'em tore me up. Still can't walk into a house a death. Nothin' like yer mother's though. Losin' her done tore me up good.

"Tried be there fer yer mother's. Fought the rage long as I could. Reckon was foolish a me to think was strong nuff to beat it down then. Still wanted to be there fer you and them girls. Honor her last way I could. Failed that too, Son. So I come up in here to visit her. Couldn't go into that damn house a death. Didn't last too long in that garden a stones neither. I reckon ya'll thought I just up n fergit her, walked out her last moments on Earth. That I done, but I never fergit, Son. Not her or those two precious girls we lost few years later neither."

"So you came here. Why? Why here hiding in the attic of the garage?" I asked

"I weren't strong 'nough do it nowhere else. Raised not to show when I'm tore up 'bout somethin'. Always just bury it till I was alone. Then most times just come out angry. I was so angry. Angry at me, and her, hell even at you kids who ain't done nothin' wrong to deserve it. Just angry at ever thing. I come here to feel something besides all that anger an rage. Helped me to remember what sad felt like. Eventually, even what was like to be happy and loved. Those took while but some a these pictures was of happy stuff. Helped me to remember those times.

"Now I kin bring myself to go into that garden a stones, sorry, cemetery and visit them graves. I go ever year on they birthdays and anniversary of day they left us. Couldn't stay long first try 'for rage come back. Now I control it better. Managed nearly an hour 'fore you drove up that day. I ain't perfect and can't never be the man y'all deserved, but I am hoping to be there fer you and yer family from now on if ya'll let me be part a it."

In that moment I watched as a stray tear fell from his left eye. And another. He made no attempt to hide them, to shield them from my view. It was the first time I had ever seen him cry, and to be perfectly honest, brought a tear to my eye seeing him finally drop his guard in front of me. Then there was an awkward silence as I realized that I had no idea what to say to the man who had grieved their losses all these years when I believed he never even noticed they were gone.

"I was wrong," I spoke barely above a whisper.

It was a simple sentence that came out of my mouth before I even realized I was going to say it.

"I mean, I always believed that you just forgot them when they were gone. That you just put them out of your mind. I was wrong about that. You mourned for them the same as I did, just in your own way. I understand that now."

"I'm happy fer that Son. Never knew how to explain to anyone. Thought showing you this here place, this here shrine a sorts might help where words fail me," he replied wiping a stray tear from his cheek.

I had been wrong about many things in my life. One of the most important might have been that I was wrong to hate my ol' man for not mourning the loss of Mother or the twins. Make no mistake about it, I hated him. It was my hatred for him that drove me to leave Thompson Station and never look back. In fact, it was that hatred that had set in motion a chain of events that would alter my life completely.

Chapter 44

There are moments in our lives we experience without realizing just how significant they are until much later on. Oftentimes it takes months or even years for the realization to hit that a single moment had a significant impact on us. The moment I watched my ol' man walk out of the cemetery during Mother's funeral for example. That memory is forever burned deep within my soul and, though I was not conscious of it then, it was the event that gave me permission to begin hating my ol' man.

Off and on for the next three years, since shortly after I was smacked into that bush on our family trip, I had used the name ol' man to refer to my father, but almost never to his face. Though there were a few times I used it, and he didn't even seem to notice or care.

Father, Pop, and Dad all carried with them a level of respect in my eyes, something he no longer had or deserved from me after watching him walk out on Mother's burial service. I was just eight years old at the time, yet wise enough to realize that my ol' man had ceased to be a father figure in my life. However, I was unaware that because of that moment in time, my path in life was now forever altered. It was then that destiny chose a path for me that would lead me from Thompson Station to a new life without the ol' man being a part of it.

It was my hatred for the ol' man that drove me to excel at connecting with people, kids specifically, in ways I once wished he could do with my sisters and me. It drove me to meet the man with two first names, David James who served as a mentor, friend, and father figure in my life for many years. It also led me to my current family, Anneliese and Beth. It was a life altering moment in every way I can imagine.

So too was the moment I watched a tear fall from my ol' man's face as he looked upon dusty old photos of Mother and the twins. In that moment, I realized that things had begun to come full circle and, if I played it right, I just might get the chance to know someone other than my ol' man. It was a chance to perhaps get to know the man I longed for most of my childhood, my father.

Chapter 45

Throughout February and March I spent three more Saturdays breaking bread across the table from my ol' man and talking about all sorts of things. Each meeting was nearly the same, brunch at the diner surrounded by chatter about life and some occasional tougher questions about decisions we had made in the past. Following brunch we sometimes went for a walk in the park across the street, or over to the baseball field near the school. Whichever direction we took, the conversation continued along the route. Upon arriving at our destination we found a place to sit and speak a little more freely, away from listening ears of passersby and often would dive into more volatile subjects. But not always.

One simple question, answer, or topic at a time I was slowly rebuilding trust, a relationship of sorts with my ol' man. We were also getting to know one another in a way that most fathers and sons never do. We were both adults, with a history of distrust and dislike, and even a little hatred on my part. We had spent so many years apart that our biology had little to do with how we regarded the other. For us, it was more about filling in the gaps in our memories and sharing things most fathers and sons never talk about.

I learned a lot about my ol' man in those conversations,

likely more than most sons learn about their fathers in an entire lifetime. I had spent eighteen years of my life living under the same roof with him and yet had no idea about simple things like how or why he came to be in Thompson Station. Sure I knew where he was born, the basic route he took to get here, and things like that. But I never knew the real story about why he had left home in the first place, or how he learned to do woodworking.

It was the first Saturday in March when he filled that gap in my knowledge about his past before Thompson Station. It was also the day I learned that he hated the small town almost as much as I did growing up and when he told me that he felt like Mother's death was some sort of punishment for things he did fighting a war in Vietnam. He blamed himself for it in a way most never would have thought of. I certainly never did, but then I was just a kid, so what did I know about how to deal with death anyway?

In turn, I shared with him my journey out of Thompson Station, riding across country with a trucker named Bob, and the chain of events that led to me working many summers at Camp Adohi. I was careful not to describe David James in a way that made it seem he had taken the place of my ol' man, in fact he filled a completely different role in my life, but I did talk about him at length often. He was as much a part of me and my story as Anneliese and Beth. I considered David James family and to speak of him in any other way would have dishonored his memory.

Eventually, I even opened up to my ol' man about working to become foster parents. Anneliese and I had talked about having more kids but both of us had worked with so many great kids during the spring and fall Foster Camp weeks. For two weeks each year, one in late May, the other in early September, Camp Adohi opened to kids in foster care at no charge. It was staffed by volunteers and David James donated the facilities and nearly half of the food while other benefactors covered the rest of the costs of running the camp. It was a way to get the kids together with others like them, out in nature, and learning life skills they would otherwise have no access to because of the cost involved in attending a session at Adohi.

Some of my most memorable weeks at Adohi each year were actually ones I spent with kids who needed forever homes. To both Anneliese and I it seemed best for us to grow our family through a foster to adopt program. It was something we talked about shortly after getting married, but then found out we already had Beth on the way and put the process on hold. Now it felt like Beth was old enough to become a big sister, even if she ended up being the younger of the two siblings.

Our plan was not to find an infant, those were far too easy to place for social workers. Instead, we thought a young child, maybe 7 or 8 was a good age. Those kids often are harder to find forever homes for and sometimes come with a little extra baggage having spent years in unfit homes or foster care placements.

Anneliese had the patience, I had the flexibility, and we had Sean to help guide us through any turbulence along the way.

"Fostering kids huh? You think that's a good idea with one a yers already?"

"We do. Beth has requested a little brother or sister many times. Money and time aren't an issue for us. So why not foster a kid who just needs a chance in life?" I asked a little taken back by his question.

"zactly what I done though you'd say. Glad some a you ain't changed Marty. You always was one to look out for ones can't look out for themselves. Proud a that in you," he said with a slight glint of pride in his eyes.

Chapter 46

By the end of February Anneliese and I were about halfway through the required classes to complete the first steps of getting our foster license. The process was slow, frustrating, and sometimes irritating but we both felt it would be worth it in the end. At least most days we did. As things with my work project began to speed up I was also forced to work longer hours which slowed our process even more. We had to cancel on a couple of classes, classes only offered once per month by the agency, because of work conflicts.

There had been some heated discussions around the house about not making progress on our licensing efforts, but in the end Anneliese understood that this project, my first solo book deal took priority. It was my career that afforded us the ability for Anneliese to be a stay at home mom if she needed to be when our family expanded. I couldn't jeopardize my career without also jeopardizing our fostering possibilities. Some nights the juggling act was too much to handle and I would find myself down at the bar having a drink or two watching Sean play for the crowd. Inevitably every night I did that, I would also find myself chatting with him between sets about work and fostering frustrations.

One night in particular, Anneliese and I had argued

about never having time for the required classes. We had just cancelled on the second one in a row, and I stormed out of the house walking the few blocks down to the bar. I was just taking a walk to cool down initially, but found myself on a stool ordering a drink about 30 minutes later. I had come in just as Sean was wrapping up his set with a crowd favorite, *American Pie* by Don McLean. Moments later he was sitting next to me, drink in hand, asking "what did you do this time Marty?"

"Nothing. Work is in the way again and she's all hell bent on getting these classes done. I just can't right now. That's all. So we cancelled. Big deal. They offer it again in two weeks. But she just flipped out on me about it, so I took a walk."

"I hear you man, work comes first. But, it also seems like you aren't really that into this whole fostering thing either. Maybe that is what she is really mad about."

"Sean, I am into it. I just don't have time now man. I really don't."

"If it was that important to you, you would make time. Like when you took time off work for Beth last January because she was sick and couldn't go to daycare. You made time to stay home with her because she needed you and Anneliese had that conference to go to. Why is this different?"

"It's not! I mean it is, but I do care about this. I just –"

"– You just need to get your ass up Saturday and meet me here by 10 a.m. I'll clear it with Anneliese but you and me got a date partner. You need to get your head straight and I know just the thing."

"Sean, seriously? It's my family Saturday. No way Anneliese goes for this idea. I've been gone every other Saturday for the last month seeing my ol' man or working on this book deal."

"I know. Trust me. I'll get her to agree and not be pissed at you. You just got to be here by 10 o'clock. Deal?" he asked hand outstretched waiting for me to 'shake on it'.

"Deal. But I don't know how in the hell you plan to get her to agree to this," I said shaking his hand.

Chapter 47

"All right somehow you got her approval, I got my ass up and out of bed, and now I am here. So you want to tell me what the heck this is about Sean?" I asked as I stepped from my car Saturday morning at 10 o'clock sharp.

"You'll see. Get in, I have an appointment this morning and you get to be my special guest."

"Special guest? Like what the hell man. I am giving up time with Beth and Anneliese today for this. This better be really good. How did you get it past her anyway?"

"Easy, I told her you were going with me to an appointment. She knows what I do. She thinks this will be a great exercise for you."

"Oh is this one of your whacky music therapy gigs we're headed to? Sean I get the therapy part, and I love music but I don't get how the two go together. Why are you dragging me into this today?"

"Hush up man! You will see all in good time. All in good time, Marty. Besides, I seem to remember not too many years ago you benefitting from a little music therapy yourself. Or did you think I would forget about that night on stage with me?"

"Oh whatever! There was more to it for sure, but I guess it may have helped that you played a song that triggered some good memories."

About 30 minutes later Sean and I were walking into a cold gymnasium attached to a church and community center in an area of Asheville I had never actually been to. I knew there were sections of the city that some called 'rough'. I mean every city has issues with low income, violence, and blight. This was Asheville's for sure. Sean had been here many times and was comfortable in the neighborhood, I was not. I was even more uncomfortable as we carried in thousands of dollars of musical equipment and set it up in the middle of the gym. Seriously there was enough stuff here for a small school band.

"Hey Sean, what's with all the gear. I mean drums, keyboard, guitars? You doing some group things today? I thought you were just a one on one guy," I finally asked as I set up the last of the three drums he had packed.

"No, just one kid. But I like to give them choices."

"Choices?"

"Choices," Sean echoed as he smiled at me from behind the keyboard he was securing to its stand.

"Yo Sean who dis?" I heard from across the gym.

"Toby! Looking good today my man. This is a friend of mine. Brought him to help me set up some new instruments for you today. Marty, meet Toby. Toby, meet Marty."

"Nice to meet you Toby," I said extending my hand in friendship. He just stared at it.

That was about as exciting as that first meeting with Toby got to be honest. He spent more time siting silent in his fold out metal chair than he did even looking at either Sean or I. I did see him checking out the guitar from the corner of his eye a few times but never got up to go play it. As part of the session Sean handed him a drum stick, and a drum, and allowed Toby to answer questions with a single or double tap on the head. In defiance, Toby began to beat the drum so violently that he eventually put the stick through the head of the drum. Sean simply told him not to worry about it, that it could be repaired. I was angry at Toby and in an instant I could see him smirk as he realized he had gotten the reaction from me he was looking for. He was testing us, or maybe just me.

Sean and I packed up the gear and headed back to the bar about two that afternoon. The ride back was mostly silent except for Sean asking me if I had gotten anything out of my adventure that day.

"uh, not really. That kid was a brat. Destroying that drum like that," I answered honestly.

"He was testing you Marty. I knew he would. Though I would have preferred he not destroy a drum head in the process for sure. He has trust issues. Comes from an abusive background. He is used to adults, adult males in particular lashing out when he makes them angry. He was testing to see if you were friend or foe."

"I am neither to him, He is a child. How old is he anyway? Looked about 10 maybe."

"He's 9 actually. And you are more to him than you might think. And he to you. I saw the connection between you. You felt it too I bet. Something about you kids that have dealt with the loss of a parent so young, something oddly connects you all together. I could see it. So could he."

"Wait what? You said he was abused. His parents died? I'm confused."

"His mother, yes. A few years ago. His father is unknown. The abuse was in the system. It happens Marty, it's why they make it so hard to become a foster parent. Trying to train people and weed out those that have no business around kids. Sometimes they miss one, or somebody comes in after the social workers have already given the green light for placement. Anyway, Toby is a good kid he has just been dealt a bad hand in life so far."

"So when do we see him next?" I asked, a smirk across my face.

"Next Saturday. Glad you are on board with this. He might open up to you. I haven't been able to make a breakthrough with him yet but it's been close. I'm hoping your weird connection with him will be the key. He's just still so angry."

"He will be for a long time Sean, a long time my friend."

Chapter 48

Sean and I spent every Saturday from 10 to 2 together for the next month. Each of them were spent driving to the community center gymnasium, setting up instruments, maybe talking with Toby or hearing him beat on a drum or two, and tearing them down again to drive home. The first few meetings seemed rather hopeless to me but Sean was optimistic that he was making progress. I felt like most of it was a waste of time but once in a while I would see something in Toby, a smile start before he caught it. Maybe the way he carefully stroked the head of the drum before impaling a stick through it, but something.

By the third meeting I had decided to take a more active role and see if I could crack his angry exterior. About ten minutes into the session I picked up a pair of drum sticks and began to tap out what I could recall of the old high school cadence. When not out on the football field, I was also a former band geek on the drumline. About seven or eight bars into the cadence, at the part where it began to repeat 16th notes alternating in rim shots, Toby turned his head to watch me play. I had piqued his interest.

When I finished playing and began to lay the sticks down on the head of the drum Toby asked, "Can you show me how you did that?"

"Did what?" I cautiously replied.

"That. I mean that thing you just played. It was cool. How did you do that?"

"Oh. I was in band in high school. Played on the drum line. It was our cadence. I could probably show you how to play it but you need to start from the beginning and practice. You ever play drums before?"

"Nope. Never mind," he replied as I watched him shut down on me instantly.

Uncertain what I had said, I looked to Sean for answers. He simply shrugged.

Grabbing the sticks from atop the drum I walked toward Toby intending to hand them to him. Instead he flew from his seat running across the room screaming "Don't come near me. Just stay away!"

I dropped the sticks immediately and stood in shock. He apparently thought I was angry, or at least was going to harm him in some way. I had no idea what to do except drop the sticks to the floor. Sean slowly walked toward Toby using his soothing counselor voice to help calm him while he approached. I watched in awe of how quickly he was able to calm Toby, and me honestly. He was a very skilled counselor for sure. This music therapy thing though, still not a true believer.

Much to my surprise, in just a few short minutes both

Sean and Toby were walking back across the room toward me. I slowly sat down consciously making myself as small and non-threatening as I could before Toby got too close. As Toby sat back in his chair he looked at me and asked a question I was unprepared to answer.

"So, Sean says your mom died when you were a kid too. What happened to her?"

Chapter 49

"So Ol' Man, now that we've had a few meals together and talked about some of the past decade or so of our lives, when do we get to the hard stuff? Or do we just not go there and try to piece together some kind of relationship just ignoring what drove us apart in the first place?" I asked doing my best not to sound bitter or condescending.

"Thought we done talked about it. Well some of it anyways. What you thinking we missed? Somethin' specific you needin' drug up?"

"Maybe. Maybe not. Guess I'm just still trying to figure this all out. I've been angry at you most of my life. No, I should be honest, I've hated you most of my life. This new communication, being adults about stuff and trying to see if we can even be a part of each other's life is a little new and kind of strange to me I guess."

"Me too. Reckon I knew you hated me but hurts me to hear ya' say it for sure. Probably deserve it."

"I don't say it to hurt you, well not anymore. At least I don't think I do. I mean I know what happened, well, happened and nobody can change it. Hell, I wouldn't even want to change it. Leaving this town was the best thing that happened to me in my youth. It opened the door for so many great things, great people I crossed paths with. I might be a little sorry that it took hating you to drive me out into the world, but I am happy that it happened. Does that make any sense?"

"Does. Ever body needs a little shove once in a while. Turns out you leavin' like you done was a good thing fur both us. Opened my eyes a little ya' see. Helped me realize what I was doing, how burnt up I was, how I done took it out on ever body around me. Took time mind you, but eventually I come round. Got my head straight. Worked through some my own stuff. Got me to a place where I could forgive myself for what I done. All of what I done. And eventually got me here back face to face wit my son. Even if he's not sure he wants be here."

"I'm here. I don't do things I don't want to. Just still so much I need to process. Seeing you again brought back up things I thought I had put behind me long ago," I replied nearly in a whisper.

"Speak up Marty. Not young as I once was. Hearing starting to go out on me. You talk to your wife about these meetings yet?"

"What? What do you care anyway? Not really your business is it," I replied quickly.

Have I told Anneliese yet? Who the hell does he think he is? It's none of his damn business if or when I talk to her. I mean I did tell her already but still, I can't believe he even asked me that. He might be my ol' man but he is definitely NOT my father!

"Whoa settle down. Was just asking"

"Yeah, but it's not your business Ol' Man. I'm an adult now remember?"

"I kin see that. Though suddenly this feels lot like you is 16 again now don't it?"

"How would you know? You were never around when I was 16. Hell you were never around when I was 10, or 8, and not even much when I was 4 or 5 were you? I helped Mother with the twins while you were off doing whatever. When she was gone I raised them myself. I stopped being a kid the day after we buried her. Thank God for Mrs. Maybelle who come in and taught me to cook, to care for them. Mother tried. She was too weak to do much good in her last months. And where was you Ol' Man? Where the hell was you?"

My temper flared out of control and thought I actively attempted to reign it in somewhere around telling him how I gave up my childhood to take care of the twins, I failed. By the time I finished I was so angry I was spitting my words across the table at my ol' man. Tossing each like a dagger aimed directly at his heart and taking pleasure in watching his pupils' dilate as he heard and processed each of them. I assumed it was in anger. I was wrong.

"I was runnin' away from you, from ever thing Marty. I was all kinds of tore up, but most all I was terrified of life on my own and how we was gonna' get by without her. I was some kind of burnt up she done got sick. I was furious she died. I was a mess and no good to you youngins then. Hell I was no good to nobody. I knew you'd be all right. You always was a fighter and you would land on ya' feet. Those girls though. They needed a mother. And theirs just left 'em."

"She left all us Ol' Man. And you did too."

"I did. I told you I got shame 'bout that. But I can't change it neither. I never dealt with death real good. Lost a lot of good men in the war. Saw a lot of death there too. When I come home, some them ghosts come with me I think. By the way, your Appalachia accent comes back when you git angry. Did ya' know that?"

"I did. What the hell does that have to do with walking out on us?"

"Nothin. Ever thing. Oh so hard to explain. Ya never been there. You can't know what is like to see death ever where you turn. To have to bury good men someplace they never shoulda' been. To leave 'em behind in shallow graves cause they was killed someplace the dagum government says they never was. You just can't know."

"Try me Ol' Man. I know you were in the war. I know you were in places the government claims we never set foot in. I know you saw a lot of crazy stuff, war is like that. I've seen movies, read books, even taken some Vietnam History classes in college. I know some of what you went through. I just don't see how that makes a man walk away from his family when they need him most."

"I couldn't keep myself together then Marty. Ever time I thought about her being gone I done broke down. Didn't want you to see me like that. When I tried to go into that building, for her viewings, I couldn't. My legs done quit working on me. I mean I tried to step in them doors and just physically couldn't. Thomas, one them workers there had to help me to the curb for a sit down. My heart was racing, couldn't catch a breath. Chest felt like my heart was gonna' explode right outta it.

"I was in bad shape. Now they tell me was all in my head but I swear to God thought I was gonna' die that day. Outside was better, in that garden a stones, sorry, cemetery. I was better but eventually it started in again. I had to leave to keep from interrupting the service. Turned out the further I got from that place the better I done felt."

PTSD? This sounds familiar. Physical symptoms brought on by mental trauma. He was in a war, sure he saw horrific things. I've seen the movies, bad shit happens in war for sure. Maybe he was reliving it? Psychology class was a long time ago but I remember something about recent trauma, like death of a loved one, can bring up old trauma like war stuff.

Sean might know more.

"And after?" I asked still sounding quite bitter and curt.

"After what? After she was gone just got easier to not deal with it. I ain't defending what I done. We done talked about this so many times already. Can't you just listen to what I is saying, not what you think I is for once?

"I mean I done messed up not being there for you youngins. I did. I own that. But I wanted to be there for them services and just physically couldn't do it. My head was all filled with war stuff, hearing gun shots and helicopters, people screaming an cryin' and junk. Think I even saw one my buddies shot layin' across the gate when I stepped out. Once I got out yonder by the curb, outside them gates, was gone, all it just gone.

"But I can't defend what I done after. I should' been there for my family and I wadn't. I was too wrapped up in my own grief. My own sorrows and fears. I let ya'll down. I deserved for you to walk out on me and I is lucky you agreed to come have a meal with me after all a this. I'll understand if we all done after today Marty. I will."

He's right, we have beat this dead horse plenty over the last few months for sure. And, there it is again. Another apology of sorts, admitting he messed up, telling me he wished he could have done it differently. Still he sounds sincere. I know I am still angry about so much stuff from our past but I might owe it to him to give this a shot. Hell I might owe it to me.

"Not planning on it being the last Ol' Man. I think we might be just getting started here," I replied with a quick smile and a wink.

Chapter 50

Sometime mid-April, Anneliese and I managed to get into the third class of the foster to adopt program. It was about two weeks after the meeting with Sean and Toby where I opened up to him about losing Mother at a very young age to cancer. I had not planned on talking about it but Sean thought it was time to play that card hoping it would help Toby begin to trust me. It worked. Something happened that afternoon between Toby and I, a connection was formed creating the basis of trust between a skeptical adult and a traumatized child.

Toby was about the same age as I had been when Mother died and going through many of the same emotions and struggles I faced. He did not have siblings to care for, or to love and be close to. Toby was all alone now without his mother where I had at least been one of three children Mother left behind.

Not long after that meeting I watched as Toby, an angry child prone to lashing out in violence, began to find a better outlet for his internal rage. Sean and I worked with him on basic rhythm and proper sticking and he was rapidly becoming a pretty good drummer. So much progress was being made that Sean began to meet with Toby one day during the week to work on basic guitar chords and strumming techniques as well.

Saturdays though, were all about learning to play that old high school cadence.

I was beginning to understand how music therapy could help in ways that talking never could. Toby was pouring himself into learning to play two instruments rather than bottling up that energy until it came bursting out in violence. Creative outlets gave him a chance to dump that energy without harming himself or others. And, it might also give him a chance to find a forever home again.

I learned through Sean that Toby had been almost adopted three times over the past year and a half but each one failed due to his angry outbursts. The families were unable, or unwilling to take on such a violent and angry child out of concerns for themselves and other children in their homes. I couldn't blame them. I had seen what Toby was capable of if pushed to his tipping point. I also saw that he was becoming less angry with each passing week and his grades in school were improving as well.

That was what finally convinced me both that Sean's music therapy was not a joke, and that Anneliese and I needed to make the time to finish our fostering license requirements. There were a lot of kids like Toby in the system just waiting for a family to understand their struggles and provide a forever home. It was time Anneliese and I were available to become one, maybe even for Toby.

By the end of April, things were looking up in many directions of my life. Anneliese and I were now just two classes and a home inspection away from becoming licensed foster parents and my ol' man and I were well on our way to a new relationship that transcended father and son into a new realm of friendship I never thought possible. There were still issues of mistrust and hurt from our past, we were by no means perfect, and I still did not think of him as a father in my life though he continued to remind me that he was in fact that, at least by biology terms. However, there was a mutual respect and understanding that allowed us to continue getting to know the other and remain in contact. I had even found myself referring to him by his first name once or twice rather than just ol' man.

Chapter 51

I was on my way home from the office when my cell phone chirped with the new voicemail alert. I had not heard it ring over the radio and was surprised to see the message light blinking at me when I flipped it open at the next red light. I was even more surprised to listen to the message and hear his voice.

"Hey Marty! I hate these dagum things. Never know what to say on them. I guess just call me back when you can. Want to talk about meeting someplace sides the diner Saturday. Thanks."

Um this is new. First he calls and leaves a message. He almost never leaves one. To top that, he wants to change the place we meet kind of last minute. I mean we have always met at the diner for brunch with zero exceptions. Guess I better call him back and see what's up.

I quickly dialed the phone number hoping he would pick up before the machine did. I hated leaving messages in a 'tag you're it' situation. Thankfully, about half way through the fourth ring he answered.

"Hello?"

"Hey Joseph. I got your message about Saturday. What's up?" I replied.

"Joseph huh? So this first name thing sticking around?"

"Well, I can go back to just ol' man if you prefer it. I just thought maybe we had moved to a first name place."

"No I reckon Joseph, or Joe, is better Marty. Don't nobody call me Joseph unless I was in trouble honestly. I always just go by Joe growing up and with my friends after that. But don't be expecting me to call you Marty all the damn time. Son is just as respectful as you given name ya know."

"Agreed. So back to Saturday?"

"Saturday. I just thought maybe we could meet a little earlier in the day. Is 9 too early? The diner ain't open for brunch then so I figured we could just meet over there cross the street if that is good witcha."

"Sure that would be okay. Is there something going on later? Some reason you wanted to meet earlier in the day?"

"No. Just thought would be a better place this time round. If it works for you I will see you then."

"Sure Joe. See you then," I said as the line clicked and went silent.

That was strange all around. He calls to change it, time and place. His voice was shaken, something is definitely up. I guess meeting Anneliese and Beth will have to hold off till next time. Better go this one alone and find out what has gotten into the ol' man – er I mean what has gotten into Joe. Man that still feels a bit strange, he's been ol' man for so long. This will take a little longer to get used to for sure.

Chapter 52

As we slowly walked along the shoreline in absolute silence, I began to wonder why today he had chosen not to meet in our usual spot. His mood was different, a little darker behind that usually warm smile of his. His call last night requesting me to meet him here rather than in one of our usual places definitely kicked my brain into high gear trying to figure out his reasoning. Many things crossed my mind, but nothing prepared me for this eerie feeling now growing deep within.

From the moment I left my house this morning to my eventual arrival not long ago and the discovery of him sitting in solitude on a bench overlooking the lake from the top of the hill, something just seemed eerily calm and right about his choice. All of our past conversations had initially begun in a public place, like this, but with far more people around. The park was empty this time of day though the temperature was easily over 70 already. It was a perfect Saturday in early May with bright blue skies and puffy white clouds filtering just enough of the harsh sunlight that it was comfortable to be outside without sunglasses for a change. Rather than the low din of clinking silverware and rattling pots and pans I was used to at the diner in town, I could hear the peaceful whoosh of the waves as they lapped against the sandy shore and then receded back into the lake. It was quiet, empty, and peaceful. This was different from every angle, and something deep inside told me that a whole lot more was about to change.

Drinking in the calmness of the scene, the sound of the waves as they lapped at the sand beneath my feet, the bright blues and greens of the sky and water stretching to infinity before me, the rustling of the leaves as the gentle breeze flowed through the branches of the surrounding trees, I bent down and filled my hand with as many rocks from the shore line as I could hold. Tossing them one by one back into the lake from which they came, I casually asked, "So what's with the change of venue? Not that I mind the scenery out here, and it's a nice day to spend a little time on the beach, but this is a first."

I could hear him slowly suck in a breath, clearing his mind of everything but the reason he had asked to meet me here today. I could see from the corner of my eye that he was nervous, hands shaking slightly as he pinched the bridge of his nose between his thumb and index finger and then lifted his head allowing them to trace the outline of his jaw line.

Finally he began, "Spent a lot of time these past few months seeing doctors, getting tests done, mostly just routine stuff, never saying much 'bout why they wanted so many dagum tests for. But lately ..." he paused, catching his breath and composure for a moment then continued, "They been saying a lot lately, one appointment after the other, all wit the same result. First that puzzled look, then they drop they head, take a long deep breath, and finish it off with some gobly gook doctor speak that I never understand but know is all just bad news." His reply was slow, each word carefully chosen and then spoken deliberately; again something new from him.

Doctors? Does that explain this scene, his unusually somber mood?

As I listened to him speak I continued to empty my hand of the remaining rocks, tossing each a little farther than the previous as the gravity of this conversation began to set in. Down to my last rock, I was tossing it lightly in the air and catching it with my right hand while I listened to him pause for a moment, perhaps catching his breath, perhaps preparing himself to utter those two words. I knew before he said them and I squeezed the rock tight in my fist as I heard him finally speak 'bad news'. Instantly, my heart grew heavy, my eyes began to sting, and I clenched my jaw as I dropped my head to hide the pain clearly visible on my face. I was certain I already knew the answer, but I needed to hear it from him. Calmly, I asked a single word question with an extremely complicated answer.

"Cancer?"

Nodding his head ever so slightly, he quietly replied, "Up in here," as he tapped his index finger against the golden brown skin just above his right eye.

I swallowed hard, staring off into the distant waves as they languidly rolled their way toward the shore just a few feet in front of me. Silence filled the air as I soaked in the news and formulated the courage to ask my next question. Finally, with limited eye contact I quickly glanced back to the face of a man I had only just begun to get to know again after decades spent estranged, and then down at the rock I had been squeezing in my right hand. Afraid to look up, to see the eerie calmness in his eyes, I continued to stare at the simple black rock in my hand while I asked, "Can they do anything?"

"Odds are bad, risk is high," he paused, swallowed hard, and then cautiously continued, "I done told 'em I ain't gonna' roll the dice," finishing the last of his words with a voice straining to hold his calm facade.

I winced trying to block the news from seeping into my brain, to keep it from registering as a reality I must now face. It was a hopeless cause and I bit down on my lower lip as I lifted my gaze from the rock still clenched in my fist, to the face of the man standing before me. He seemed so normal, so healthy and fit standing in the cool brown sand, water lapping at his feet. He didn't look sick, let alone like a man who had just told me he was gravely ill. As our eyes made contact, reality set in and I could see it in his eyes. This was not a joke, not something that had just happened overnight. He had been struggling with this for a long time, seeing one specialist after the other, all with the same conclusions. The man now standing before me was nearing the end of his journey, and he was almost at peace with that reality.

"How long?" I bravely asked, hoping to hear something positive for a change.

"Hard to say. Reckon it could be months, a year maybe, two if I is lucky," He answered back as if he had been rehearsing that very line in his head for the last few moments, and maybe he had. It was an obvious question to anticipate after delivering this kind of news, and I am certain it had been one of his first questions when the doctors finally told him the very same thing he was now telling me.

Months, two years at most, that's all I have left with him? How long until he gets sick, starts to deteriorate, to fade away? How much longer will he be the same man I've gotten to know over these past few months, the improved version of the man I remember growing up? How long has he known? Is this what is behind his new view of life, the world as I know it?

Silence filled the air once again while he waited for my next question and I wondered what to say. I tossed the rock from hand to hand before eventually dropping it into my pocket and picking up another from the beach near my feet. I lost all track of time as I flipped back through the years of memories in my head. I knew eventually that would be all I had left of him, just memories of things we once did, of laughs we once shared, and stories we once told. There were huge voids in my mental scrapbook. There were years spent living my life without any contact between us, not even knowing if the other was still alive. I wondered if there were enough time left to help fill some of those voids, to right some wrongs and undo some of my mistakes.

"You awful quiet over there. What you got running through that head a yers?" he finally asked breaking the silence between us.

"The years I wasted. The time I missed out on with you. I can never get that back and pretty soon I'm gonna' want it all back, the years I should have been here plus all the times I was!" I said before throwing the rock I now held in my hand as far out into the lake as I could make it go.

I stood, tears filling my eyes, hands shaking, and heart pounding in my chest, facing the water before me. I wished I could simply slip beneath the waves peacefully and return to find that this was all just a bad dream.

"Wouldna changed nothing, certainly not this," he said placing a hand gently on my shoulder as a comforting gesture, "and we both know it needed to happen," he finished.

"You still buying that cabin in the woods?" I asked

quickly changing the subject away from my own inner guilt trip.

"Depends on what the bank says, but I sho am hoping to."

"Guess you'd better take that offer on the house after all," I blurted out with a cry in my voice.

That was when I finally let go, allowed myself to feel the enormity of the situation, allowed reality to sink in completely, and gave up trying to keep my reaction to this news internal. With a heavy heart, I began to process the news that one of my greatest fears was coming to life before my very eyes. I had spent most of my adult life not caring one way or the other about my ol' man's death. I swore I wouldn't shed a tear, and certainly wouldn't bother with the funeral. Six months ago that began to change. I knew then that letting him in was risky, that I was putting myself out there to get hurt again, but I never dreamed that it would be like this.

I guess I always knew someplace deep inside that one day I would be faced with the reality of his death, I think we all understand that on some deeper level from birth. When I allowed myself to begin a relationship with him again, I knew he was near the end of the road, but I had always hoped that finish line would be much further in the future. Still, here it was staring me in the face, looming in the not-distant-enough future, bearing down on me faster than I was prepared to see. Our days together were now limited. A tangible, yet arbitrary number now cast a shadow over them on some cosmic countdown chart, crossing them off one by one as each sunset arrived. I was losing him, this time forever, and there was nothing I could do to prevent it.

Chapter 53

My visit with Joe was cut short that day, a mutual decision I might add. As I climbed back into my car leaving him standing on the beach staring out over the lake, I felt as if the whole day had passed me by in those few hours we were together. We had spent some time after his bombshell landed talking about odds and ends, the cabin in the woods he was hoping to purchase, the offer he was considering from the development firm to buy the home he currently resided in, the same one I had spent the first eighteen years of my life in. We even talked about sports and politics, two subjects we rarely if ever spoke of because when they did come up it generally didn't go well.

My ol' man and I were on opposite sides of many things, he was a NASCAR fan, and I never understood the point of racing anything, especially cars. His political views were a little to the right, mine a little to the left on most things, especially when gun control and equal rights were involved. Football was my favorite sport to watch, and play for that matter, and Joe had not seen a game since I was a junior in high school. Somehow in the gravity of that conversation, or more likely the desperation to not talk about his diagnosis, we managed to hold intelligent conversations and respectful debates about all of those things and more. It had been an eye opening time together in more ways than one.

Eventually I ran out of things to say, as did he, and the silence began to settle in between us again. I found myself staring off in the distance wondering how many more days like this he would have, how many we would have together before he began to disappear. Other than Mother, I have never personally watched someone deal with or die from cancer and I was so young I had no idea what she was going through at the time. Unfortunately, I had heard plenty of horror stories from friends over the years that had gone through it as a caregiver.

Then there was Kevin, one of the authors I worked with closely in my early days as an editor and who I considered a friend of mine long after he moved on to another publishing house. A few years back I had watched him gradually become ill and eventually suffer the cruel fate of a man diagnosed with HIV/AIDS. In his final days he suffered from dementia, didn't remember to do simple tasks like eat and bathe, and had to be placed in an end of life care facility where he eventually died. I would go visit occasionally, but often it was only for a few minutes at a time because he rarely remembered who I was and would instead carry on conversations with people not even in the room. I knew it was the disease, and I saw with my own eyes what it did to his body and mind. He became a shell of his former self. Someone that looked like the man I knew, but contained none of his wisdom, compassion, or knowledge. All those things had slowly died when the dementia set in and in the end, when Kevin finally breathed his last breath, I was relieved to get the news. His suffering had finally ended and he could rest in peace.

What little I did know of brain cancer, I was aware that it carried with it the same symptoms that Kevin had suffered. Eventually Joe would suffer from dementia and become a shell of his former self. Eventually it would ravage his mind to the point that nothing of him remained and only then would it finally allow him to rest peacefully.

"Here I go again! God, Kevin died like seven years ago after that two year battle with AIDS and David James hasn't even been gone that long. That loss is not even five years old yet and still feels like it happened last month some days. I've barely begun to heal from that. Now I get to watch what I saw with Kevin all over again in a much shorter time span and feel that stab of death's sharp knife in my chest before too much longer. Or do I?" I asked my reflection in the rearview mirror as I pulled my car from the parking lot and began to head in the direction of home.

Chapter 54

I remember the sun was barely peeking through the clouds as I made the right turn onto Highway 80 just outside of Thompson Station. The sky was blue behind the low cloud deck and it certainly looked like a storm was rolling in from the north. How fitting would that have been, to have the sky cloud up and dump buckets of rain on my physical world like the news of Joe's condition had done to my mental state. Sort of a cheesy effect from any number of Hollywood movies I know, yet fitting just the same. But I was headed south, and driving into a beautiful bluebird day.

Inside my head I was simply spinning in tighter and tighter circles toward a deep black nothingness. Since hearing the news I had been only going through the motions of life, not actually living it. I was walking, talking, breathing, and now driving like I was still alive and well. Inside I was far from okay and more numb than I could remember feeling in a very long time.

This feeling was familiar, I knew the sense of dread and loss well in my life, but this somehow felt very different. Not loss, or depression, or grief. It was something that blended the worst of those into one strange feeling and tossed in a growing rage to top off the volatile mixture inside me.

"Get a grip Marty! Clear your head enough to pay attention while you drive this damn car!" I screamed at myself in the silent car as I whipped the steering wheel to the right guiding the car back into my own lane just seconds before coming head on into a large SUV honking its horn at me.

"Too much to stick around for here to do something stupid behind the wheel and wind up dead. Calm down! Concentrate!"

With slow deep breaths I gradually calmed myself and managed to clear enough of my mind that I arrived in the parking lot of Adohi Park about two hours later. I was not certain I set out to come here, or even what exact route I took to get here. But I had arrived and felt the need to go for a cleansing walk along the High Ridge Trail.

Before setting out on foot I made a quick phone call home to let Anneliese know where I was. We had decided to meet up here later today for a picnic dinner with Beth, it was a family activity we tried to participate in at least once a month when the weather allowed for it. I was a few hours earlier than I had planned to be and Anneliese reminded me that she had a full afternoon of errands to run on her way up here. She was going to try cutting a couple of hours off her schedule so that we could spend a little extra family time in the Adohi Park since I was already there.

Chapter 55

Exhausted, more so mentally than I was physically, I finally crested the ridge entering the clearing that looked out over the bluff to the land below and beyond. The hike up here, much like the drive from Thompson Station to Adohi Park, was a blur of images, sounds, smells, and haunting words circling in my brain. I desperately needed to clear my head, to purge what I could, and bury what I was not yet ready to deal with.

All of the disappointment, hurt, and guilty feelings swarming inside my head had reached well over my tolerance levels. Those were familiar feelings and belonged in this situation, though I needed to purge them for my own sanity. Even the sense of helplessness fit. I was helpless after all. I was not able to change fate, or time. I was certainly not able to fix what the best surgeons and physicians in modern medicine could not cure. All of that made sense to me as I took up my post along the face of the ridge and began to process the swarm inside my head. What didn't feel right here was the anger.

Since shortly after climbing into the car leaving my ol' man on that beach alone, I could feel it in the pit of my stomach. As I drove, it grew from that small seed of anger into the foul taste of rage. As I hiked my way along the High Ridge Trail, I focused my brain as best I could on the hike. Along my path rocks were kicked, even roots and small trees were victims of my growing anger. More than once I found myself grabbing hold of low hanging tree branches and stripping them of their leaves as I yanked my hand downward. Clearly my rage had bubbled to the top of this emotional stew inside my gut.

"What is it I am angry with? With cancer, or time? With life, or death? No, those are nothing to be angry at. They're out of my control. Anger doesn't make sense, nor will it resolve any of them. So what is it Marty? What are you so angry at you feel like you could snap at any moment and take this rage out on the nearest moving object?"

As I sat pondering that question, sorting out the day's events and conversations into neat little stacks to be dealt with one by one, it suddenly occurred to me.

"Son of a Bitch! He knew. He knew all along that something was wrong. Maybe not what, but something big for certain. He kept it quiet, lured me back in. All just to rip it apart again. He hasn't change a bit has he?" I screamed to no one in particular. No one was there to hear it, or to refute my logic.

"Hey there Martin, long time no see. What brings you to my neck of the woods, literally, old friend?"

I turned abruptly to see David James crest the final

approach to the clearing from the trail and walk toward me on the edge of the cliff.

"I, um. Well I come here to think, clear my head. Always have since that first time we hiked up here together back in '96," I replied easily.

I must be dreaming this. The man is dead. He did not just hike up that trail. But this feels so real, The sun warming my skin, the breeze against my cheeks. I feel all of that. Just go with it Marty, see where this little adventure takes you.

"How you been Sir?" I asked trying to hold back the smirk knowing I already had the answer.

"Always Excellent!" That was his response to anyone who asked him how he was feeling, or doing. In his terms it meant that as long as he was able to provide an answer he was good enough.

"How about you Son, how has life been since I saw you last?"

"Well, I'm not certain how to answer that. I mean you're dead and have been for a long time now. It's been hard to adjust, to accept that I can't just drive up here and go for a hike with you anytime I need to sort out something. You would always provide those nuggets of wisdom. But I have managed."

"So what is troubling you now Martin? I can see the

heartache on your face. Talk to me."

"It's my ol' man. The one I told you I never wanted to see again, not even at his funeral. A few things have changed since then. Ran into him, he apologized, tried to make up for some lost time, sucked me back into his world. Then he dropped a bomb on me that he is dying. Makes me wonder if his supposed change of heart was all just to bring me in close, open me up for one last slam dunk of emotions."

"Glad you listened to that advice I gave. You kept in touch with him even when you wanted to just run away again. I doubt he intentionally set you up on this though. When did you run into him again?"

"You know. When I went to visit Mother and the Twins graves. Last fall."

"Right! And how long has he been sick?"

"I don't know for sure. He says he has been seeing a lot of doctors trying to figure out what is wrong. Seemed like he only recently found out. Like he wasn't sure how to tell me even. He just seemed so matter of fact that this was it, the end of his road. He is choosing to do nothing about it, to just pretend that it isn't there and let it kill him."

"Pretend what isn't there?"

"Cancer. Oh God, he has terminal brain cancer. He

wormed his way back into my life and now he's going to leave it again. That Son of a Bitch is just going to walk out of my life again!"

"Whoa Martin. Slow down a second. So he has cancer. I am very sorry to hear that. Is there anything that can be done to cure it?"

"No. Non-operable. There are treatments that might help but nothing that can cure it."

"He's your father Martin –"

"– Don't call him that! He ain't, hell never was my father. Being a father is a whole lot more than just biology. A father is there for his kids, takes care of them, knows them, and helps them grow to be adults. My ol' man never did any of that. Truth is you were more of a father to me than he ever was. I never did tell you that did I?"

"I knew."

"Of course you did," I said with a chuckle.

The man with two first names always knew far more than I ever said aloud. Of course he would have known that I felt like he was a father figure in my life. Even if I never once said it to anyone.

"But at least set your past anger aside for a minute and think about this logically Martin. Even if he is the vindictive man you remember from your childhood, does it make sense that he would hide his diagnosis from you, plan to run into you again at the cemetery, apologize his way back into your life, and then just when you think everything has evened out decide to tell you he is dying just to hurt you again one last time?"

"Yes!"

"Really? Think about it with you head, not your heart Martin."

He's right. It doesn't make sense. And the timeline doesn't either. I saw him last fall then went months with no contact over the winter. That was my choice. Maybe he knew something was up, maybe that is partly behind his change of heart but this isn't some elaborate scheme to suck me in and stomp on my heart again. I'm not sure he is even capable of that kind of planning if I have to be perfectly honest. And the man I have gotten to know over these last few months just seems far too genuine to be the same vindictive jerk I remember as my ol' man. He has honestly changed.

"I guess that is pretty impossible. But he is leaving me again anyway. There is nothing I can do to stop him this time, and he seems oddly okay with it. Maybe that was just an act but I think he might have already decided this is his time to go. That is not okay with me!"

"It doesn't have to be okay with you Martin, it will

happen no matter what. Why don't you spend the time you have left getting to know everything you can about him, the man he is now. Maybe it will help explain the man he was to your daughter when she starts to ask questions."

"Ahh Beth, my pride and joy!"

"She is beautiful, spitting image of her mother, thank goodness. Hate to see what she would turn out like if she got your looks," he teased as he elbowed me in the ribs.

"Ouch! Man that hurt!"

Wait if this is a dream would I have felt that? Yeah maybe. I feel pain in that nightmare about the car accident. But nobody else is in that dream. Just me and a whole lot of silence.

"Sorry, I forget my strength sometimes. Hang in there Martin. Spend some time with that father of yours and learn from him for a bit while you still have the chance. Most kids like you don't get a second chance to get to know their distant ol' man. Mine never had the change of heart like yours seems to have. Take advantage of it or you will regret the missed opportunity when it's gone."

"Marty! Marty you up here Babe?"

"Anneliese? Is that you?" I shouted back turning my

head away from the man with two first names, David James and toward where the trail opens up to the clearing.

Anneliese emerged with Beth in the Kiddie-Pack backpack smiling from ear to ear. Careful not to slip I scrambled to my feet and met her halfway across the clearing with a gentle kiss for both of my precious ladies.

"Hey I thought you had a full afternoon today?" I questioned.

"I did but it's after 6 o'clock. I saw your car in the parking lot and figured this is where we would find you. It's such a beautiful day I thought maybe we would join you up here for a little bit before that picnic I brought with me. You okay Marty? You're pale, look like you've seen a ghost."

"Funny you should say that actually. I think I just did," I said helping her shed the Kiddie-Pack and setting it on the ground so that Beth could enjoy the view alongside us, a lot further from the edge than I had previously been sitting.

"What do you mean?" Anneliese asked her voice riddled with concern.

"Not sure really. I must have fallen asleep. I was the weirdest dream! Sat right there on the edge of that cliff and had a conversation with David James himself, in the flesh. It felt so real."

"Really? So what did you two talk about in this dream of yours?"

"My ol' man."

"Ol' Man? So you've backed off the first name thing again huh? What happened this time Marty?"

"You know I went to see him today, this morning. He didn't want to meet at the diner, wasn't the right place to tell me the news I guess."

"Yes. What was his news Marty? You're shaking," she said reaching for my hand.

"Apparently he has terminal brain cancer. He's choosing not to treat it. He's dying Anneliese. We just started to get to know one another again after all this time and now he's checking out on me."

"Oh Marty, I am so sorry to hear that. You haven't talked much about your visits with him but what you have told me was so positive. Felt like you two were getting to a good place. Any idea how, um … "

"Long? Could be months, maybe a year. Two seems like a real long shot. So many things could go wrong and change it all. Hell he could be dead tomorrow for all I know."

"Yeah, that's life Marty. Cancer or not any one of us

could be dead tomorrow babe. It's why David James always told us to 'live for the here and now, let tomorrow take care of itself' remember?"

"She is right Martin. Listen to her!" I heard almost as an echo in my head. The voice of David James again.

"Did you hear that?" I asked Anneliese.

"Hear what?"

"I just heard his voice again. This time at least I didn't see him standing in front of me saying it but I swear I feel like I am going crazy and talking to his ghost now."

"Marty, you're a little over emotional right now. Stress can play tricks on you for sure. Maybe you just need to take it easy and relax a little. Though, I have to tell you that I believe in ghosts, and some people's ability to communicate with the dead. Maybe you are more connected to the universe than you think."

"Oh now who sounds crazy!" I laughed playfully pushing her away from me.

"C'mon lets go back to the picnic area and have some of that dinner you packed us. Haven't eaten much all day, lord knows I could use some food right about now!" I said getting to my feet and extending a hand to help Anneliese from the boulder she was sitting on.

Chapter 56

I blamed my first vision of the man with two first names, at the bar on stage with Sean a few months after his passing, on grief. I passed it off as a result of high stress, a little alcohol, and a lot of grief. I never gave it much more thought than that initially. I eventually settled on the idea that perhaps spirits are real and present in our world all around us. Perhaps life does not cease to exist after death but rather, we are just no longer in a visible form to those still alive. I mean haven't we all had an encounter with someone we knew was passed and yet felt so very much in the room with us?

I do not choose to debate the existence of spirits or ghosts however, I simply accept that something happened both in that bar years ago, and sitting on the bluffs along the High Ridge Trail. Something I cannot explain or rationalize in any way. I was there, I know what I saw and felt. I know most reading this now will simply think I am insane in some way. It matters less than you know.

What does matter is that because of a short conversation with a very wise, and admittedly deceased man, I managed to make peace with my ol' man and his past transgressions more than I thought I ever could. I realized that my journey in life for the next while, maybe months, maybe more, would involve being far more of a son to him than I ever thought I could be. Eventually, he would need me to be there for him in a way I never dreamed was possible.

I could not walk away from any dying man knowing it would mean he was left to finish his days here on Earth alone. Not even my ol' man. No matter how much I once hated him, and maybe a time or two secretly wished this fate upon him if it meant Mother could be returned to me.

It took me a few days to settle all this in my brain, but eventually I made a phone call Wednesday afternoon that would forever change my life. Dialing the phone felt right, and the relief in his voice as he answered confirmed that, maybe for the first time ever, we were of the same mind on the subject.

The call was short, mostly to apologize for the delay in calling him back. He had tried to reach me both Sunday and Monday. I was honest, not making excuses for why I had not answered or called him back. I told him his news had taken a few days to sink in and settle. I needed the time to get a handle on all that was racing in my head before I reached out to let him know that, no matter what was ahead of us, he was not alone in this fight. I intended to do right by my ol' man in this journey, and I admit it was at least in part driven by my own guilt for the way I left things so long ago between is. That was less relevant than my desire to help him tackle this challenge in his own way, to live out his last months however he chose to, and to be there in the end when his card was punched one for one last day. The man had helped to give me life, I owed him that much even after all that had happened between us already.

Chapter 57

"Martin, I have news maybe you ain't gonna' like."

"Martin?" I questioned.

"It's yer name aint' it?"

He's never called me Martin that I remember. Memory issue? That thing in his head to blame?

"It is, but you always call me Marty. Mother called me Martin, she hated when people shortened my name, but –"

"– She had a bug up her butt bout using full names didn't she? She refused to call me Joe like ever one else done. No. To her I was Stephen. Hell, my own mama called me Joe. Easier to separate me from my pappy, where I done got my name, but you Mother, God rest her soul, she done told me once she was raised to call people she cared for with they full name. A show a respect. To her I was always gona' be Stephen."

"She told me something similar when I asked why she always called me Martin instead of Marty like you did. I never let anyone call me that after she died. Well not until many years later when I met David James, who also refused to call me Marty no matter how many times I tried to correct him."

"Sound like a wise man. Right happy you done run into him when you did Son. Lord knows you needed someone to show you how be a proper man after the mess of a father I was."

"He was for sure. So what's this news you have I might not like? Is it doctor visit news?" I asked apprehensive that it could be about his health.

"No. No. No. Nothing like that. I just selling the house. End a the week. I got more than I thought she was worth and it done been paid for since you was back in school. I just don't need the space no more. Found me a right good two bedroom cabin up the hill I think be perfect for me."

"Finally selling huh? I knew you were looking at a cabin further up and that developer was tossing out numbers. That house has so many memories for sure but not all of them are good. It is your house Joe, do what you want it does not affect me really."

"How'd you know that?" He asked in a vaguely angry and extremely suspicious tone.

He told me about it. How does he not remember?

"You told me –"

"– Oh. When I done told you?"

"While back. Not sure when exactly but it was during one of our first few lunches together."

"Well, you can help me move then. There's a lot stuff that just needs to get gone. Some might be stuff you want. I know there be a whole box of clothes from them girls up in there. Might be worth keeping for that little girl of yers, something from her aunts."

I hadn't thought about that honestly. I mean him moving into something smaller means having to get rid of things we packed up and moved to the garage after Mother died, the twins too. All those boxes will need to be opened, and dug through. There might be treasures in there worth keeping, but most of what we will find is memories and tears for sure.

"Yeah for sure. I can help go through things. Most will just get donated though I bet," I carefully replied attempting to hold in my feeling if impending grief.

We were only 10 minutes into our first visit since he broke the news about his condition and already the mood was sad and retrospective. This was going to be harder than I thought to spend time with him and not think about what was coming at us down the road.

"So where is this little place you are planning to move Joe?" I asked trying to get to a more positive conversation path.

"Oh it's a little ways up the road, still close enough

to town I can come in for groceries and supplies. But is out in the woods with a right pretty view of them hills out the bedroom window and back porch. Perfect place to call my last Marty."

His voice cracked a bit on that last sentence but he caped it with a smile and a wink hoping to keep the conversation from going that direction.

"Sounds like it. Two rooms you said? Going to use one for storage or you planning on a house guest?"

"I don't know. I reckon it might be good to have a bed there case time comes I got to have someone stay with me. You know this here thing in my head eventually going kick in and make me forget things. Doc says new memories be the first to go, but eventually might forget things like where is the bathroom, how to hold a fork. Might be needing someone there to make sure I don't go blowing up the place 'cause I done forgot how to light a dagum stove."

And there it was, the elephant in the room was now in full view and part of the days conversation. I had no idea what to say to his honesty other than to agree with him. It was all true. Eventually he would need a caregiver, someone to look after him and a room for them to stay in was important. So was getting him into a new place while he could still learn a new house layout and commit it to a place in his memory that would not be immediately affected by the mass growing in his head.

Our conversation that day drifted back and forth between his impending move and the reasons behind it. We managed to stay on the positive side of his condition for the most part. We spoke of the eventual outcome only once, and the darker side of what we could expect between now and then only a few times. We were both trying our best to concentrate on the fact that other than the occasional headaches that over the counter medications could not begin to tame, he had no symptoms. Being that he was choosing not to treat it, we both knew that it was only a matter of time before they began to show. For now though, he appeared healthy and was handling the headaches well with the prescribed pain killers. Even his appetite was unaffected as he polished off his meal and followed it with a rich piece of homemade cheesecake.

Chapter 58

It had been two weekends back to back of sorting boxes and making trips to the donation center for usable clothes, toys, Christmas decorations, even kitchen items. Today I was supposed to be spending in the fourth of five required foster parent training classes with Anneliese. Instead, I had backed out. I had a decent excuse of needing to help Joe move. But it was really just an excuse. I could have found a way to get both done, if I had really wanted to spend most of my Saturday in that class.

Anneliese agreed that it was more important right now to help Joe, but it was not my only reason. Since learning of Joe's diagnosis all I could think was that my life was already complicated enough. I didn't have any room to bring in a foster kid with baggage that could tip the apple cart if they had a bad day. Hell, some days I was the one tipping it over all by myself as I worked through my own grief and anger about things happening around me. I kept that to myself. It would only upset Anneliese and right now I didn't have the energy to deal with that too.

I had also stopped going with Sean to see Toby. In fact I had stopped seeing Sean at all and had not even told him about Joe. Mostly because I didn't want him to immediately go from supportive friend to trained counselor, then make me talk to him about all the crap swarming inside my head. I wasn't yet ready to talk to anyone about it, not even Sean. I'm sure he would have understood why I was not available to meet with Toby and finish teaching him that drum cadence if I explained what was really going on. Too many questions would be asked, so I simply told him I was too busy and ducked his occasional phone calls. Real adult of me, I know.

On a positive note, this was also the second weekend in a row of conversations with Joe and getting to know the man he had become since I walked out of his life. We laughed, joked, and even cried at mementos and photos we found among the boxes. They spawned memories, stories, and conversations I never dreamed would be possible with the man I had stopped thinking of as my father when I was a young child.

I had started just calling him ol' man because father, dad, and pop no longer seemed right. He never showed that he cared about the name change when I first timidly tried it out one day at dinner, so I stuck with it. Lately, I had stopped using it almost entirely opting instead for what his friends use to call him, Joe. He was definitely feeling more like a friend than a stranger in my life because of biology. However, as I began to get to know more about him, his past, his present, his strength for moving forward in life when he lost everything he once loved, including me, I realized how much we were alike. He was my father, by biology, and recently he felt a little more like one by choice. And he didn't seem to mind when I referred to him that way either.

"Hey Pop, where was this photo taken? It's of all of us, Mother and the Twins, me, and even you are in it," I asked from across the dusty garage attic.

"Well let's have a look see. This here look like that zoo trip to me. Boy that was a darn long time ago. You mother and me been having a rough go with bills and such. I worked a awful lot of overtime and done got us caught back up on most things. Turned out we had extra. So we decided to pack up you youngins and head over to that there zoo up in Asheville. Was a little place, mostly just a petting farm with some a them wolves and a few reptiles out back aways from the other stuff. I remember you mother asking some stranger a take this here picture long side the barn. She always said we don't ever got enough vacations or pictures of the whole family."

The zoo trip? I remember it being a rainy miserable day where I was stuck with my baby sisters doing what they wanted to do. I also remember my father's temper when I asked to go do something I wanted to do. No scars left but I definitely remember landing in that bush hard after his hand met my face. Was this even the same trip?

"Did they have bumper cars or something? I remember a trip with bumper cars," I timidly asked trying to clarify if my memory was of the same outing.

"No not at the zoo. I think them bumper cars was at the county fair. They had them a petting zoo part too. You probably don't have much good to remember about that trip."

"County fair with a petting zoo attraction. That does make sense. Was not my best day for sure."

"Mine neither Son," he added with a shrug and eyes darting to the floor.

He looked momentarily ashamed, and it was clear we had the same memory of that day.

"I guess I just don't remember the zoo trip then. It was a long time ago but sounds like we all had a good day."

"Yes indeed. Was one of the last before you mother got sick. Maybe is why I remember it so well. She was so happy and looked so healthy. Oh if only we'd known what was going happen ... " he trailed off in thought.

"Would you want to change it? I mean if it was a good day for all of us, and a happy memory isn't that enough?" I asked.

"I reckon it is Son. I guess it has ta be."

"You know I have never taken Beth to the zoo. Perhaps we should do that over the summer. The five of us."

"I'd like that Marty. I'd like that very much."

Chapter 59

Quite likely the best day of my adult life, outside meeting my little girl for the very first time, happened on July 4th 2012. I of course did not realize it until much later on, but it was the day that my family became one again. Anneliese and I had opted to spend it at Joe's new cabin on Lone Pine Trail a few miles up the mountain from Thompson Station. He'd been moved into the place only a few weeks by then, but managed to unpack nearly all of the boxes I helped him move from the old place. It felt like it had been lived in much longer. The place was nice, tucked up under the trees to keep it cool on hot summer days, and had a view of the mountains in the distance from every window on the back side of the house.

The cabin was actually a two bedroom house with a decent sized kitchen, big enough for two people to be working in and not always bumping into one another. It also had a dining area off the kitchen that was really more of an enclosed porch. Since it was insulated and heated he should be able to use it all year long. The living space was a moderate size and came complete with a pellet stove for extra heat on colder days. The stove sat in front of what used to be a wood burning fireplace the previous owners had closed in saving the chimney for the pellet stove to vent through. It was a wise upgrade eliminating the drafts of an old fireplace and allowing for extra heat on days when the furnace just wasn't enough to take the chill from the damp mountain air.

All in all it was quiet, just the right size for him and the few material things in life he treasured. It also freed him from the familiar space that carried with it so many memories, good and bad alike. It had the added bonus of not giving me the willies every time I pulled into the driveway like my childhood home had. I now had one less excuse for not coming to see him on those days when he was not up to a drive into town for conversations over brunch at our booth in the diner.

This trip was an exception of course. I was a nervous wreck as I parked the car in front of the large oak tree along the drive and took a slow deep breath to steady my nerves and untangle the knot in my stomach. I had been here many times over the last month helping Joe to clean, move, even to unpack some of the boxes. However, today was the first time I had brought Anneliese and Beth here, or anywhere within sight of Joe to be honest. I was finally ready to share them with Joe, and Joe with them. I knew it was time to see if we really could be just one happy family together one day at a time, or if my fantasy would fizzle into bitter childhood memories of holidays spent as a family.

"You go on and let him know we're here Marty. I'll get Beth out of the car, let her run some of that pent up energy off in the yard, and you can come outside when the two of you are ready," Anneliese calmly said as she gently rubbed a hand across my right knee.

"Yeah. That sounds like a good idea. Let me go see if he is ready for this after all."

Chapter 60

"Hey there Marty! Happy Independence Day Son," Joe greeted me cheerily as I stepped into the kitchen from the mudroom.

"Back at ya' Ol' Man! You look like you are feeling good today. Any more of those mind numbing headaches?"

"Nope, not a one on 'em. Not for couple a days anyway. Doc done got me on some new meds said should help keep 'em from knocking me on my ass like happened last week. Not sho if he meant keep 'em from a-comin' or just keep 'em from being so dagum painful. Didn't bother to ask. Just glad he got something thought could help one way or the other."

"It's probably to help keep them from being so bad, Pop. But I am glad he had an idea too. I hate to see you in pain like that. Especially when nothing we tried even seemed to help ease it."

"Enough talkin' 'bout my dagum health huh? Thought you was bringing me a surprise this time. How long you gonna' keep me a-wonderin'?"

"Depends, how you feel about meeting a couple of people today?" I asked with a wink and cheshire cat grin across my face.

"You mean you. My daughter-in-law? My grandbaby? Oh that make my day Son, hell my whole dagum lifetime. They come with you?"

"Sure did, look out there," I said as I gently turned him to face the front windows where Beth was running around under the shade of the tall hemlock trees.

We stood there in silence for a minute or two as he watched her through the window. The smile on his face was all the proof I needed that I had made the right choice to bring them with me today and spend it as a family here at his cabin.

After allowing the reality of his growing family to set in, I helped him find his shoes and lead him out the front door toward where my wife and daughter were now sitting at the picnic table on the small patio. Joe wasted no time in kneeling down to be eye level with Beth and saying hello after I made the introductions. She looked at him a little curious, then at her mother and me for a second before wrapping her little arms around his neck and gleefully declaring her joy of finally meeting him. It brought a tear to the eye of every adult there for sure, though none of us would admit it until much later in the day.

It was the first time both of my families, the one from my past life in Thompson Station and the one I had created after leaving, met one another. The anticipation leading up to this day was intense, almost nauseating right up to that first step into the house today. Then things just sort of fell into place. It seemed like it was meant to be this way. Maybe it was. While Beth played in the yard, Anneliese and I worked to prepare a lunch fit for the day and occasion. Joe played with Beth taking breaks on the picnic table near the grill occasionally and striking up conversations with Anneliese and me I never would have dreamed were possible just a few weeks ago.

At one point, I left Anneliese and Joe in charge of the grill while I ran off to play chase with Beth. As I staggered up out of breath toward the picnic table I overheard Joe telling Anneliese, "Never had me much a relationship wit my own pops. He just worked. Kept on me when I done messed something up or forget do something he done told me get done."

"That sounds familiar," I managed to puff out while gasping to catch my breath.

"Sho it does Marty. Maybe I was bad as him wit you. Wadn't no better."

"You weren't easy to live with. But it's in the past. Time to move forward," I cautiously replied.

"Forward's good. Good to see you learnt from my mistakes stead a repeatin' 'em."

"I do my best. Looks like the burgers are done. Beth come on and wash your hands, time to eat!"

Over dinner we told the stories of how Anneliese and I met, our wedding and honeymoon adventures, even stories from my childhood. We ate, laughed, and enjoyed our day together until well after the sun went down and the fireworks ceased to light the night sky in the distance. For the first time in longer than I will ever recall, I spent a holiday with Joe and did not hear or participate in a single argument other than who would wash the dinner dishes. Joe claimed that since it was his house he should do them, Anneliese and I disagreed and beat him to the sink before he could take over the task.

Chapter 61

Nearly two weeks after spending the July fourth holiday with Joe at his cabin, I pulled into the parking lot of the diner in town on a Thursday evening for our first ever "dinner date". Things had gone so well with Joe meeting my family on the fourth that I realized now was just as good a time as any to expand our family. Even with a child who might have some serious baggage to deal with.

Our weekend would be spent jumping through more hoops in the process of becoming foster parents. Anneliese and I planned to drop Beth off at Sean's house after dinner so that we could be ready to go to the training retreat as soon as I was done with my meetings Friday afternoon. It was a good plan, but I still had my doubts about the whole thing. I did my best to ignore them.

Sean had remained working with Toby doing music therapy and I had gone with him a couple of times recently. It had definitely helped rekindle my desire to work with kids who needed a break in life. It also reminded me that I could help Toby deal with his anger, something he had gotten more of a handle on but not complete control over. I knew his pain, I lived it once.

I knew Toby was a good kid outside of his outbursts. Anneliese and I had even talked about maybe fostering him once we got our license squared away. Beth's safety was a concern but we agreed that if Toby could control his outbursts on a regular basis, we were willing to at least try.

Anneliese and I hoped to be on the final stages of getting our license after this weekend's training retreat. It was a full Saturday and Sunday event to complete both of our outstanding parenting courses along with a CPR and first-aid certification refresher and the last of our pre-licensing interviews. The only thing left in our way would then be the results of our finger prints search, something that should be completed in the next few weeks, and a final home inspection that was already scheduled for the following Wednesday evening.

Because this was the weekend that Joe and I would normally have gotten together for a Saturday morning brunch, Anneliese and I decided to make this one a Thursday evening dinner date with the family instead. I swear I could hear him smile over the phone when I made the suggestion and he jumped at the chance to get together with his 'two favorite girls' as he had begun to call my wife and daughter.

"Hmmm. That's odd. I don't see his truck here," I said aloud as I pulled around the back of the diner.

"Maybe he's running late."

"Maybe. But that would be a first for sure. Maybe he parked out front on the street and I just missed it when we drove in. Let's go in and get a table. Beth looks like she might start eating that seatbelt if we don't feed her soon," I joked.

"Nuh uh!" was her only response as she reached down to unbuckle it.

Stepping through the heavy glass door I scanned the room looking for Joe. My initial surprise began to turn to concern when table after table turned up no sign of him. Obviously I had not simply missed seeing his truck in the parking area. I decided to go with my wife's theory that he was just running late and the three of us took a table in the middle of the diner. I intentionally positioned myself so that I could monitor the door looking out over Main Street while we waited.

Where is he? He might have stood me up a few months ago, or even if he had not made such a strong connection to Beth when he saw her on the fourth, maybe. He might consider not showing if he thought he would be in for bad news I guess. But he sounded like he was looking forward to this when we last talked two days ago.

I have a bad feeling about this. He is never late. He's never been a no-show. Maybe I should call him.

"Hey, I'm going to step outside for a minute and give him a call. Maybe something came up," I said as I stood from the table, pushed in my chair, and headed toward the door already reaching for my cell.

"C'mon Joe. Pick up," I whispered aloud as I called first the house phone and then the cell I had given him recently for emergencies.

"Hey Pop, it's Marty. We're here at the diner for dinner. Hope you are on your way. See you soon."

Voicemail! I hate voicemail and I know he won't bother to check it. Heck I am not sure he even remembers how to check it. I'll give him another ten minutes before I drive up there and check on him. I hope everything is okay.

Dropping my phone back into my shirt pocket I stepped back inside the diner and returned to my waiting family.

"Anytihng?" Anneliese asked as I pulled out my chair and sat back down across the table staring out at Main Street through the glass door.

"Nothing. I left him a voicemail on his cell. I am not sure he will remember how to get to it but I called the house and got no answering machine. I figure I'll wait here another few minutes and then maybe drive up to check on him. Just to be sure everything is all right."

"You look concerned Marty. Why don't you go now. Beth and I will stay here, in case he shows before you get back. Go check in on him and lay those fears to rest."

"You sure?"

"Absolutely."

"You are the best. What would I do without my rock, and my beautiful little angel over here?" I asked kissing them both on the cheek as I hurried out the door.

Chapter 62

The drive up the mountain felt like it took hours as I dialed and re-dialed the house phone, then the cell in turn hoping to reach Joe. Each time ended with me hanging up after multiple rings and trying the other number. Luckily the road was not heavily traveled in either direction because I was also taking some of the blind mountain curves much faster than I should have. Between speed and staring down at my cell phone to dial the numbers, I definitely crossed into the oncoming lane more than a few times. Only once was I met by another car who blared their horn while I swerved back into my own lane. It was a close call for sure but I managed to safely arrive at Joe's house without wrecking my car. However, by the time I reached the end of the drive I was convinced something was very wrong. When I laid eyes on his old truck parked in front of the house, I went into full blown panic mode.

Crap! His truck is here. I knew something was wrong. Park the car, get in there and find out what happened. Breathe Marty. Take a deep breath before you go busting in the house like a crazed lunatic.

Trying my best not to jump from the car and rush through the door, I took a deep breath and casually walked toward the house while calling out "Joe? You here Ol' Man? Pop? Anybody home?"

As I reached my hand to knock on the door, it swung open revealing Joe standing on the other side with a confused look on his face.

"Marty? I thought I heard you out here making a ruckas. What'r you doing up here today?"

"I came to see you Pop. We had a dinner date in town. It's Thursday."

"What? Dinner? Oh yeah I must've forgot. We usually git together Saturdays. Got me all turned round. Let me git my dagum shoes and you kin hitch me a ride," he apologized as he shuffled off down the hall leaving me standing just outside the door.

Odd, he never invited me in. Oh well, I'll just step into the kitchen and wait for him anyway.

"I called here to find out where you were. Your cell too. It went right to voicemail. No answer here. Something wrong with the machine?" I asked skeptically as I looked about the kitchen for the answering machine that was on the counter last time I was here.

"Dagum thing up an quit on me. Need to gift me a new one. And I can't get that new fangled speak thing to give me my dagum messages. Thing keeps telling me I got 'em but not how to git to 'em."

Gift? Speak? Man even for his broken Appalachian English

those words sound like odd choices.

"I can show you again, maybe write the steps down this time so you have them if you have trouble. Did you not hear the house phone ring? I called at least 20 times," I questioned

"It rang, weren't nobody there when I answered first time. Just ignored it after that. Sorry if it were you."

"Maybe you need a new phone as well then. Hold on a sec, let me see if it answers now," I said as I dialed his home number on my cell.

Joe picked up the ringing phone and placed it to his ear.

"Hello? Hello? Nothing again! This dagum phone busted too. Stupid phones. Stupid made in China techno-crap. Why they gotta' make such CRAP and sell 'em you like they is all 'new and improved'? Damned thing wont' tell me who is calling. Won't even let me talk to who it is. I HATE THIS GOD DAMNED PHONE!" Joe screamed as he threw the cordless phone down scattering pieces of metal and plastic across the floor.

"Shit! Dagum thing can't even fall to the floor without gittin' all busted to pieces! Let me finish the damn job then!"

Stomping his foot down on the largest part of the phone, the sound of crunching plastic made it clear the device would never work again.

I stood in shock watching the spectacle in front of me. Before the phone hit the floor I could still hear my cell ringing in my ear. It was clear that the phone was not to blame for failed attempts to call Joe. He had picked up the cordless receiver and placed it to his ear without hitting the 'talk/on' button. The phone never answered and was still ringing when it was thrown to the floor. In fact, it did not stop ringing until the battery separated from the device as it broke into multiple pieces.

Wow! That is the temper I remember. That is the ol' man I remember from my childhood. He is back for sure. Maybe being around Beth and Anneliese is not such a good idea after all. Hate to have him blow up like this with them. Hell Beth would be terrified of him right now, like I used to be when he went into a rage. Not good for her at all.

"Hey Joe, calm down. It's just a phone. We can get a new one, maybe we can find one that is not made in China. Okay?"

I kept my tone calm and level, as if I were talking to my daughter after one of her tantrums. That is what had just happened. Joe had thrown a tantrum at the phone he thought was broken. He was so angry that it would not work he destroyed it before finding out that the phone was fine, he just had forgotten to push a button allowing it to work.

"Hey Marty! When you git here? I thought we was a-meetin' in town for dinner. Did you bring my two favorite girls with you?"

What the hell? He doesn't remember the last ten minutes? His mood is the ol' man I have gotten to know these last few months, all after the monster I just saw crawl out from my childhood? Am I going crazy here? I guess just roll with it?

"Hey Pop. I've been here a few minutes. Don't you remember me coming up to see if everything was okay when you didn't show up to the diner?" I carefully asked.

"I didn't turn up? It's Thursday right? I didn't miss dinner did I?"

"No, no we can still get dinner. Beth and Anneliese are waiting for us. How about I clean up that mess on the floor while you get ready and I will give you a ride."

"Sure. What happened to my phone? Did I drop the dagum thing like that there machine used to be over in the kitchen? That sho made a hell of a mess on the floor too. Not sure what happened but it turned up all in pieces on the floor a few days back. Looked lot like this here mess. Sure don't make stuff like they used to. Dagum flimsy 'made in China' plastic crap now days."

"Yeah looks like maybe the same thing Pop. Go get ready."

The answering machine and the new phone? He doesn't remember either one? It's like some multiple personality thing. I wonder how long this has been going on. Dinner, a new CORDED phone with a SIMPLE answering machine and a call to his doctor are definitely on the list for this weekend. He warned us of erratic behavior but I never expected this.

Shit this weekend, I can't cancel. Anneliese will kill me. Or will she? I mean this is Joe's health, she might understand. Ugh I just don't' have time for this fostering stuff now. I have to call the doctor first thing tomorrow and I guess we'll go from there.

"All righty I is set! Let's not keep them precious ladies waiting no longer Marty. We kin clean up this here mess when we git back."

"I got it all cleaned up Pop. You got your house key with you or should I leave the door open?"

"Oh I lost that dagum key weeks ago, I just leave it open. Who's gonna' bother me up here anyway?

Add new door locks and multiple hidden keys to the list now too I guess.

Chapter 63

We had traveled a mile or two in silence on our way into town when I finally managed to build up enough courage to ask Joe a question. It had been rattling inside my head since I witnessed him slam the phone to the floor in a fit of rage and frustration, but had taken time to formulate the right words. I wanted an answer, but didn't want one all at the same time. I also didn't want to alarm him, or anger him by asking. I knew what his temper looked like and suffering its wrath while operating a motor vehicle was not a pleasant thought.

Marty you have to ask him. You need to know what is going on, how long it's been going on at least. It could be just meds. It could be a new development in the process. But you got to ask! All right here goes nothing!

"So, um, back at the house, I mean the deal with the phone today, and the answering machine before. I mean, have there been any other, uh, strange things that happened recently around the house? Like finding the phone on the floor today and not remembering how it got there?"

"No! Well – no nothing important."

Any lapse in memory is important damn it!

"Joe this is important. Are you sure there was nothing else? I mean you said the machine in the kitchen was on the floor and you didn't remember it even falling. Today the phone. Anything else recently, even if it seems minor?"

"Well, yeah they was something I guess. I think they might be a spook in the place or something. You know I saw a show on the TV once where these people they dies in a house and they ghost stayed there. Hung around breaking stuff, leaving water on, that sorta' thing."

Shit he's gonna' flood the house! Is that stove electric or Gas? Is he still safe by himself? We haven't had that conversation yet but he can't live alone forever. He's going to need someone to be there. To be sure he is safe and following doctors' orders. Are we there already? I thought we had so much more time than this.

"Water running?"

"Yes. I took me a nap few days back, don't member what day it was but not too far back. Anyways, when I git up, I had to pee so bad almost didn't make it out the chair. Running water does that you know. Git up to find water on in the kitchen sink. I didn't turn it on. Think my cabin might have it a spook. Trying a make me crazy or something."

Ghost. Oh how I wish that could be true. I saw him today. He flew into a rage then seconds later was confused about what had happened and had no memory of the incident at all. The only ghost here is an alter ego inside that head of his.

"I'm sure it's not a ghost Pop. I'll call your Doc later and see if he can get you in for a checkup, maybe tomorrow. Maybe it's a side effect of some of your meds –"

"– or this damn thing in my head!"

"That too."

Chapter 64

"Marty think about this, please. I know you are concerned about Joe. I am too if I have to be honest. But canceling this weekend, these classes means another month before we can get them completed."

"Anneliese I know. And I'm sorry it keeps getting delayed. But I just can't. I can't do it this weekend. I called his doctor. He sees us today at 3 o'clock. That means I am ducking out on half a day's work on this book project and I'm already nearly an hour late to the office. I need to work this weekend to make up for that or we'll never hit this deadline. I'm sorry babe, but with this new development with Joe, now is just not a good time," I attempted to explain to my upset wife.

I'm not sure there will ever be a good time to get into this mess, but this is definitely not one! No way can I miss that appointment. And I do have work deadlines to meet. But I also don't want to ditch Beth for a weekend to run off these classes when there is no way we will be taking in any new kids while this thing with Joe is going on. I can't handle their issues and his at the same time! Not now that Joe seems to be getting bad so much faster than we thought he would.

"I understand about work, and the appointment. I

just want you to understand that we are delaying it another month if we can't do this weekend."

"I know. We are still in limbo for the fingerprints stuff anyway. State is sure taking their time with that aren't they? We can get the final house inspection out of the way, get registered for the next classes, and wrap this up. Just not this weekend. Okay?"

"Okay," she replied sounding defeated before walking out of the kitchen leaving me alone to wonder if I would ever be honest with her about my doubts.

Chapter 65

"Hey there Marty, didn't expect to see you in here tonight! You ain't hiding from those girls of yours are you? You know I will just rat you out next time I talk to Anneliese," Sean joked approaching the barstool next to mine.

"She's still pissed I cancelled last weekend to get the foster parent classes and first-aid stuff done. She'd love to hear I was with you, hoping you'd talk me into registering for the next round instead of 'dragging my feet' as she keeps telling me.

"Not why I'm here tonight though. I just thought it might do me some good to talk to a friend tonight, 'bout something else. You got time now?" I asked hoping Sean could spare a few minutes to chat outside.

"Sure do. I only have one set tonight, early nights for me now that my music therapy business is beginning to spread its wings. Reminds me, I'm supposed to tell you that Toby says hello and he is ready for a lesson on all those stick tricks and rim shots for the cadence when you can find the time."

"Yeah, I'll see if I can find some time to go with you to a session in the next couple weeks. Assuming I am not about to enter the world of full time caregiver for my ol' man that is."

"Uh oh. C'mon outside Marty. You can fill me in. I assume that's what you wanted to talk about anyway."

I followed Sean outside, grateful for his time and counseling abilities, and hopeful he could help me figure out what my next move would be. The initial Friday visit to Joe's doctor led to some tests done Monday. The results had come in yesterday. The news was not good, but did have a silver lining. According to his doctor the tumor had increased to about the size of a quarter. It was about the size of a dime when first diagnosed only a few months ago. The good news though was that it had apparently skipped over the Brocas area of the brain.

That part of the brain is responsible for speech production and, once affected would produce a rapid onset of difficulty expressing words before eventually rendering a person mute. So far, Joe showed no signs of this portion of his brain being affected. However, the tumor was now affecting a larger portion of the frontal lobe and had spread into the adjacent temporal lobe as well. It was only a matter of time before his symptoms would worsen.

Already he had shown signs of short term memory loss, trouble controlling emotions, and some minor language difficulties like using the wrong words or names of objects. According to the doctor we could now expect those to worsen and broaden to include what he called 'sequence issues'. When I asked for him to clarify that he explained that often patients will perform daily tasks like brushing their teeth but do things out of order. He has one patient who would use the dry brush on his teeth, then put the paste on the brush, and finish by rinsing the unused toothpaste from the brush right away. Sort of like the toothpaste was cleaning the brush not his teeth. In another case, he had patients who would get dressed but put on their pants before their underpants and then become angry when others tried to correct the behavior.

The news of new symptoms was the tip of the iceberg I knew. It was proof that Joe's condition was deteriorating faster than I had expected, and I suspect faster than he had as well. His tumor was aggressive, we knew that from the beginning, but it now looked like he might be on the shorter end of those predictions for how much time he really had left.

In part because the doctor said routine was more important now than ever and in part because I was concerned about leaving Joe alone for the entire weekend, my plans changed again. Saturday, the day after our visit to the doctor's office and our usual monthly brunch meeting day, Joe and I had brunch at the diner again where what seemed like a new symptom emerged.

The song *Earth Angel* came on the old juke box in the corner and it was like Joe had been instantly transported back in time. He looked right at me and asked "Where is she? Where did your mother run off to now? She knows we got to dance to this here song no matter where we is when we hear it."

It took a full ten minutes after the song ended to calm him down and remind him that Mother was dead so she could not dance with him. That was what I really wanted to talk to Sean about.

"Funny thing about the brain is that music tends to unlock secrets we keep otherwise hidden Marty. He heard a song that reminded him of something important to him. His brain went right back there and relived it. Maybe you and I would not get so sucked into a memory because our brains are healthy. But you take one that is damaged, from injury or like Joes with a tumor on it affecting how it processes information, and you get what you saw. I'd bet it will happen again and the trigger just might be that song for him. But it also means that he could become unpredictable or unstable when he hears it too. Something you can't really know for sure because his brain isn't working the way it should be."

"So maybe we could try playing for him, see if we can help him find some happier memories not related to Mother?" I timidly asked Sean.

"Would be happy to. He didn't take the news so good huh?"

"No. I've never seen him this quiet. After the doctor's

appointment and then the incident at the diner with him looking for Mother, he's kind of shut down on me now."

"Would be happy to help, or at least to give it a shot. Remember I can't promise anything. Music therapy works when it can, but in his case there is no way to know if it will, or what might come of it."

"I know. So many unknowns here, but it's worth a shot."

Chapter 66

"Hey Pop, the ladies are in the car ready to hit the road, you got everything you need for this little family adventure?"

"I think so Son, but of course you know I will forget something. Always happens. Hopefully ain't anything important."

"What happened to your face? " I asked wiping a drip of blood from his left cheek.

"Cutting. Razor was rough on me today I guess," he said.

"Cutting? You mean shaving?. Come on in the bathroom for a minute let me help clean these nicks up before any get infected on you. Sure do have a lot of them. Maybe you need to use more shaving cream next time. It'll help the razor glide on your skin easier, not be so rough."

"Cream? That stinky white foam stuff? I used plenty of that. Burned a little and left a mess. I had to wash my face again. Ain't using that stuff again," Joe said shaking his head violently.

"Maybe we need to try a different brand. Shouldn't burn at all. It just helps the razor cut the hairs without tearing up your skin too.

"You did put it on before you used the razor right Pop?" I cautiously asked.

"Why would I do that? Used it after like I always done. Been shaving since for you was born Marty I think I know how to git it done. I done it like I always do. That green stuff, razor, white crap I ain't never using again, then washed my face two times. Shoulda' only had to do that once."

After? Why would he do it after? He should know the right order for shaving. Order! Sequence! Doc warned us about this.

So here we are, Joe did all the right shaving steps but in the wrong order. Worst part, he's convinced he did it right.

Keep calm Marty, we can work through this. Remember what Doc said, acknowledge but don't challenge.

"Well then maybe it's time to try using an electric razor. They are a lot easier on your skin. I use one from time to time when I have trouble with regular razors."

"I never like those things. But this thing hurt today," he said tossing the safety razor into the trash can next to the sink.

"I guess I could try one a them electric ones if you say it'll be easier on this mug."

"Okay Pop, looks like you're all cleaned up. Let's head out to the ladies waiting in the car. Maybe we'll stop by the store and pick you up a new razor on the way home. How about that?" I said patting him on the shoulder trying to hide every ounce of my concern behind a broad smile.

"Sure thing Marty."

"Everything okay, you were in there a while?" Anneliese whispered to me as Joe climbed into the back seat alongside Beth.

I subtly nodded yes as I checked in the mirror to see that Joe was in the car okay and able to securely latch both the door and his seat belt.

Anneliese had already offered to sit back there so he could make the couple hour trip to the zoo in the more comfortable front seat. Joe refused. He claimed this would give him more time to hang out with his granddaughter. I think he just didn't want to feel like he was putting Anneliese out. In any case the ride to the zoo outside of Asheville was comfortable, energetic, and entertaining. Beth and Joe passed the time by making silly faces and playing simple games like finding letters on road signs in the order of the alphabet. I spent the ride glancing in the rearview mirror once in a while looking for any signs of memory or temper issues. I was still on edge after the phone incident, the follow up meeting with Joe's doctor about what had happened, and now today's shaving mishap.

At the doctor's visit I was hoping for a quick fix, a solution to keep him from flipping out like he had with the phone. Instead I walked away with the knowledge that the tumor was growing, time was fleeting, and he could make no promises.

Some pain medications were changed, in case they had caused the rapid change in temperament or memory loss rather than the growth of the mass. Some new tests were run, all of which came back inconclusive. Joe was not willing to take more medications than required so anti-psychotic medications were not an option at this point. Though a prescription was ordered, filled, and in my bag just in case there was a need. For now, everything seemed as normal as could be. No memory lapses, no wrong names said, no signs of anything but a grandfather playing in the back seat with his granddaughter and having the time of his life.

Our day at the zoo was enjoyable. It was the first full week of August and the weather was as perfect as you could expect for this time of year. The sun was shining brightly but not too hot, the clouds and slight breeze kept it comfortable even in the hottest hours of the afternoon. We enjoyed a picnic lunch, carousel rides, bumper cars, and the Ferris wheel together more than once. Beth's favorite part was the big cats, lions and tigers sleeping in the shade all afternoon. I think my favorite part was watching Joe carry her around on his shoulders so she could see over the heads of the adults. Smiling from ear to ear they both looked like they were having the time of their lives.

"This was a great idea honey," Anneliese whispered in my ear at one point.

We were sitting on the park bench waiting for Joe and Beth to finish their fourth or fifth carousel ride in the latest marathon. Beth was determined to ride each animal, and Joe was determined to let her. Anneliese and I were content to sit under a large shade tree on a beautiful sunny day watching the two of them build a bond that could never be replaced or broken. I wished for a moment that I could have had the same chance with Joe at Beth's age, but I quickly put that thought aside and concentrated on simply being happy that I was given a chance to get to know my ol' man over the past year, to actually meet Joe so to speak.

We had come a long way and I knew that each day we spent in one another's lives meant one less left to spend. I was determined to find the happiness in all of it. I would need those memories to squelch my grief soon enough. Sitting there on the park bench, Anneliese tucked under my embrace, sun shining down through the leaves of a giant shade tree, Calliope music and children's giggling filling our ears was most definitely going to be a cherished memory of watching Beth as a child. The cherry on top of that memory would be watching Joe, a man I once thought incapable of feeling any emotion but anger, enjoying the carousel almost as much as the beautiful little girl at his side. Both of them were grinning ear to ear.

"This was indeed one of my better ideas lately,

maybe ever. Perhaps this can finally replace the awful memory I have of my last family trip. I was about Beth's age, Kera and Kylee were just babies still. Mother and I tended to them all day while he sulked off to do something else. I don't even remember where he went or why, but I remember him smacking me so hard I landed in a bush across the path. That was the first day I risked calling him ol' man. After Mother died a few years later, it is all I ever called him, until recently."

"You know, that's the first time you mentioned why you called him that for so long. Do you realize you don't use it much anymore?"

"Guess I never gave it much thought. He doesn't seem like the same guy I remember from my childhood, except when I saw him get so angry at the phone and destroy it. That's what scares me. What if he flips out again like that and Beth has to see his temper? She is so young she won't understand that it's not his fault, that he is just having another episode he can't control."

"Only time will tell Marty. We just need to keep an eye on them. To make sure one of us is always nearby in case it does happen. Nothing we can do to prevent it for sure."

"No, I guess there isn't. You know I always thought that family trip we took, the one where Joe smacked me into a bush for asking him a question he didn't want to answer was here, to this zoo. Turns out I was wrong. It was to a fair instead. I guess my young mind confused the petting zoo and bumper cars of that fair with this place. Amazing how our complex minds can tuck away such detailed memories and yet mess up simple things like location. It's actually why I never brought you and Beth here before," I rambled aloud.

"When did you figure out you were mistaken?" Anneliese questioned.

"Helping Joe pack. He found some photos of our trip here to this zoo. I was too young for it to have been the same memory I had burned into my mind. He remembered the fair trip vividly too. Turns out he hated how he acted that day, almost as much as I did my entire life. That one moment in time set the tone of our relationship right up until the day I walked out of his life. As important as that memory was to me, every detail of it, I still got it wrong. Makes me wonder how much else about my childhood, about Joe I remember wrong."

Chapter 67

Not long after our day at the zoo, the following Saturday actually, I met up with Joe at the diner in town for another Saturday morning brunch. As I drove into town I cruised the street in front to be sure that his truck was not parked there before pulling into the lot behind the building. It was a habit I had picked up after the first time he forgot about meeting me for a meal. It had also saved me from unnecessary worry once when he did park out front instead. Today, his truck was parked in the back lot, a little crooked and not between the lines as it should be, but it was there and looked to be mostly in one piece.

Strolling into the diner I quickly spotted Joe at our usual booth in the back and waved to Miss Maybelle behind the counter as I passed. Nearing the table it was clear today would be different than past dates with Joe. He sat with his elbows on the table, head resting in his hands. I cleared my throat as I approached but Joe did not even look up as I sat down.

"Everything okay Pop?"

"Just got me a doozie of a headache ain't nothing can touch. Be fine after some coffee I reckon."

"Cup's right in front of you Pop. Have you taken any of those pain meds the doc gave you last week?"

"Yessum, well ... I think so. I mean I took something this dawn when I git up. Just can't learn what it was. Felt fine all the way here but this racket. The noise in here is makin' my head feel like when you was learnin' to beat that drum a yers."

This dawn? Morning maybe? Learn? What is he saying? Learn, remember maybe? Decrypting these wrong words is getting more and more difficult. Or is it because he does it more and more?

"You order –" I was interrupted by Miss Maybelle delivering a piping hot western omelet for Joe and my usual stack of hotcakes, eggs, hash browns, and toast.

"Here ya go you two. Had ol' Jimmy whip these up soon as I saw ya come in. I figured you would order the same thing you always do."

"What if I wanted something new? Ever think 'bout that? Take this here back dagummit! I kin make my own damn decisions! Ain't no, no – damn it can't never find words when I is mad!" Joe screamed at her.

"Sho thing sweetie. What kin I git for ya' then?" she said shocked but with a smile as she picked up the plate in front of Joe.

Grabbing the plate back from Miss Maybelle Joe snorted "Oh never you mind. I'll just eat this."

"Hey, Pop. We can get you something else if you want.

No big deal."

"Always eat this anyways. Thanks, Maybelle. Sorry I done snapped at you. Just not feeling myself today."

Minutes seemed to pass like hours as I sat across the table from Joe, not eating his food, not even touching his silverware. I was wondering what to do.

His moods are growing increasingly less predictable and often very dark and scary. I know he doesn't want to make people uncomfortable, or to make a scene in public places that leave others thinking he is just some crazy old man. He hasn't told anyone about his diagnosis in town. It is a pride thing with him for sure but he is at a point in his life that he could be a recluse, except for these meetings in town with me. Maybe it's time to move these to a more private location, for his safety and privacy.

And then there is the driving. I mean the front bumper of the truck has new dents and scratches, and it's barely parked. Is it time to take the keys? Oh God, what if he snapped like that while he was driving. He could kill someone! I'm not ready for this, but I guess it's time to start making some permanent changes.

Excusing myself from the table I collected a couple take-out boxes from Miss Maybelle and paid the bill before returning to the table with Joe. I no sooner sat back down across from him when he had another outburst of what looked to be anger at the noise level of the diner. I quickly packed our meals into the boxes and stood next to the table saying "Come on Joe, let me take you home where it is not so noisy. Maybe we can get another of those pain meds in you and take the edge off this headache that is behind your foul mood today."

"I ain't in no dagum foul mood. Just pissed off and my top hurts. They is a difference dagumit!"

"So there is Pop. But let's get you someplace a little quieter and see if that helps the head at least. I don't know what I can do about you being pissed off."

"Nothing Marty. They is nothing you can do. But home does sound right good about now. Eat my food in peace. Maybe I kin be up to talking at you next."

"No problem Pop. Bill is already paid. I'll take you in my car and we can worry about getting your truck home when you feel better."

That was the last time we met at the diner in town for a meal on Saturday, or any day for that matter. Joe's condition was deteriorating and he was no longer up to meals in places with a lot of background noise. In fact he was not up to anything with a lot of noise period. Anneliese and I returned the following day with Beth to pick up Joe's truck from the diner and park it in the driveway alongside the cabin.

As I climbed out and locked the doors of the truck, I wondered if it would ever be driven again, or if it ever should be driven by Joe again at least. I had been making bi-weekly trips to the grocery store for him for nearly a month now. Taking the keys to his truck just meant he would need someone to check in on him more often in case there is a reason for him to go into town.

The medical alert system was installed into the house already and set to call him once a day as a welfare check. If he doesn't pick up or call back within the hour they call me. So far I've never had to dispatch help because we couldn't reach him. But how much longer will that last? It's time to have that conversation with him. He can't be on the road with a temper like I saw yesterday. He shouldn't be driving if his head is hurting that bad. If he needs to get to the hospital and has keys to that truck will he try to drive himself or call an ambulance like he should? Marty, you know this needs to be done, for his safety, and for everyone else's too.

Thankfully Joe was in better health and spirits when we entered the house that day. Seeing Beth running toward his chair in the living room and jumping on his lap made me momentarily forget why we were back here and the conversation that needed to happen. I decided to give them some time together before Anneliese took Beth for a walk outside and I had a chat with Joe about driving his truck. It went better than I thought it would. He was reluctant to agree, but did eventually hand over both sets of keys.

"You got a spare stashed someplace I need to know

about Pop?" I joked.

"No. Those the only two I got. If I can remember how I might be able to turn her over with a screwdriver job though."

"Maybe. But you will have to break a window to get in and with winter coming that will be one cold joy ride into town don't you think?"

"Sure would Son. Sure would. Guess I will just accept my driving days is done. Upside is I git to see you more I reckon. Who else will bring me groceries and my prescriptions?"

"Thought maybe I'd get Sean to come by for me. You know he loves to come play music for you, he can bring groceries with him."

"Sean is a good guy, and we do have some fun when he plays, but why you ain't gone be wit him? You play still?"

"I do, and I will. But we are about ready to release this book I have been working on all year. So for the next month I may be tied up when you need me. I'll still make it up here though, I promise you that. If you are up to it maybe we can make them a whole family visit and I will bring the girls along with me. Sound good to you Pop?"

"Sounds just about perfect Marty!"

Chapter 68

As I stepped from the car I could smell the damp chill of fall in the air. It was mid-September now and the leaves on the hardwoods had long since begun to lose their green. The forest on the hills beyond the house was now ablaze with orange, red, and yellow. Before long the first snowflakes of the season would begin to fall, and winter would not be far off.

Since surrendering his truck keys to me nearly a month ago, Joe had begun to develop more complications from his condition, mostly in the form of headaches that prevented him from getting out of bed some days. He had made some changes to his diet, his routine, and his medications that seemed to be helping. But it was becoming clear to everyone that his better days were behind him.

I knew it was time to begin to make decisions about end of life things, caretakers, and final arrangements. I knew it was, but really who wants to have that conversation with anyone, ever?

For now, Sean and I had set up a schedule each checking in on Joe two times a week. Sean came Tuesday and Thursday while I came up Wednesday and Saturday. We would each bring groceries with us, prepare meals that could be tossed into the microwave or oven to be warmed up, and occasionally just eaten cold if Joe wanted. It was working for now but I knew it was not a permanent solution. My work schedule was going to have to give a little so I could rely on Sean less, or we would have to hire a live-in caretaker. That was a last resort as far as I was concerned.

Sean and I had also managed to come up together a couple of times to deliver groceries and play music while Joe listened, and remembered stories of his youth, my youth, and sometimes just recent history. I always wondered how much of what he remembered was true or just the fabrications of a decaying memory, but it all seemed so real to him when he would get lost in telling the stories that I never dared to ask.

On Saturdays Anneliese and Beth always came with me, though each time I opened the door I wondered what version of Joe would greet us. Even on his bad days Joe would spend time in the recliner with Beth on his lap telling her stories. Some days you could see the pain on his face as he struggled to push it aside, others he was chasing her around the living room and playing 'tickle monster'. Brain cancer is as unpredictable as it gets I think.

Today was Saturday, the second Saturday of the month to be exact. It was once the day each month that Joe and I would meet for brunch in town at the diner. I never thought I would miss those mornings in the beginning of this journey spent with bad coffee and decent food over sometimes forced conversation.

Today would be another brunch over homemade coffee in the comfort of his cozy kitchen here on this mountain followed by a difficult conversation about the future, and the end. A conversation nobody wants to have but that needed to be done while he was still in a place to make decisions.

Pulling the key from my front pocket I let myself in trying to be as quiet as possible in case he was having another of those super bad mornings. I was surprised to see him not only up and about, but also dressed and waiting for me at the kitchen counter.

"You're looking good today. How's the head?" I asked.

"Not bad for a change. I took one of them Norco things last night and I think it mighta knocked the damn thing out this time. You got omelets?"

"Sure do. Your favorite one with biscuits and grits to go with."

"Oh yeah? Smell me something good for sure. You too good to me some days ya' know that Son? I know I don't deserve this chance after how I was when you was growing up. But I sure appreciate you giving it. Chance to get to know you and yer beautiful family. Means the world ya' know?"

"To me too Pop," was all I could say while I choked back the tears stinging my eyes.

I should have done this years ago. Should have come to see Mother and the Twins long before I did. Might have run into him then. Had more time to spend with him. Might have even been enough for him to be part of Beth's life from the start. Oh if I could go back and change just one thing. STOP! Crazy thoughts Marty. You know it happened this way for a reason. You don't have to like it but you do have to understand and accept it.

We ate in virtual silence both seeming to be lost in our own thoughts. It was a peaceful yet eerie silence for sure. One of those where you really wish you knew what the other was thinking. I wondered to myself if he knew his time was coming to an end. If he thought he could beat this tumor out of his head with a positive attitude, or if he had just decided to let go and take whatever life had left to throw at him.

After brunch we talked a bit about his plans for the house after he no longer needed it, what arrangements he thought about for his remains, funeral, that sort of thing. We also talked about what should happen when his time was nearly up, if he wanted the doctors to try to keep him alive as long as possible or just let him go. He very clearly stated he wanted a 'Do Not Resuscitate' or DNR order in place as quickly as possible. It was not a conversation I wanted to have, nor one I wanted not to happen at all. I knew it was important to honor his wishes once he was no longer able to voice them.

I agreed to have my lawyer draw up some paperwork for him, granting me medical power of attorney and guardianship of his estate along with getting a DNR order on file. What that would mean long term, I was not certain. It was obvious to me that Joe was beginning to see that he was nearing the conclusion of his journey and wanted to tie up some loose ends before it was too late though.

It was the most honest and difficult conversation I had ever had in my entire life.

"So how them classes you two takin going? I get me some more grandkids for I die?"

"What?" I asked shocked at is question. I had not said anything about classes, or fostering for that matter, to Joe.

"Them classes you got take for that Toby kid. Sean told me bout them while back. Said you was gonna' take in some kid like you, lost his mama and got no other family take him in."

"Sean told you about Toby? About Anneliese and I working on our foster license?"

I'll kill him!

"Yeah. Said you was dragging yous feet too. Best not be on account a me boy. I ain't no reason fo you let some kid sit in a home wit no parents. Git it done and help a kid out. You is a good dad to Beth. Be a right good role model for this Toby kid too I reckon."

Great! Now he thinks I'm dragging my feet too. I'm not. I have a lot going on right now. Does no one see that but me?

"I'm not dragging my feet. We've had some schedule conflicts, but we're getting them wrapped up. It's not the only thing we are waiting on anyway. Fingerprint results are still not back and nothing moves forward until that is done. Though that should be soon, I hear the summer backlog is about cleared so we should be hearing something soon. Anyway, Sean should have kept his mouth shut. I would have told you once things were in a more final place. Right now there is still a lot of stuff up in the air, with our license and with Toby. But we're working on it," I calmly replied.

"Good ta hear Marty. I meant it, you is a good dad to Beth and I reckon this Toby could use a pops like you too."

Chapter 69

"Marty? You there? Kin ya' hear?"

"I can hear you Joe. What's wrong? You sound panicked."

"Smell me some gas. Cooker ain't been on in days. Don't know where it comin' from but I smell me some gas and afraid will blow up this here house a mine."

"Go outside and turn off the tank. I'm on my way over to see if we can find the leak. But you need to turn off the gas to the house, and open windows to let it air out Joe."

"Tried that. Can't git the thing off. Spun that wheel thing round far as it goes but still smell me some gas."

"I'm on my way Joe. Stay outside, away from the house. Go have a seat on the picnic table up on the hill," I said ending the call and heading back to the main trail where Toby and Sean were sitting on the rock ledge.

Sean was still Toby's therapist, though it seemed more and more like music was Toby's required therapy and Sean was just a partner to play music with. I joined them as much as I could, but with Joe's condition worsening I had less free time to spend with Toby than I liked. It was now nearly October and Toby was back in school for the year, doing well for a change. Sean and I decided that rather than a stuffy indoor music lesson this weekend we would take him on a hike along the high ridge trail up at Adohi. It was a beautiful early fall color hike for sure.

I was proud of how far Toby had come with his anger issues and knew that some family would be lucky to adopt him one day. He was on his way to controlling his anger outbursts, earning straight A's in school so far this year, and even planned to play on the drum line in the school band as soon as he was old enough.

I wished that I had the time Toby needed, and that Anneliese and I required to complete the foster parent certification process to offer him a forever family with us. Unfortunately, it looked more and more like I had my hands full with Joe. I also didn't think it was fair to bring Toby into that mix knowing Joe would only require more and more of my time as his journey drew closer to its end. Not to mention him getting attached to someone who was certainly not going to be around for too much longer. Toby had suffered enough loss in his life.

"Hey, guys!" I called out to Sean as I reached the trail intersection.

"I got to go. Need to head out to Joe's house, said he smells gas and can't tell where it's coming from. I'll catch up with you later."

"I have that gig tonight Marty. You were supposed to give Toby a ride back to the group home," Sean reminded me.

"Crap! Okay, well I guess you are just going to get a grand tour of Thompson Station and the surrounding woodlands on the way then Toby. I can drop you off after we stop to check in on Joe and be sure he isn't blowing up the house on me."

"Okay, I guess. Who's Joe anyway?"

"My only living kin. C'mon we need to get moving. It's a ways from here, but I can probably make it in about an hour if there aren't too many idiots out on these mountain roads. Let's make this a 5 minute hike down to the car if we can. Okay?"

"Beat you down old man!" Toby shouted as he ran past me down the High Ridge Trail toward the Adohi parking lot and my waiting car.

Chapter 70

"Joe? You out here Joe?" I called walking around the back of the house toward the picnic table on the hill where I told him to wait for me.

Where the hell is he? I told him to sit on this picnic table and wait for me damn it! Did he go back into that house? Guess I'd better go check.

I was stopped in my tracks by a sight I never would have expected as I rounded the corner of the house. Toby had apparently gotten out of the car and was currently being embraced by Joe. The two of them were hugging in the middle of the driveway. I wiped my eyes in disbelief before I said "Hey, I see you two have met."

"Sho have. What was you thinkin' leaving dis here boy in the car all by his self? And what you doing up in here today anyways Marty? Not that I ain't glad to see ya' or nothing but thought you was coming back Thursday. Today ain't Thursday is it?"

"No Pop. Today is Sunday. I'm here because you called me about smelling gas. Toby and I, this is Toby Jameson by the way. He's one of Sean's patients and my little drummer prodigy I guess. Been teaching him to play the old high school cadence since Sean isn't that great at advanced drum techniques. Anyway, the gas? Where is the gas smell at?"

"I done fixed it. Don't remember calling you. When I did that?"

"About an hour ago Pop. Called me on my cell. I told you to shut off the gas outside and I would be over to help. You don't remember that?"

"Why would I shut it down outside? Was just the cooker top. I musta' bumped one them knobby things. Gas was on but not lit so it smelled up the place. I opened windows and aired it all out. Ever thing's fine. Sorry you run all the way up in here for nothing Marty."

"I'm just glad you're okay Pop. Let's go in and take a look around as long as I'm here anyway. Make sure everything is all good before I take Toby back to the group home."

"Group home? What for? Why he ain't staying with you. Thought you and Anneliese was getting all them classes done so you could take him in? Ain't you got that straightened out yet Marty?"

"You were?" Toby shyly asked.

Crap! Stay calm Marty, explain it to him. To THEM.

"We are actually. But right now is not a good time to talk about this," I replied watching Toby's face go from wide eyed grin to sullen in an instant.

"Oh. I get it. You changed your mind. It's okay. Happens a lot," Toby said as he scuffed the toe of his shoe along the gravel drive.

"No Toby, we did not change our mind. This is why I hadn't said anything to you about it. I didn't want to get your hopes up. It's complicated. Very complicated, but I am working toward possibly becoming your faster parent. Maybe even long term if you are interested. Now is just not good timing."

"Why it ain't good Marty? This boy need a home, a father. He need you dagumit! Why you dragin yer feets boy? Best not be 'cause a me. Done told ya' that for. I kin still smack you upside that thick skull a yers if you needin' some sense knocked in ya'," Joe sternly replied.

Damn it I wish he hadn't said anything! I can't handle taking on Toby right now with everything that is going on with Joe. How do I explain that to a ten year old? A ten year old who has already lost his only family, gone from foster home, to foster home, to group home because his adoptions kept falling apart before they can be finalized. How do I make him understand that this is not because I don't care about or want to help him? I just have to keep my own sanity in check and take care of a dying man. I'm not sure I can also take care of another child, especially one who has already lost so much and has a history of violence when he loses control of his emotions.

"It's complicated Joe. And now is not a good time to

talk about it. Let's get the house checked out so I can get him home. We'll talk about this later."

Chapter 71

Toby was silent all the way back to the group home outside of Asheville. He stared blankly out the window clearly lost in thought, or just avoiding any possible moment of conversation I might find. He was not himself, at least not the happy boy I had gotten to see recently. No, this was much more akin to the angry secluded boy I witnessed destroying instruments the first day I met him. He had retreated inside himself again, and this time it was my fault.

How did this go so wrong so quickly? I didn't want to get his hopes up so I never said anything about it. Now he hears from Joe that we were working on it, gets all excited, and then this because I just can't take him on right now? I mean I have my hands full with Joe! How can I also take on the responsibility of Toby? We don't even have our final license yet! I couldn't take Toby in now even if I did have the time. After today it's pretty clear Joe will need a caregiver full time, and I feel like it needs to be me but there are things to get worked out before I can even do that. For now I just need to get someone lined up.

"Toby? It's not that I changed my mind about you. You are a great kid and I think my wife and I could offer you a lot more than you have right now. But it is complicated with Joe right now. I just need some time to get him settled with a caregiver. Then I can talk to our caseworker again and see what the status of our license is now, if we still have a path forward."

"Don't bother. Just go back to your family, push your pops off on some stranger, go back to your life. I'll be fine on my own."

"Stranger? I need someone who is qualified to care for his needs right now. He is –"

"– dying. He's dying Marty and you are not even going to be the one to be with him. You're just going to find someone else to do it so you don't have to. Go ahead. Do that. But not the kind of family I want, so just let me be," Toby said slamming the door and walking into the group home as fast as he could.

I never said Joe was dying. How did he know that?

"Kids are smarter than you think Martin, especially that one. He is wiser than his age and can see the signs. And he's right you know. You are pushing the care of Joe off on a stranger, or at least thinking you should. Is that really what is best for him, for you?"

"Oh David James – you always pick the worst times to show up in my head, you know that?" I said to myself in the empty car as I pulled out onto the busy street.

"I want to be there for Joe, but he needs a caregiver right now. I am not qualified and even if I was, I have to handle stuff at work first."

"Martin, he needs someone to help him live out his last days in dignity without causing an accident. In the end he will need more, but he is not there yet. So find someone to check in on him for now when you can't. But it has nothing to do with why you are dragging your feet about Toby," David James replied.

"I just can't do this right now. Not with Joe dying. That kid has lost so much already. Why put him in the middle of this?"

"Because he wants, no needs a family. Joe comes along with that. Give him a chance to get to know your family, even Joe if he wants to, before it is too late. Push him away now and you might not get the chance when you think you are ready."

Chapter 72

"What's he doing here?" Toby shouted at Sean from across the room refusing to come any further than the doorway.

"He's the reason I am here Toby. Can you please come over, sit next to me? Marty and I would like to talk to you for a few minutes."

"I'll sit but I got nothing to say to him," Toby replied as he moved the chair to the other side of Sean, further from where I was seated, placing Sean between us like a gate keeper.

My 'conversation' with David James after dropping Toby off at the group home was the catalyst for all of this. He was right, he was nearly always right. I spent the entire drive home coming up with one reason after another why this was a bad time and we should hold off. Then I ran every one of them by Anneliese and Sean that evening over an unplanned dinner gathering. Both of them shot holes in each excuse until I simply couldn't come up with a reason not to move forward with fostering Toby. The following day, I reached out to our licensing worker to find out what was left to complete.

What I discovered was that we were at the final step.

A home visit for our 'final inspection', the signing of a few more papers, and the arrival of our cleared background check with fingerprints moved us from the status of 'working to get licensed' to 'waiting for a state approval'. Our licensing worker said it could take up to a month, but that since we had a specific child in mind, and he was also a permanent ward, things could move much quicker than that. After all, placing Toby in our home would free up a bed in the group home for another child that may need it.

It all felt so fast considering it had taken months to get to this point. I knew it was for the best and was working to handle my growing fear that I was somehow making a mistake with Toby. Sean was helping me with that part. Anneliese was too, my rock reminding me that helping out a child was worth the minor inconveniences of lost time, even with everything that was going on with Joe to consider as well. Now it was time to talk to Toby.

Shifting my weight from side to side, attempting to get comfortable in this very uncomfortable chair, room, and situation, I finally cleared my throat and began, "Toby, you don't have to talk to me if you don't want to. I do have a couple of things I need to say to you though. Just some things I think you should know.

"First off, Joe says to tell you hello. He was very happy I was coming here today and wanted me to tell you that. He didn't spend much time with you, and knows almost nothing about you to be honest, but he figured out very quickly that you are a pretty awesome kid. He wants you to know that no matter what happens, nobody can take that away from you."

"Yeah? His nurse tell you that or you bother to go see him on your own?" Toby snapped at me.

It was quick, venomous, and said to get under my skin. It was progress!

"No actually, told me that himself this morning when I was getting ready to come here. Over breakfast. Anyway, it is partly what I wanted to tell you. I know you were concerned that Joe would be left in the care of some stranger. I just wanted to tell you that while he does have a caregiver that stays with him a few days a week right now, I have worked things out with my job so that when he needs it, I can be his full time, live-in, caregiver. For now, I still see him two or three days a week and the whole family spends weekends up there with him to keep him company and make sure he has whatever he needs for the rest of the days when we're not there."

"Good. He's your pops, you should be the one taking care of him when he can't."

"I agree. And that is the main reason why I was 'dragging my feet' as everyone kept telling me about finishing up the requirements for Anneliese and me to get our foster care license. I knew that eventually this time would come, when I would have to care for Joe and not be around to care for Beth and any other kids we brought into the house. I talked to our licensing worker, she happens to also be your caseworker by the way, and shared my concerns with her. She assured me it was not something that would prevent us from getting licensed, or a placement."

"So, you didn't want me cause of Joe?"

"Yes. No. It's more complex than that. Toby, Anneliese and I do want you to come stay with us, if you want to. Beth is crazy about the idea of getting an older brother and I think you two would be great together. I was concerned that because of Joe's, um, condition it might not be good to bring you into the situation. But I've realized I was wrong."

I paused, glancing from the floor to Toby and back to the floor. I was nervous and ashamed at how I had handled my own emotions about Joe and bringing Toby into a loving family that was going through a tough time. I thought I was protecting him from losing someone else in his life. I was really just making excuses to push Toby away and prevent myself from getting too close to someone else that I might also lose one day.

"So you was wrong. What's that mean?" Toby softly asked leaning forward in his chair enough that he could see me around Sean.

"Joe is dying Toby. I thought I was protecting you from

getting close to him and then watching him die. You have seen so much of that already in your life I didn't want to be the cause of any more. What I didn't think about was that Joe is a pretty neat guy who might even teach you a thing or two in the days he has left.

"You brought him joy in those few minutes you talked to him in the driveway, and judging from the smile I saw on your face that day I would say you enjoyed it too. Who am I to get in the way of what could be months of joy spending time with Joe? Not to mention, living with a family who would love and care for you, and provide you with a pretty awesome and adorable little sister to follow you around?"

"Yeah, I knew he was. Still, he was funny and talked about all the fun stuff we would do at his cabin on weekends after I moved in with you. Then you said he was lying, that I was stuck here –"

"– you're not stuck here, Toby. That's what I'm trying to say, well that and apologize for being such a dunce the last couple months," I interrupted.

"Toby what Marty is trying to say is that we talked to your caseworker. The last class they needed was done a month ago, she was just waiting on their background checks and fingerprints to come back. That has happened now. Their license was approved Thursday, The day I called to set up this meeting in fact. Marty and Anneliese have the space, even with Marty not home much because he is staying with Joe to care for him more. If you want to, your case worker is willing to place you with them," Sean explained.

The look on Toby's face was priceless. It was clear he was excited about the possibility of moving in with my family. I was still reserved, in case he decided not to join our family even short term. I took a deep breath and slowly exhaled while I waited to see what his response would be.

Eventually, he nodded his head and replied with a simple "Sure. It has to be better than this place, even if it's not a forever place. We can try it."

Chapter 73

"TJ? Beth? Anneliese? Anybody home?" I shouted as I hung my coat and dropped my work bag on the bench by the door. I could hear giggling not far off. Beth's little girl giggles could make anyone smile from ear to ear even after the worst of days.

"Daddy home!" she screamed as she came tearing around the corner and leapt into my waiting arms.

"Hi baby girl. Did you have a good day today?" I asked.

"I did! TJ and me we got to play when he got back from school. We played cars, and dollies, and bikes, and it was the bestest time Daddy. I like TJ. Thank you for giving me a big brudder Daddy!"

"You're welcome Beth. But remember he is only here visiting for now. He might have to go away again. Though, Mommy and Daddy hope he doesn't have to."

"Beth hopes too!" she said running back to the living room to resume her play time with Toby, her new big brother TJ.

Toby had officially moved in a little over a week ago.

Sean agreed to continue working with Toby as a music therapy student. I agreed to have the sessions at the house in the rec room of the basement. I arranged for the nurse caregiver to stay with Joe Monday through Thursday so that I could be home more with the growing family for now. Joe was doing well. Well enough that he really just needed someone there in case he forgot to turn off the water in the sink or the gas on the stove. Most days anyway. Anneliese and I agreed that when it became more than that, when he had more bad days than good, or that it was more severe memory issues, I would spend more days a week with him as long as it was safe to keep him in his home. Eventually even that would have to change.

I had previously arranged for my work schedule to allow remote work three days a week, with Toby moving in I was now up to 4 and only traveled to the office on Tuesdays. This allowed me to spend the weekend, Thursday evening through Monday morning at the cabin with Joe. Anneliese came up with the kids Friday after Toby got out of school and stayed through dinner on Sunday. Monday, Tuesday, and Wednesday nights I was home so that I could both spend time with Beth during the day while Toby was in school, and spend time with Toby doing homework when he came home in the afternoon. That left Joe with his caregiver just Monday night through Thursday mornings.

It was not perfect, but it was working, for now. As excited as Beth was to have a big brother to play with, Anneliese and I were excited to see Toby bonding so well with the entire family. I was still concerned about allowing him to get too attached to Joe, something else

Sean was helping me work through, but I enjoyed his addition to the family enough that I hoped he would choose to allow us to adopt him eventually.

Chapter 74

As I sat staring out the window, eye level with the low hanging grey clouds of that chilly fall day, I was lost in thought. Not one common thought or memory, but rather thoughts so random and uncoordinated it felt like my brain had been split into hundreds of independent pieces, each running to catch a different thought train. I was remembering our time together over the past year. It had now been a little more than a year since we stumbled back into one another's lives. I was also thinking back on the decades we spent apart, and the day he first broke the news about this condition.

God even today, so many months after I first heard the news I can't bring myself to say that awful word. A condition it is for sure, the 'Big C' as we've not-so-lovingly referred to it lately. Cancer damn it! He has brain cancer! And, as it nearly always does, it is --

The doctor had just left the room, delivering news I didn't want to hear with his typical positive spin on things. Now a full six days after I checked him into this place, he was still not able to go home. A place he so desperately wanted to be. Joe had been asking for days when they thought he might be able to leave. To go to a place with hot food, a comfortable bed, and the simple luxury of knowing his surroundings, where things were, how things felt. He was hoping for tomorrow, I was just hoping eventually.

The last few days had been tough, watching him slide backwards into the grips of this disease. He had all but stopped eating, slowed his drinking, refused to get out of bed except for trips to the bathroom, and spent much of the day asleep. It was clear he already had, or was at the very least on the verge of giving up his fight.

Can I blame him? Can I force him to eat, or drink? Can I make him get up out of bed, move his tired bloated body about, and begin to feel a little more like himself? Of course the answer to all of it is no. All I can do is support him, in whatever decision he makes. No matter if it is to increase his calorie count and liquid intake to give his body a chance to fight off this pneumonia, or if it's simply to allow it to consume both of his lungs, to shut down his liver and kidney functions, and to slowly but painfully fade from existence. I know it's his choice, but I'm not yet ready to let him choose the latter of the two.

Slowly I turned from the windows back to face my reality, to face his withered and worn out body. It was time to have the dreaded discussion about his nearing end, to make my peace with his decision, and to be the son I knew I had to be. Like it or not, I could not save him, and neither could the doctors. I knew what needed to be done, what had to be said. What I didn't know was how to begin, or even if I could.

"Son, come sit here next to me," Joe said in his whisper of a voice between shallow rapid breaths.

I honored his request leaving the solitude of the bank of windows behind, carefully stepping over the IV and Oxygen tubes lying across the floor beside the bed. As I slipped into the chair at his bedside and leaned back to brace myself for what I knew was about to take place, he began to speak again.

"Got me a question. Maybe dumb I know, but still a question. Could be I is wrong, but I'm a ask anyways."

"Ask away Pop. No question is dumb," I interjected while he struggled to catch his breath.

"Just give me minute. Please don't talk, or make me laugh again. That hurts Son. I want to get through this without coughing up my dagum lung again."

"Okay. I'll do my best. Let me know when it's my turn to speak."

"Smart Ass!" he coughed at me.

The room was silent while he struggled to catch his breath. The hum of the IV pump, the fizzing of the water bottle for his oxygen line, and the occasional beep of the heart monitor he was hooked to kept me company. They also masked the raspy, shallow sounds of his lungs as he struggled to breathe, and to speak.

"That doc was just here. He says no cancer, just

pneumonia. What he mean by that? Does it change my um, you know?" he asked and paused for my response.

I waited to be sure it was my turn to speak before offering a slow, evenly paced response.

"No. It means that you can fight this battle with pneumonia, and you can get strong enough to recover from it and go home, where we both know you would rather be. But, your diagnosis is the same."

"So I can go home to ... I can get stronger and go home if I can manage to eat and they can get these here meds all sorted. Right?" he asked just for clarification.

I knew what he was asking me, I knew what the pause and sudden change in his words really meant.

"Yes Pop. If you can manage to get your strength back, to eat, to drink, to move your body in a stronger direction, you don't have to die in this hospital room. Or, if this is going to be it for you, if you are tired of the battle and ready to let it go, we can check you out A.M.A. and take you home tonight. You won't last a week.

"Did you hear what he said, 'right now you're losing ground. Every day you don't take in enough calories you lose ground and you are losing this battle?' those were his exact words Pop. And he is right. So now it's fish or cut bait time. You tell me what you want to do.

"You chose to not have surgery. You chose to not have radiation or chemo. You chose to let it take its toll on your body and ride it out until the end. Now you are so weak you landed here with pneumonia. It's time for you to choose how it ends. Are you going to try and fight the pneumonia? Or are you going to let the pneumonia be the end? It's your call."

His body language told me he had already given up hope. He had given up hope the day before when he woke up to raspy shallow breaths and swollen limbs. His body was giving up on him as far as he was concerned and it was time for him to decide if he was going to let it, or if he was going to fight back and at least try to win this battle.

Chapter 75

"Pappa!" Beth squealed from the front door all the way to the living room where Joe was sitting in his recliner.

"Hello there Sunshine. Looks like you are happy to see me today," he softly spoke as he helped her climb to his lap and snuggle in.

"I am! I am! Daddy said you were better. Are you? I wanted to come see you. I had to wait. We brought my new big brudder too."

"Yes dear, I'm a feeling better now. Going to try staying out that dagum hospital since they ain't let the most beautiful girl in the whole world come see me. Wadn't much fun a place anyway. I like it here much better," Joe said as he winked at me from across the room.

It was Thanksgiving Day and the family was together again. Joe had been home from the hospital for a whole 24 hours by now after nearly eight full days spent tied to machines. He still had a long way to go to recover all the strength the pneumonia had stolen from him, but he was at least making an effort to do just that. He was eating without much argument, small portions every few hours at least. He was drinking more water than I had ever seen him drink, and he was getting up and around on his own most of the time. His new cane sat by his chair and he occasionally remembered to take it with him for stability. He was able to move slowly from room to room in his own house as he needed.

As a condition of his release from the hospital I was now staying with him full time. I had taken a leave of absence from work, just two weeks so far but I was prepared for it to be a much longer term if that's what it took to get him back on his feet. Assuming that was even an option. I hated that it also meant I was now away from Anneliese, Beth, and Toby, them coming to see me now because I couldn't leave Joe alone by himself for long periods of time. I hated most of the situation, but I was determined to do what needed to be done. I was also determined to enjoy my Thanksgiving Day with my family and not dwell on the knowledge that it was very likely the only one we would spend all together.

Hours of laughter, storytelling, and the simple enjoyment of spending time together in the same place made it by far the most memorable Thanksgiving I will ever experience. Joe was happy, smiling, and eating. He took his medications as prescribed without being reminded to. He used his spirometer, that little thing you blow into to make the balls float. They give them to nearly everyone in the hospital, especially those at risk of or who have pneumonia. He used it every few hours and only had one or two coughing fits that left him white as a ghost and gasping for breath. He even managed to go outside for a short walk, mouth and nose covered of course, with Beth and Toby while Anneliese and I finished the dinner dishes. It was the way holidays should be spent and another of those happy memories I will forever cherish and think of often when the road gets rough.

Chapter 76

By the end of the first week of December, Joe was looking much more himself. He was staying on top of taking his medications and eating regular meals with me three times a day. His portions were still smaller than I would have liked, but he would often have small snacks between meals. It helped ease my concern about him not taking in enough calories to properly heal his tattered body. Once a day, the two of us would walk to the end of the drive, nearly a quarter mile round trip, to collect mail from the box. Joe would follow it with a nap in his favorite chair looking out over the mountains from the front windows. While he slept, I would try to get some work done on my laptop.

I had the cable company install an internet connection the first week he was home from the hospital so that I could still work and stay with him. My company was very understanding about the situation, and the writers I was working with were more than sympathetic enough to work around my new schedule for meetings. A few days a week I would spend the morning in conference calls in the spare room, what had now become my bedroom and office, while Joe read a book between his naps. We'd found a rhythm that was working and his health was continuing to improve almost daily. I was optimistic that he might pull through this and see the New Year after all. Something that just a few weeks ago sounded impossible.

On weekends Anneliese would bring Beth and Toby for a few hour visit. The three of them would play games, sing songs, and tell stories to one another for hours while Anneliese and I sat back and enjoyed the view. It was wonderful to watch them together, but also bitter sweet knowing that it could not last for long.

As optimistic as I was about Joe's health improving, I was also reminded almost daily about the growing mass in his head. Most often it was by forgetting simple things, like what day it was or my wife's name. Other days it would be more frequent, more important things like that he had to get out of the chair to go to the bathroom, or use water when taking a shower. Those were the harder days for sure but thankfully, for now at least, there had only been a few. There had also been no more temper tantrums since a few days prior to taking him to the hospital with pneumonia.

It was however, obvious that life had come full circle now. I was once a burden on Joe as a child. I was someone to care for daily, clothe, bathe, and feed. On his bad days, Joe was now very much like an infant requiring assistance with dressing, bathing, and eating. There were not many of those days, but I knew that it would not be too much longer before there were more of them than days when he was entirely self-sufficient. For that reason, on December 15th I made a call to my wife that would be the first of a string of difficult calls.

That morning Joe had refused to get out of bed for breakfast and instead chose to sleep another hour before I came in to wake him again for his morning meds. I no sooner opened the door and was forced to shut it again to protect myself from whatever flying object Joe had hurled in my direction. It made an awful sound as it crashed first against the door, and then to the floor. I suspected it was once a mug he kept full of water by his bedside for late night medication requirements.

"You need to get up and eat something. You have meds to take."

"I don't take me any medications. You trying to poison me again. Always shoving food in my face and them little pills that do God knows what to me. Who you anyway?" he shouted back through the closed door.

"Pop, it's me, Marty. I am just trying to help you get your strength back."

"Marty? My son? You can't be him. He left long time ago. Never sayin' so much as goodbye. Self-absorbed little bastard that one. Just because I worked lots he think he was better than me. Him an all that proper speakin. Learned him too much in that school a his I reckon. You best not be him anyways. If in you is, you ain't welcome no wheres near me!"

Self-absorbed little bastard? Is that how he really feels about why I left. I know it's just another 'episode' but he has never talked about me that way before. At least not to me. Stay calm Marty, remember what the doc said when he gets like this. It's just his memory playing tricks on him. Remind him who he is, who you are, where he is. Keep him calm and ride it out best you can.

"Pop, I have an omelet for you if you are hungry. You want some breakfast today?" I tentatively asked through the small crack between the door and its frame.

"I ain't you Pop. Even my son would know that. Little bastard been calling me his ol' man since he was eight. You think I wouldn't know that you pill pushing bastard?"

"That's right Joe, I used to call you that all through my childhood. But I outgrew it. Got to know you again this last year together. I am your Son, Marty. I love you Pop, even if you can't remember that today."

Those were my final words to whatever bitter man was inside my father's room that day. Anneliese and the kids were supposed to come up for a visit. I called to tell them not to come before I spent the rest of the day trying to keep busy with work and ignore the occasional rantings from behind the closed door of Joe's bedroom. It was the beginning of the end.

More to calm myself than Joe I suspect, I eventually picked up the guitar and began to play songs I thought he might remember from our lunch dates at the diner.

Most of that juke box was filled with old country classics like *Walk the line*, *He Stopped Loving Her Today*, and *Two Wooden Crosses*, which I did know how to play and enjoyed on occasion as any boy born and raised in Western North Carolina would. They didn't feel right for this situation though so I focused more on the oldies upbeat songs it contained like *Rockin' Robin* and *Crocodile Rock*. When I finally gave in to temptation and began to strum the opening chords to *Earth Angel*, a song I knew he would remember and hoped might bring him back to the present, or maybe a more peaceful version of his past self, I had finally picked a winner.

Partway through the first chorus Joe stumbled to his door, peaked out into the hallway where I was sitting, and asked "Marty, when did you get here. I thought you was gone today. I'm starving and can't remember how to make me nothing to eat."

I stopped playing immediately, smiled at him, and headed to the kitchen to make us some dinner. The power and magic of music on the human mind had shown itself to me once again. Sean as a music therapist was not a crock, he was a genius!

Chapter 77

Sometime around 4 A.M. I sat vigil at his side watching the life slowly drain from his frail and tattered body. We brought him here to this place, the Weaverville End of Life Care Facility, yesterday as the snow softly began to fall in the high country on one of the last days before winter. Fitting I suppose that the new season would begin as his life was drawing to a close. Fitting too, that the long awaited flakes of white, those joyful little flakes of snow that only arrive in the season of death, of winter, here in North Carolina would too make their delayed arrival on the same day in which Pop's body was just too far gone to care for him in his own home. That is where he had spent the last three weeks.

Joe had spent them in his home, his new cabin in the woods never seeing the outside world thorough more than a frosted window pane. He sat looking at the grey skies and brown grass that desperately needed to be covered with a fresh blanket of snowy white flakes if only to help protect those plants that were not too far gone to survive the colder temperatures of the winter months, and to improve the view of the landscape immensely. Winter is as much a part of the life cycle as is spring and summer. Spring brings with it longer days filled with warming rays of sun while summer provides the perfect opportunity for plants to thrive in its glory. Winter provides a chance for Mother Nature to rest and rejuvenate herself for a new cycle of growth an opportunity. The irony of the cycle of life ending in the cold winter months coinciding with the nearing end of Joe's life cycle was not lost on me in the least.

Within half an hour of me calling the hospice number, an EMT unit was at his front door looking for the best way to get Joe from his perch, a place he refused to be removed from as usual. It was partly to blame for me making the phone call to begin with. His featherweight frame of a little over 120lbs was more than I could manage to get up and about anymore as his condition deteriorated.

The memory incident on Dec. 15 was the first of many. Each grew longer and more difficult to shake him from. His mood had worsened over the course of the last 48 hours. As of 6am this morning, Dec.19th, he had barricaded himself in front of the windows of his bedroom. He sat upright in his wheelchair with the oxygen tank flipped over across the narrow passage between the bathroom door and the small section of his room that allowed the best view from the windows to the snowless outside world. It was done intentionally, a last stance claiming his rightful place as king of his domain, and a futile one at that. His rants from atop the perch he had claimed as his throne told me his actions were brought on by the growing mass in his skull rather than a strange but far too often seen side effect of his medications. It also told me it was time.

I could no longer manage this battle alone, nor could I manage his worsening pain. As much as I hated to admit it, I could not take care of Joe by myself. When I had moved in full time to care for him after the bout with pneumonia, I had agreed that when it became too much for me it was time for residential or end of life care. It was up to me to make sure that Joe was taken care of in his final days. I owed him at least that much based on our rather rocky past and how far we had come over the last year together.

It was at least an hour ride down the mountain, into the valley, and across town to this place, the in-patient hospice facility he and his doctor had chosen when he made the decision to not treat his cancer. It snowed the whole way as I followed behind hoping I would not lose track of the EMT unit. The roads were snow covered and travel was hindered by the often blinding snow squalls as we passed the large patches of open farm land near the upper portion of the valley. It seemed like an eternity.

Though it was certainly long enough, I made not one single phone call to my wife letting her know what was going on. I don't recall why now, but I was afraid she would somehow talk me out of this decision, try to convince me I could handle it on my own for a bit longer, delay this inevitable move a few more days. I would have been wrong.

Our arrival was quick and rather uneventful. The nursing staff had a room waiting, complete with all paperwork pre-filled out and awaiting signatures. They had his DNR order on file already and simply asked if it was still in place. They reviewed the names, birth dates, and photo ID I provided. They cleared him through the admissions process in his new room-at-the-inn in under 30 minutes and were already preparing his first dose of pain medications in no time flat. This was nothing like the previous hospital visits we had endured where the first 24 hours were often spent on a gurney in the ER. This was so much better than that, and more of an at-home feeling than I ever expected. But it wasn't his home, or where he wanted to be.

"How's the bed Ol' Man? Has to be more comfortable than that wheel chair you have refused to get out of for the last 3 days," I said trying to goad him into a response, even if it would be an angry one.

"Maybe. We back to that ol' man crap again now?"

"Maybe. You feeling better now that you are settled in a bit or was that just because you don't want to get the nurse here all riled up?" I said winking at the nurse currently checking his vitals after giving him the first dose of pain medications.

"Well this ain't where I wanna be. That you know. Nobody never wants be here. But I reckon we both knew was a coming. At least the nurses here nicer than that last place you done take me!"

And there it was, a lucid understanding moment where we actually agreed that this was best for him. We had not had one of those in weeks, maybe as long as a month. Not since I agreed to take him home from the hospital that last time. Between the pain, the meds, and the growing mass in his head he had not been terribly lucid since he almost died from pneumonia 6 weeks ago. There were good days, Thanksgiving was one of those for sure, but there were not very many of them after that first week home. I was beginning to think it was no longer possible, that I would never again have even a moment of understanding with him when it came to decisions about his care, or his life.

"Hey I need to go make a phone call Pop, let Anneliese know what is going on and where we are. The house is not far from here, if the snow lets up a bit I'm sure she will be over later to stop in and check on you for herself. I'll be right back okay?"

"Yeah sure thing. Tell her to give them grandbabies of mine a great big bear hug for me okay?" he said trying visibly to hold back tears and appear to be a stubborn old coot refusing to show emotion right up to the end of this journey.

I knew better. I knew he was stubborn for sure, I mean I got it from somewhere right? But I also knew it was more of an act now, to appear strong for me. I knew in his lucid moments he felt like a burden on me. Truth be told, he was. But he was a burden I chose to carry. No matter how many times I tried to explain that, it never seemed to get through to him that I was there by his side because I wanted to be, not just because it had to be done.

Over the course of the next few hours we talked about many things, some things we had discussed time and again, some so generic and general I can't even remember what they were now. What I can remember is that he was the calmest, the most like himself I had seen him be in months. He was lucid, in only moderate pain, speaking, alert, and genuinely happy to have my family and me at his bedside.

Anneliese and the kids came almost as soon as I made the phone call to let them know what was going on and, except for a quick leave to go grab pizza for dinner, it was at Joe's request of course, had not left. There we were, the five of us, one big family sharing stories, laughs, and pizza. It is one of my better memories of my ol' man, Joe, my father.

Chapter 78

Anneliese took Toby and Beth home around 9:30 that evening so they could get some sleep and come back the next day, if Joe was up for visitors. I decided to stay by his side sleeping in the recliner the facility provided for family and guests to use. His first night was peaceful. Both of us managed to get some much needed rest between the pain meds and vitals checks every few hours. I awoke early to the soft sounds of a guitar being strummed and a voice humming along to the tune in the corner of the room. I didn't recognize the melody, but the voice I knew well. Sean had come and brought with him a guitar. The music therapist was in the building.

I arose quietly smiling my appreciation in his direction but not interrupting. He had done this countless times before for other patients who had reached the end of their road. Sean was a professional who always seemed to know the right melody or song for the occasion to help patients remain calm and allow nature, and life to take its course. I left the two of them alone hoping to get out of the room before either of them realized I was crying.

I'm not ready for this damn it! He was doing so good for so long. Now it's just all over. This is not fair! Why him? Why now? Why like this?

"Martin, you know the answer to all of that. There is a plan, a reason for everything. That is why him, why now, why like this. That has to be enough my child."

Mother! Oh how I have missed the sweet sound of your voice. It has been months since you spoke to me, even in my dreams. Of course it would be you who stepped in to remind my head what my heart already knows.

This was meant to be, why does not matter. I know I have to accept this, to deal with it somehow, and to allow Pop to complete his journey. I can only hope that you are there to guide him on his way. I believe you are, I mean that when he is ready he will join you wherever you are now. I have to hold onto that faith. There has to be something positive out there on his nearing horizon!

"Hold fast to your faith dear Martin. Faith can help you through your grief," she spoke again this time much more of a whisper as I finished my walk around the complex and headed back to Joe's room. It took less than 10 minutes before I was standing just inside the doorway listening to the slow melody of Sean's voice soothe Joe as he drifted in and out of consciousness in the pre-dawn hours of that morning.

Joe was relaxed, drifting in and out of consciousness for much of the day. He woke only briefly, once when Anneliese stopped by with the kids in the afternoon, and again near the end of the cycle between pain medications from discomfort. Sean came and went a few times, making rounds to his other patients in the area before coming back to check in on Joe, and me after dinner. When he left for the evening he laid the guitar case on the window bench next to me and said, "in case you feel like playing a little" as he patted me on the shoulder.

I did not feel like playing. I felt like closing my eyes and transporting myself back in time to undo some of the mistakes of my youth. To right some wrongs and take advantage of times I had missed out on with my father. That was neither possible, nor practical. Missing out on those times had provided the opportunities to meet David James, Sean, and Anneliese. They had opened doors in my life I did not wish to close. My past had formed my future and, though I longed for more 'good days' with the man I had spent most of my life hating, I was quite happy with how things had turned out otherwise.

The nurses changed shifts as day bled into night and the morphine doses were increased both in amount and frequency. It was an effort to keep Joe as comfortable as possible. He would occasionally stir in the bed shifting his thin frame from side to side or mumbling conversations to people I could not see nor hear. His words were garbled as if simply talking in his sleep though his eyes remained open, staring at the window, seeming to look at whomever he was conversing with. I held on to my hope that it was Mother come to help him let go of this life and move forward to whatever happens next. It was clear that his lucid moments were behind him now, only time remained.

I drifted off to sleep listening to the gentle rhythm of Pop's raspy breathy and the hum of the morphine pump sometime after the sun set that cold December day. I did not dream that I remember, and sometime around midnight awoke feeling rested and oddly peaceful for the first time in weeks. Pop was peaceful in his bed as I quietly checked to see that he was still breathing. His chest barely moved with each shallow raspy breath now. He was still clinging to this life, but in my heart I knew that my stubborn ol' man just needed to let go.

Picking up the guitar Sean had left for me, I began to play softly. I started with his favorite, *Earth Angel* hoping he was aware enough of his surroundings to hear even just the melody and be reminded of better days. Finishing that I just let my fingers find the chords and did not think about what song would be next. Some of the notes were wrong but out came things like *Amazing Grace*, Pop's favorite church hymn, *On the Loose*, my favorite camp song, and what would be the last song I ever played for Joe.

It was during the final chorus of *The Dance*, a popular country song by the artist Garth Brooks that speaks about how life is full of risks we must take knowing they may break our hearts in the end, that Joe took his final breaths of life.

Stephen Joseph Taylor passed away somewhat

peacefully just after midnight December 21, 2012. I remember it well, a little too well at times, and even today it strikes me as odd, yet somehow fitting that it should be on the 26th anniversary of Mother's passing. They were star-crossed lovers according to Mother, and somehow I know without really knowing that she was there to greet him on the other side.

I've not yet made up my mind on what really lies out there for us when our journey in this lifetime ends, but having felt the presence of both Mother and the man with two first names, David James many times since their journeys came to an end, I know there must be something out there for us. What exactly it may be I'll find out soon enough. For now, I'll let it be and find peace in the knowledge that time really can heal most things, even something that I thought was too far gone, too broken to ever find all the pieces to put back together, a relationship with my father!

A Note From The Author

After finishing my first novel *Unconditional,* a work of fiction that also happened to pull in many elements of my own childhood and coming of age, I set out to write a novel that in no way could be confused with a fictional version of my life. That was the goal as I crafted a story of a boy who faced hardships and eventually grew to hate his life so much that he one day left it all behind him in search of something completely new. That was very much not my childhood, thank goodness, though I understood fully the desire to fledge the nest after high school and set out on a life that would allow you to spread your wings.

Initially I thought the story would go in a different direction, something maybe a little more fantasy based. I was thinking something like the boy as a child receives email from his future self, offering advice he hopes will change the path he travels down. I mean who wouldn't want to send an email to our younger selves warning of impending danger, or bad choices so we could alter the decisions we made? It sounded like a cool idea to me at the time. Then I sat down and tried to hammer out the 'rules' I would need to follow to make that plot line work, and make sense, and also get across the point that changing our past changes the people we become down the road.

I abandoned that plan, and the story I began sat idle on my hard drive while I went in search of a new story to write. It would be nearly a year before it was dusted off again and worked on hoping I would find some way to make it work.

In the mean time I was still writing. Mostly it was journaling, but some of it was good. The chapter where Joe reveals his diagnosis to Marty is one example of this work. The piece was originally called The Dream. It was penned as a journal entry describing a dream I'd had the night before. That one entry in my journal spawned a new idea for a book. I began writing it a day or two later. The journal entry had to be tweaked to fit into the final product, but much of it remains intact.

Now I had a new story to tell, and since I had never had to deal with cancer, or memory loss, or things even remotely related to this in my life, it was still a story that would in no way be reflective of my life. Six months into working on this new story of a boy learning that his very close friend has a terminal brain tumor, I learned that a family member who had been battling lung cancer had just been told that it metastasized to his brain. Suddenly life was getting a little closer to mimicking art. I continued to work on the book, but refused to talk about it to anyone, including my wife who only new I was writing something.

In October of that same year we learned that my mother-in-law, LeAnn had stage IV breast cancer. I stopped writing. Life had officially gotten too close to mimicking art and though not an expert about stage IV cancers of any kind, I had done enough research for this project that I knew the odds were not in her favor. From October 2009 until November 2011 I wrote almost nothing. There were a few long winded emails to a friend where I filled him in on events of my life, blew off some steam, and tried to carry on conversations that in no way reflected how hard it was to watch someone so full of life and joy slowly decay into someone who battled every day just to get out of bed not letting anyone around her know how much it hurt just to take a breath some days.

LeAnn improved, handling chemo remarkably well and giving me a glimmer of hope that she might actually beat the odds. For a year and a half she remained in good spirits and relatively good health having little to no side effects from the aggressive chemo outside of losing her hair and sense of taste. The family was cautiously optimistic. I dusted off the project I had started after finishing *Unconditional*, the one about a boy getting emails from his future self. I still was not about to write about cancer.

Knowing that the email thing was just not something I could pull off, maybe another author has those skills to make it flow and not seem just plain weird. I do not believe I do. I still liked the idea of a boy leaving his rocky childhood behind him in search of something his own, but also making it somehow come full circle and realize that what he hated about his childhood also made him who he is. Good or bad, it needed to happen.

I didn't know how to make that work, but I continued developing the story of his childhood and running away from it all. I began to wonder if the two stories, the one about brain cancer and the story of running from the past could possibly become one.

I had an idea, a little inspiration to write again despite everything going on in my real world life. Inspiration is exactly what I had lost when that cancer diagnosis hit. Now it had returned in a small flicker of an idea, but it was there and I pounced on it.

I began with a time line for the two very different stories and brainstorming ways to tie them together as one cohesive book. It was harder than it seemed at first, but I knew it could work if I took the time. I had a new project, same as the two old projects. Reminds me of a song lyric most of you will have never heard "meet the new boss, same as the old boss" It's from a 70's song by The Who *Won't Get Fooled Again.*

Late in 2010 my writing had a few more setbacks. The family member who had been told his lung cancer metastasized to his brain passed away in November. In December of that same year, I learned that the wife of a very good friend, the same friend I had spent time writing lengthy emails to when I was writing nothing else, had been given a grave diagnosis. This time it was not cancer. Instead it was a disease equally if not more cruel in its symptoms and outcome, a very aggressive version of Alzheimer's.

At the time I was working on what became Part 2 of *Meeting Joe*. Specifically, I was crafting the chapters dealing with the symptoms Joe exhibited as a result of his growing brain tumor. I stopped writing again. Life and art had collided full force and it was no longer possible to finish this project without it in some way resembling events now taking place in my life.

I would spend the better part of a year writing nothing. From December 2010 through the summer of 2011 I don't think I wrote anything longer than a Facebook status! It was not all due to the events of late 2010. In March of 2011 we got the news that though she handled chemo like a champ, LeAnn was having what she referred to as 'episodes'. A trip to the doctor confirmed that her cancer had also metastasized to her brain. It was a reality I knew was inevitable in the beginning. My research for the book project told me that if the chemo didn't cause life ending complications, a stage IV cancer would nearly always find its way to the brain. It was still news that caught us a little off guard.

The family did what families do best, we rallied the troops, planned gatherings, camping trips, did whatever we could to make as many happy memories as possible in the time we had left. I had no time to write, at least that was my excuse when anyone would ask. The truth was that I had lost my inspiration again, and I wasn't certain I could write a story about a dying man whose disease and symptoms would closely resemble both that of LeAnn's and those of my friend's wife with Alzheimer's.

It was at one of the many planned family gatherings when someone, I have forgotten who, asked if I thought I would ever write another book. I mentioned that I had started one long ago but tabled it a few times over the last couple years. LeAnn asked why. I replied something about not having enough time and was told almost in unison by everyone in the room to "make time". I had no response. I hoped it would be the end of it. It was not.

In November 2012, while LeAnn was in the hospital with pneumonia, my wife and I spent a lot of time keeping her company. She was there for over a week. At least one of those visits I took a notebook and pen with me and began to pen a journal entry. It became chapter 74. Again it took a little tweaking to make it fit this story but honestly not too much of it was changed other than names and pronouns.

While writing that evening, LeAnn asked me if I was working on my book again. At the time I was not, I had no idea that it would become part of *Meeting Joe*. I didn't want to let her down so I said "maybe" hoping she would let it go. She did not. I don't recall the exact words but she more or less told me that I should be working on it and that she didn't want to be the reason I never got it done. I'm not certain if she meant because I was spending so much time with the family that I had no time to write anymore, or if she had a clue that I had stopped writing at least in part because she was dying of cancer. I suspect the latter.

It took a lot of effort on my part but when we found ourselves sitting by LeAnn's side at the hospice facility in the first few days of January 2012, I wrote. I spent some of those sleepless nights with my laptop, hammering on the keyboard trying to pour my emotions into a story LeAnn would be proud to have dedicated in her memory. It was her insistence that I write again, that I not use her as an excuse not to write, that forced me to at least try. I knew she would never get to read the finished work, but in her final moments of clarity before the morphine drip and the end of life cycle left her in a mostly unconscious state, she made me promise to finish and publish the story. In fact, it was the last private conversation we had where I was certain she was fully coherent.

It would take some time for me to get back to writing again, but in late 2014 I finally had a first draft in the hands of a couple people who provided basic feedback on what worked, didn't work, and was just plain missing from the story. That's when things began to make huge steps forward. *Meting Joe* had now been in progress for more than two years, with large blocks of time where it was never worked on at all, and I knew it would take time to apply the suggestions I got back after the initial drafts were reviewed. I was determined to take as long as I needed to make it the best story it could be. After all, I was doing more than writing a novel. I was fulfilling a promise to LeAnn, and also honoring her memory along with all those who have been taken far too soon by diseases like cancer and Alzheimer's.

Timmy Meets His Match

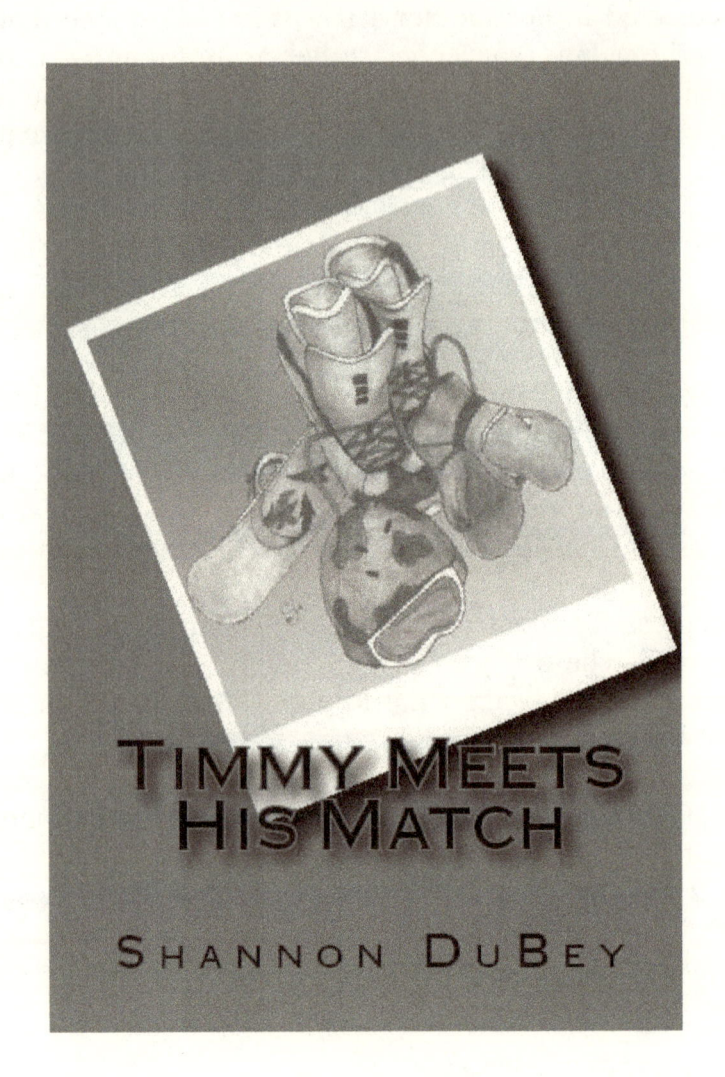

Shannon DuBey

UNCONDITIONAL

SHANNON DUBEY